I0660798

Lucretia P. Hale

The Struggle for Life: or, Board Court and Langdale

A story of home. Fourth Edition

Lucretia P. Hale

The Struggle for Life: or, Board Court and Langdale
A story of home. Fourth Edition

ISBN/EAN: 9783744747585

Printed in Europe, USA, Canada, Australia, Japan

Cover: Foto ©Andreas Hilbeck / pixelio.de

More available books at **www.hansebooks.com**

THE STRUGGLE FOR LIFE:

OR,

BOARD COURT AND LANGDALE.

A STORY OF HOME.

BY

MISS LUCRETIA P. HALE,

AUTHOR OF "SEVEN STORMY SUNDAYS," "THE QUEEN OF THE RED CHESSMEN," ETC.

WITH AN INTRODUCTION BY REV. EDWARD E. HALE.

FOURTH EDITION.

BOSTON:
A. WILLIAMS AND COMPANY.
1868.

Entered, according to Act of Congress, in the year 1867, by

A. WILLIAMS & CO.,

In the Clerk's Office of the District Court of the District of Massachusetts.

PREFACE TO THE FOURTH EDITION.

THIS book attempts to illustrate two familiar things, which seem to the author and myself to require constant illustration, and, though evident to all men, to be very often forgotten. They are certainly matters of the first importance in the daily life which we are leading.

The first is the contrast presented in the sad lines of Miss Procter which follow this preface, and which were themselves the only preface to the first editions. In the charities of a large city especially, this contrast forces itself upon the attention at every step. At the drawing-school or social party or evening dance of some well-regulated chapel, you meet forty or fifty fine young men and women, cheerful, intelligent, prosperous, and with fair prospects for useful and happy life. After the party, you bid them good-evening, and, going to another section of the town, put yourself under the protection of a police-officer, who takes you through a sad round of public dance-rooms, drinking-shops, and various other offices of lust, where you see a hundred or two more young men and women, recruited from just the same ranks of society, from just the same races of men, from just the same pecuniary circumstances, from which came the young ladies and gentlemen from whom you parted an hour before. Ten years ago, when they were all little children, those of them who grew up in Boston sat on the same seats in the primary schools. What has made the difference in present fortune or in future destiny between one of these groups and the other?

Grant all that any man dares claim about the transmission of vicious and virtuous propensities in the blood. Grant all that is demonstrated so sadly about the low type of life, and the weakness of the stock, from which the pauper and criminal classes are bred. After every such concession, the general truth remains but little affected, that, in such a contrast as that I have described, the young persons who appear to be successful and prosperous have had the watchful sympathy and oversight of personal friends, who had heart enough to wish to take care of them, and wit enough to know how. These two requisites are more essential than is money, which is, however, a convenient auxiliary. Those who are going to ruin, on the other hand, have had no such friends: they have grown up in the rooms, it will not do to say in the houses, of parents who have not wanted to watch over them, and have not known how if they wanted to; or, probably enough, there has not been even parental affection: they have been orphans or vagrants, attached only to some distant relative. Of the poorest stock, so far as inherited capacities go, they who needed the best treatment and care get the worst, if they get any. Yet in such experiments as that described in this book, and as are possible wherever there is one person with constancy and faith enough to carry the trial fairly through, the result shows, as Miss Procter's poem shows, what might have been in a thousand experiments. Only the thousand experiments cannot be tried by any great society, or in the tumult of what people call a " moment." To take the figure which Maffei uses when he speaks of Xavier's mission in Japan : these fish cannot be swept into a net, they must be caught by a hook one by one. And you need about as many fishermen as you have fish. To any person of either sex really doubting how to be of use in the social problems of our time, this process of saving from almost certain ruin a single child of God is always open. The book takes its title of The Struggle for Life from Dr. Darwin's celebrated chapter, which bears the same name. That chapter shows what seems sad enough when we think of unconscious vegetables only, — how, of a thousand elm-seeds, all but one die, and only that one struggles into the life of the full-grown elm. The difference between elms and men is, that the souls of men are immortal, and that men are conscious of suffering in the failure of their struggles for a higher existence.

We dare not turn away, therefore, from the struggle for life of a human being, if it be a struggle in which we can lend a hand.

The other point which this book tries to illustrate is a simple encouragement to a large class of persons, who, without knowing it, are doing an immense service in this world; and who ought to be reminded, were it only by the simple machinery of a story, of the dignity and amount of service which they render. In the last thirty years, this country has received from Ireland several million of emigrants. They were, generally speaking, the most ignorant, inefficient, and hopeless representatives of the most unsuccessful tribes of that great Celtic race of which the general destiny has been, that it has steadily been driven to the wall by the advances of stronger races. These millions of emigrants arrived here, perfectly unacquainted with the conditions of their new life, and equally unfitted for it. Most of them were trained in the humblest lines of life of a semi-barbarous agricultural peasantry. Their destiny here, in general, was to live and work in the higher lines of manufacturing, commercial, and domestic industry. Never was a more difficult problem presented to any people than was the absorption of this horde of untrained laborers. Never has any social problem been wrought out with higher success. The contrast is marvellous between the raw Irishman or Irish girl on an emigrant-ship in New-York Harbor, and the children of the same persons, thirty years after, in their new home.

Of the transformation which works this marvel, the credit is chiefly due to the courage and the long-suffering of the Christian women of America, who have taken these peasants into their houses, and trained them to the requisitions of a higher social grade. No process can be conceived so admirably adapted for facilitating the transplantation of a race. The ignorant domestic has learned something every day, in the home-school, of the methods and the responsibilities of a new life. So soon as she has learned enough to stand alone, she has left her mistress, who has to enter again on the same unending and apparently thankless duty. But, by this constant process, the great work is accomplished, which seems clearly to have been intended in the providence of God, of the safe absorption and regular uplifting of millions of an inferior race into the duties and dignities of American citizens. At this moment, when, without the same resource, we have a like problem to solve, in elevating and assimilating four millions of freedmen at the South, we may well render tribute to the sacrifices, the trials, and the energy of half a million homes, which, in thirty years past, have in the Irish race wrought out such a remarkable victory.

In these homes, however, as that victory has been wrought, there have silently lived, suffered, and died thousands of patient and faithful women who have distressed themselves daily with the thought that the agonies of household care left them no opportunity to enter on the higher service of their God. They have thought that they were unprofitable servants. They have supposed that the great Christian missions were for others, but not for such as they. There has been no moment of vision even, in which they have seen, that, by just this martyrdom of their daily cares, God was educating a race, and, in the transformation of an inferior race into a generation of larger grasp and power, was working one of the great miracles of history. Such women die and go to their account, supposing that here they have been left on one side in the arrangements of the Master's service. They open their eyes upon the nobler spheres of another world to find ten cities assigned to them in the calendar of its service.

> "Unconscious Genius, who shall try to tell
>   Its blush before the Lord who knows it well!
>   How strange upon its ears, the great award, —
>   This servant's pound has ten pounds gained, O Lord!"

My sister and I have hoped that the lesson of this book might give some encouragement to those who are struggling on in the tedious details of such thankless duty.

The book has long been out of print, and a new edition is now published in answer to a request from the Ladies Commisssion on Sunday-school Libraries.

EDWARD E. HALE.

SOUTH CONGREGATIONAL CHURCH,
    Boston, Nov. 11, 1867.

CONTENTS.

ix

" GOD gave a gift to earth:—a child,
   Weak, innocent, and undefiled,
   Opened its ignorant eyes, and smiled.

" It lay so helpless, so forlorn,
   Earth took it coldly, and in scorn,
   Cursing the day when it was born.

" She gave it first a tarnished name
   For heritage, a tainted fame,
   Then cradled it in want and shame.

" All influence of good or right,
   All ray of God's most holy light,
   She curtained closely from its sight;

" Then turned her heart, her eyes away,
   Ready to look again, the day
   Its little feet began to stray.

" In dens of guilt the baby played,
   Where sin, and sin alone, was made
   The law that all around obeyed.

" With ready and obedient care,
   He learnt the tasks they taught him there;
   Black sin for lesson,—oaths for prayer.

" Then Earth arose, and in her might
   To vindicate her injured right,
   Thrust him in deeper depths of night.

" Branding him with a deeper brand
   Of shame, he could not understand,
   The felon outcast of the land.

———————

" GOD gave a gift to earth:—a child,
   Weak, innocent, and undefiled,
   Opened its ignorant eyes, and smiled.

"And Earth received the gift, and cried
Her joy and triumph far and wide,
Till echo answered to her pride.

"She blessed the hour when first he came
To take the crown of pride and fame,
Wreathed through, long ages for his name.

"Then lent her utmost art and skill
To train the supple mind and will,
And guard it from a breath of ill

"She strowed his morning path with flowers,
And love, in tender, dropping showers,
Nourished the blue and dawning hours.

"She shed, in rainbow hues of light,
A halo round the good and right,
To tempt and charm the baby's sight.

"And every step, of work or play,
Was lit by some such dazzling ray,
Till morning brightened into day.

"And then the world arose and said:
Let added honors now be shed
On such a noble heart and head!

"O World! both gifts were pure and bright,
Holy and sacred in God's sight:—
God will judge them and thee aright."

A. A. PROCTOR,

From Legends and Lyrics

STRUGGLE FOR LIFE

CHAPTER I.

THE CORNER OF THE STREET.

"PLEASE give me a few cents for to-night's supper! It's almost night now; I have been out all day, and it is just a few chips I have got now, and how shall I go home?" So pleaded a youthful voice, and so it went on till it drew the attention of one of the passers-by.

The voice came from a poorly, thinly clad girl. She wore an old shawl and a short dress, which displayed large feet, scarcely covered by the worn-out shoes. The whole dress was faded in color, and faded, too, was the thin face beneath the old bonnet. There was no youth in the face; no room for a happy dimple in the cheeks. Its expression, as well as the words which accompanied it, pleaded sorely, and kindly Miss Elspeth could not help stopping to answer it.

"It is a cold night for you to be out in the

streets, child," she said, as she stopped; "haven't you a warmer shawl than that?"

"And, indeed, I shouldn't have this, if it hadn't been for the kind lady round the corner."

"Come home with me to my house," said Miss Elspeth, "I haven't any money to give you, but I may find you something warmer to wear."

On the way, Miss Elspeth asked Hannah O'Connor what was her history, of her family, and where she lived. Hannah told her how many children there were, and how her mother was sick, and her father couldn't get work. But Hannah was not much of a talker, and Miss Elspeth did not yet understand how it was they were all so poor and must suffer so much, when they reached her own door.

She went in, and leaving Hannah in the entry, she entered a room that opened upon the first floor. "Sister," she said, a little timidly, as she went in, "I have brought home a poor little Irish girl I have found in the street. She is half shivering, and poorly enough dressed for so cold a night; she is a pleasant-spoken child, and her mother is sick and all. Eleven years old, she says, but she looks worn and anxious enough to be twice that. I have been thinking what we could give her. There is that old brown shawl of yours, — there is some warmth in it still, but I don't think you'll ever wear it again. It is not fit for you to go out in, and even on a sick day—"

"You've given away all your own clothes, Elspeth, and you must come to me now," was the answer. "A poor child in the street! You can't turn the corner but what there's a poor child; and if you were to bring them all home, where in the world are we going to put them all?"

"While you are thinking of that, I'll go up and get the shawl," answered Miss Elspeth.

"It's in the right-hand drawer of my closet," said Miss Dora, "the second from the top. There's a cloth with camphor lying over it, and my best shawl on top of it. But you may as well ask that child in. There's no need of her freezing out in the entry when there's a good fire here."

Miss Elspeth opened the door for Hannah to enter, and placed a chair for her by the fire.

As soon as Miss Dora set her eyes upon the child, she exclaimed,

"You've been here before? I thought as much. Give once, and you are sure to have to give again! It's that same child I gave the petticoat to last Monday! Didn't I tell you not to come again for a week, at least? And here you are —"

"But I asked her to come now," said Miss Elspeth, "and I did not see her here the other day, you know; and how could I tell it was the same one? Poor child! how can you speak to her that way? She looks forlorn enough!"

"Well, go and get the shawl; there's no need

of waiting any longer," said Miss Dora, "only I
advise you to keep my best one for next time she
comes. I should like a Sunday's wear out of it
myself."

The girl had meanwhile looked from one to the
other,— a little defiantly at Miss Dora, imploringly
at Miss Elspeth. She took the seat towards which
Miss Elspeth motioned her, and turned towards
the warm, cheerful fire. Miss Elspeth left the
room.

Miss Dora softened a little towards the child, as
she sat silently looking at her. There was something to her touching in the contrast between the
disorded, tattered, unneat dress, and want of dress
in the poor girl, and her own carefully arranged
garments, and the clean, prim order of everything
in the room. Only the blaze of the fire lighted up
the room, and this was cheerfully reflected from
the highly polished furniture, from the shining
brass knobs on the doors, and closed window-
shutters. Into her complaisance, at her own comfort and ease, there stole a feeling of pity for the
poor, destitute child, who must be looking at all
this unwonted luxury with wonder and envy.

So when Miss Elspeth came down with the
shawl, she herself got up and went to the closet,
and in a few moments brought out a little packet.

"Here's some tea for your mother; Elspeth
said she was sick."

Hannah looked pleased.

"Where is it you told me you lived?" asked Miss Elspeth.

"In Board Court, going out of Barter Street. It used to be No. 45, but they've changed the numbers now."

"Perhaps the neighbors will show me the house," said Miss Elspeth.

"There's three O'Connors live in Board Court," said Hannah, "and there's two Dennis O'Connors. But you'll tell the house, because the gate's off the hinges, and there's a barrel by the door, and it's on the right-hand side, half way down the court."

As Hannah left, Miss Elspeth slipped a piece of money into her hand. She was hardly sure if it was right, and did not venture to tell Miss Dora of it; indeed, she hardly ventured to think of it herself. She did not think it a good practice to give money to poor people when she did not know them enough to be able to guess how it would be used; but this poor girl looked very destitute, and the night was very cold.

Directly came in Miss Dora's neat maid, — for Miss Dora took all the charge of the housekeeping, — and she set the little table with its clean cloth, and she put on the little old-fashioned cups and saucers, and the steaming teapot. About this time, waked up Ralph, the cat, who had been fast asleep till now, curled up in an easy-chair, not far from the fire. In his dreams the flavor of the tea had reached him, and he stretched himself, and prepared to beg for his wonted saucer of milk, rousing himself to the duties of life.

Tea-time passed along silently, for neither Miss Dora nor Miss Elspeth were in the habit of talking at the hours of meals. After the tea-equipage was taken away, Miss Dora drew up to the fire with her knitting, and Miss Elspeth seated herself by her basket of stockings.

"Mr. Coke called this afternoon," began Miss Dora.

"Does he continue in the same mind about the house?" asked Miss Elspeth.

"They are going to pull the house down, and Mr. Badger's too, and the whole row. He says he told us he'd give us till spring to think about it; and now it wants a month to spring, and they are in a hurry to go to work. For my part, I'm sick of Boston. If they are going to pull down all the old houses, I don't care how soon I leave it. The old trees and gardens went first, and now the houses must go. Ours is the last wooden house in the street. Mr. Allen's brick stores fill up our little dooryard, and now the house must go, too!"

"How pretty the dooryard used to be," said Miss Elspeth, "and the strip of border that led up from the gate. About this time the earliest cro-cuses would be out. I remember one spring they were up quite as early as this. Don't you remember that spring—"

"I told Mr. Coke," interrupted Miss Dora, "that I didn't care how soon we moved; if the old house was to go, we might as well leave it sooner as later. He told me of a quiet house in Townsend Place. But I told him that they would build us up wherever we went, and I would quite as soon go out of town —"

"I'm glad you've come round to that," said Miss Elspeth. "There's that pretty little house at Langdale, near the Rothsays and Amy. Amy Rothsay settled we should go there long ago, you know."

"I don't much care where we go now," said Miss Dora.

"Then the rent is much lower than we pay here," suggested Miss Elspeth.

"Well, what does that matter?" answered Miss Dora; "we have enough to live upon comfortably as it is. There's no necessity of scrimping."

"But then, sister, there's our little plan: we could afford to have Martha and Margie live with us out there."

"It's easy to say we'll have Martha and Margie," said Miss Dora, "but it means something more than to have them live with us through the summer or winter. It means that we shall take care of them, and provide for them till they can support themselves; and who knows if that will ever be?"

"But if we decide not to keep a girl," interrupted Miss Elspeth, "but do the work ourselves, we can provide easily for more than ourselves."

"And what's to become of Nancy?" asked Miss Dora.

"Why, Nancy would never go out of town, you know," answered Miss Elspeth, "especially if she marries Aaron, as she hinted; and I was thinking at tea-time, since perhaps we couldn't do without some help, why couldn't we take this Hannah O'Connor? She is older than Martha and Margie, and for a year or two till they are old enough to help us —"

"That comes of thinking at tea-time, Elspeth. You always are inventing some plan while you are eating. It is not healthly to eat and think at once. One thing at a time is enough for me, and you, too. And pray don't say any more of Hannah O'Connor to-night; she makes me think of my poor brown shawl. How handsome it was when it was new! I wore it to church the first day, and Mrs. Brigham noticed it."

"It has worn well," said Miss Elspeth.

"Yes, I've had it about for a sick shawl many a day, and there's warmth in it yet. Well, I shan't lose sight of it, if your Hannah O'Connor should go out with us to Langdale. Not that I can think seriously of that. How will you ever get our furniture into such little rooms? And how are you going to take Ralph into the country? The cat is fond of me, but more fond of the house, I'm afraid. If you had a procession of Irish girls to take Ralph away, he would be back the next week. You know we couldn't leave Boston, on Ralph's account."

CHAPTER II.

MARTHA AND MARGIE.

MISS DORA was decidedly conservative. She loved Boston with an inflexible love. Yet it was the Boston of her younger years to which she had always clung. She loved the old parts of the town. Its narrow streets, with here and there an old wooden house, among its newer and statelier rows of brick buildings. She loved even the sidewalks, and the rattle of wheels upon the pavements. She did not often venture into the country; when she did, she complained of its stillness that rung in her ears. Frank Rothsay had often said, Miss Dora would rather have a brick tree than an elm or oak opposite her window, any day. To move Miss Dora out of Boston would seem like moving the State House itself.

But many things had been a long time at work upon these old prejudices. In spite of Miss Dora's remonstrances, Boston had gone on enlarging, — in her mind, not improving. The old wooden houses were fast disappearing, the quieter streets were becoming noisy thoroughfares, Miss Dora was

jostled and elbowed at every corner, and almost
run over in Washington Street, and there was a
threat of making a railroad even there. A large,
fashionable shop was opened in their own door
yard, and there was a row of carriages every day
in front of her quiet windows.

Miss Dora's expressions, too, were always
stronger than her feelings. In spite of Miss Dora's
strong words, Miss Elspeth, small and meek as she
looked, had the rule in the end. The two Misses
Elton had lived long undisturbed in the little house
which seemed so exactly fitted for them. But an
inroad had been made, a few years ago, upon their
peace when the dooryard had been built upon.
Their own front door had been opened upon the
street, and their already little parlor had been cut
smaller. Miss Dora had declared then she would
leave Boston, and never set foot in it again; and
when, this spring, the landlord began to talk about
pulling down the house, both Miss Dora and Miss
Elspeth listened more willingly to what their friends,
the Rothsays, had to urge about going out to Langdale, to live near them.

"As well move there as anywhere," said Miss
Dora, at last; "there won't be but one more
move !"

Miss Elspeth inclined to the plan of moving out
of town, since it might include her favorite wish of
taking Martha and Margie home to live with them.

Many years before, Barbara, a favorite cook, had

left the Misses Elton's service, with the injudicious
purpose of being married. This was one of the
unpardonable sins with Miss Dora; and that Barbara should have the folly to give up a comfortable
home for the uncertainties of married life, shook
her faith in women. Barbara had married a carpenter who was apparently getting on in the
world; but he and his wife again sinned in Miss
Dora's eyes, by leaving Boston and going to live
in New York. Years passed on; and after the
sickness of her husband, and other troubles, Barbara returned to Boston, but did not venture to
intrude her poverty upon Miss Dora and Miss
Elspeth.

By accident Miss Elspeth had fallen upon her.
One of her neighbors had begged her to go and see
a poor woman who was struggling along with three
children and a sick husband. Miss Elspeth went to
the place she was directed to, — an out-of-the-way
court, — up some shackly wooden steps. She
opened the door, and in a poor-looking room, she
found Barbara. She had not expected to find her
in the Mrs. Smith who had been recommended to
her charitable cares.

Poor Barbara! She, who had been married from
Miss Elspeth's house with some pomp and ceremony, and had been used to cooking dainties and
luxuries, if she did not share them, was sitting now
in a forlorn, unfurnished room. She held her
youngest child in her arms, and sat close by a small

stove, scarcely larger, Miss Elspeth thought, than
her bread-pan.

Barbara was filled with wonder at seeing Miss
Elspeth again, and was soon willing to tell over her
troubles. Her husband had just gone out to find
work again, after an attack of rheumatic fever.
Her two girls were at school, for she still could
keep them decent enough for school. But, though
she had gradually parted with all the little treasures of housekeeping she had possessed when she
had married; though the poor destitute room
showed only a barren neatness; yet Barbara
seemed to think she had quite a jewel left in her
baby. With pride, she opened a drawer in a little
chest of drawers, that served many purposes, to
show the little wardrobe she had managed to prepare for it. Miss Elspeth was deeply moved when
she compared it with one she had seen a few days
before, prepared for a little child no more tender
and helpless than this one, — its countless cambric
dresses, flannels, and blankets, with embroideries
and displays of knitting, — all that was rich, and
fine, and luxurious, — presents from those who
could give with little personal sacrifice. Mrs.
Smith showed the one little white dress she had
made of the cambric of her own wedding dress, and
the blanket of coarse flannel, in a corner of which
she had found time to embroider one little sprig.

This was in the autumn. All through the winter
Miss Elspeth went to see Barbara, and care for

her. One or two visits had shown her that Barbara's strength was failing, and she was dying from the over-work and cares of the few last years.

Before the spring she died, and the baby soon followed her. The little baby went before it was old enough to bear the long name its father had given it. But Mr. Smith married again, before the year was out, a widow with three children. Here was a double enormity in Miss Dora's eyes; and the greater was her pity for the two little girls, Martha and Margie. Their stepmother had little time to devote to them if she had the will, and Miss Elspeth often brought them to spend days with her, when Miss Dora was gradually won by their quietness and gentleness.

So all through the last winter, it had been the subject of Miss Elspeth's thoughts, how best she could provide for Martha and Margie, and whether it were possible for her to take them into her own household. Whenever the subject had been brought up, Miss Dora had always said that they could not afford to take care of two children, especially since Mr. Coke had increased the rent the last two years, in spite of his having cut the house up smaller. But now the house itself was to be left; and, with the great inroad of change this event must throw open, Miss Dora was willing to let other innovations pour in.

Amy Rothsay came from Langdale with glowing accounts of the little house to let just next to them.

2

All its charms she brought out rapidly and vividly to Miss Dora's listening ears. It was not at all a desolate country place, with the nearest neighbors half a mile off. There were pleasant people all round,— cosy old Mrs. Bunce, the Lees, the Paxtons, who had a son who came home from India every year or two, and brought home pretty things, so that their house was all filled up with fascinating Canton furniture and boxes and tables, and all such, and the Fays, and the Carltons, and then the Rothsays—

"And then the Rothsays," Amy went on; "dear Miss Dora, you don't know what treasures the Rothsays are for neighbors. Here I come in and see you once a week,— mamma not oftener than once a month,— and papa, I'm sure he does not come more than once a quarter, to tell you how stocks are, and what has risen, and what has fallen——"

"Nothing has risen, that I know of, lately," interrupted Miss Dora.

"Wait till you get to Langdale," said Amy; "papa will stop and see you every night on his way up from the cars, and give you the papers, and tell you the news."

"Where are we going to find the time to read the papers?" asked Miss Dora. "Elspeth is going to set up an orphan asylum, as far as I can see. You don't know that we are to be overrun with all the poor children of her acquaintance."

But Amy did know all Miss Elspeth's plans, and was deeply interested in them.

"Oh, dear little Martha and Margie," she said; "I shall be so glad to have them near us! Such a notable little person as little Martha is! And what large, grave black eyes Margie has! I remember seeing Martha, one day when I was dining here, help Nancy set the table, and the little thing was very useful, putting on the forks and spoons, though her eyes came up no higher than the table. She's a little born housekeeper!"

"She's just like Barbara in some of her ways," said Miss Dora. "She moves round just as quietly. She was the last person, Barbara was, that you would ever have thought of being romantic; getting married and going off, and having a family of children and dying——."

"Everybody dies," suggested Amy.

"Everybody does not die of hard work," said Miss Dora; "and Barbara, if she'd stayed here, might be here now. There's our Nancy; I don't so much wonder at her. She always had a flirty air. I knew she was fond of being looked at. I concluded from the first she would marry some time or other. And now she's going! Everything comes upon us all at once! The house is pulled down, and Nancy must needs marry; and we're going to leave Boston and all."

Miss Dora admitted that she was going to leave Boston. This was a great point gained.

CHAPTER III.

TWO INSTEAD OF ONE.

WITH this encouragement, the house in Langdale was visited, and preparations made for leaving the Boston home; in the midst of which, and during the frequent discussions before the final determination, Miss Elspeth did not neglect to inquire about Hannah O'Connor. She found that she was well known among her acquaintance. Mrs. Badger, the president of the sewing circle, knew that she spent her days going about begging for anything and everything; that she had a never-do-well mother, and that the father was now in the House of Correction; that they lived in the lowest degradation, while it seemed hopeless to give them anything, for money and food and clothing were squandered in the most reckless manner. Miss Elspeth was not dismayed or discouraged by these representations. Hannah O'Connor's moving face had made an appeal to her heart, and she was not one who would forget it. The child had made its claim upon her, which she could not throw off with words that others would use. She could not say to her.

self, these people are not worthy to be helped, it
is no use doing anything for them, what is given
them is worse than thrown away ! Hannah O'Connor stood before the eyes of her memory, and
would not be moved away. Even if she should go
hundreds of miles off, she would know still that
Hannah O'Connor was in the world. She was put
there to grow up in it. And she was growing up
in worse than poverty, in worse than destitution.
Miss Elspeth directly felt that she was responsible
for her, the more so, perhaps, that no one else was
sensible of the same feeling.

So one morning Miss Elspeth and Amy Rothsay
set forth for Board Court. They stopped at Mrs.
Badger's for more particular directions than Hannah had given. Miss Elspeth confided to her
in part her plans with regard to Hannah, if she
could persuade her to leave her mother.

"It will be a real charity," said Mrs. Badger,
"though when you've seen the other children,
you'll want to take Bessie rather than Hannah. I
never could see much to like in Hannah ; but Bessie is a pretty little child. She is younger than
Hannah."

"Then it would be more important," said Miss
Elspeth, "for me to have Hannah. She is too old
to stay in such a home longer. By-and-by it would
be too late to do her any good."

"Well, you have not seen Bessie," said Mrs.
Badger. "Perhaps you'll decide to take them

both. I know you won't have the heart to leave Bessie behind."

"What would Miss Dora say to that?" asked Amy, as they walked on.

Miss Elspeth was looking very thoughtful.

"I know I wish our house were a little larger, and things were a little different," continued Amy.

".I am more able for such things than you," said Miss Elspeth.

They reached Board Court. It was fortunate they had Mrs. Badger's direction besides Hannah's, for the landmarks she gave were not decisive; almost every gate in the court was off its hinges, and barrels were plenty. It was perhaps in the forlornest of all the houses that they found Mrs. O'Connor was living. A troop of noisy children were playing in the unpaved dooryard, across which some clothes were swung to dry. Miss Elspeth and Amy made their way up stairs, through dirt, close air, among noisy women and children, into a room that seemed at first quite filled.

Mrs. O'Connor lay upon the bed ill, and three or four of the neighbors had come in to visit her and entertain her. Hannah was in the room, holding one of the twins in her arms, the other was lying upon the bed. There were two boys in a corner quarrelling over some marbles. These were "Stee-vie," an older brother of Hannah's, and a friend of his. Then there was a smaller boy playing on the floor, who was "sister's son" to Mrs. O'Connor.

Miss Elspeth and Amy seated themselves in two chairs that were left vacant by two of the neighbors, who then took their leave. Hannah recognized Miss Elspeth, and came forward to speak to her, and from behind Hannah's dress peeped out the little face of Bessie.

Mrs. O'Connor began a long detail of her sorrows and grievances, of the mischances that had befallen Dennis, and of her distress at what she should do, now that he was shut up, and cut off from helping the family. Miss Elspeth was discouraged by her tone and manner. She could see in her whole appearance the source of all the wretchedness of the family. There was a recklessness and a shiftlessness that showed no desire for a better position in life, especially if it required to be worked for.

Amy, meanwhile, was making the acquaintance of the baby, and presently of Bessie. Bessie had been very shy, but ventured at last to come near Amy, and to ask:

"May I smell of one posy?"

Amy held in her hand two or three English violets, that had been given her as she came into town in the morning.

Amy drew Bessie near to her, and gave her one of the violets. Bessie's eyes glistened with pleasure. She was a pretty child, when her face could be distinguished through the dusky veil that concealed it. She had thick brown hair, and clear, trusting blue eyes. Her cheeks glowed, and looked more

healthy than Hannah's. Amy longed to wash her
and make her clean, and discover the clear complexion beneath. Bessie was the little pet of the
family, the little favorite in Board Court. Her
timid ways made her shrink from playing with the
noisy, rude boys who seemed to people the place,
yet not one of them would have wished or have
ventured to hurt Bessie.·

Amy saw why it was that Mrs. Badger was sure she
should want to take Bessie out from such a home.
It seemed impossible to leave her to struggle with
such wretched and hopeless poverty. Hannah,
too, was the useful member of the family evidently.
No doubt she brought home every day, from her
wanderings, enough, or more than enough, to support the family for the day. Amy found herself
really hoping Miss Elspeth might be moved to take
Bessie, even if she left Hannah behind. Hannah
was already used to the discomforts and the hard-
ships around her, while it would be a great pleasure
to take the little Bessie out into a better home,
that seemed more fitted to cherish so attractive
and tender a child.

They walked away from the house a little while
in silence, when Amy exclaimed, " That dear little
Bessie, her pretty face haunts me ! "

" I have been thinking of it. I have been wondering if I should be justified in taking her away
from her mother," said Miss Elspeth.

" But her mother," said Amy, " could hardly

object so much as to have Hannah go away. Hannah must be her dependence."

" Oh, I cannot let Hannah stay !" said Miss Elspeth, " it would be worse for her in the midst of such influences than for Bessie. Those lovely ways and charms of Bessie are just what might protect her in such a place. I am only wondering whether I am not wrong in taking away such an influence as hers is, from the rest of her family. It is what makes even those rude boys more gentle."

" I know it," said Amy. " The boys in the corner stopped quarelling when Bessie went near them. But it makes me shudder to think of her living always in such a home."

" Yes, indeed," said Miss Elspeth; " if I could make sure it were right, I don't know why we should not have them both; it might be good for Hannah."

Amy almost embraced Miss Elspeth at the corner of Hanover Street.

" Oh, do take them both !" she exclaimed; " and we will help you,—mamma and I. I will take care of all of Bessie's clothes. I cannot bear to think the little thing should grow up in such a place. Will you do it ? Only Miss Dora !"

" Only make sure it is right," said Miss Elspeth, " and Dora will see that it is right, too."

" It's a responsibility," said Amy, fearing that her eagerness might be bringing too much care upon good Miss Elspeth.

"There's more responsibility with a few duties than a great many," said Miss Elspeth. "One cannot do more than one can; and it is very easy to do less."

"Everybody does not think so," said Amy. "Dear Miss Elspeth, it won't do to tell Miss Dora where we saw the brown shawl."

"Wrapped round one of the twins," said Miss Elspeth, smiling.

They stopped again at Mrs. Badger's.

She was rejoiced to hear that Miss Elspeth thought of taking home the two children. "I am very glad," she said. "I have been thinking, while you were gone, if I could not help you. Some ladies, some of my friends, would agree with me, I have no doubt, to clothe Bessie; and Hannah, too, perhaps. You ought not to have the charge of all that, when you have so much care besides."

"There'll be a contest," said Amy, "I have no doubt, as to who shall do the most to help you. We will try not to stop in mere professions."

CHAPTER IV.

THE EMIGRATION.

Miss Elspeth found no obstacles to her benevolent endeavors. She sent for Hannah one day, and broke to her the plans that were formed for her. The matter was easily decided, when Mrs. O'Connor willingly gave up both Hannah and Bessie. For Miss Elspeth had already decided that it would be no charity to Hannah to take her away from her home, while she left Bessie behind; and that it would not break off all Hannah's home ties if she had the child still with her. Hannah listened to her silently. She expressed no pleasure or sorrow at the proposal.

Hannah was eleven years old now, but she looked far older. Miss Elspeth told her she wanted her to stay with her five years. At the end of that time, she would have learned a great many things; and Miss Elspeth promised, then, to put her in as good a condition as she knew how. And she told Hannah that she might then have her own choice as to where she would go. Hannah decided she would follow Miss Elspeth now. Five years was an

unknown period of time to her; the home that Miss
Elspeth offered her was unknown, too; and the
unknown was attractive to her. It had always
been her pleasure to wander in distant parts of the
town, in search of something different and new;
and now it seemed as if the world were opening
before her. There was a secret reservation in her
own heart, all the time, that no one could bind her
anywhere; and that whatever she promised Miss
Elspeth, or whatever allurements were offered her,
she could come back again, any day, to Board Court.
Miss Dora and Miss Elspeth little thought, the one
so satisfied with her own position, the other filled
with pity of Hannah's, that Hannah was looking
forward to a home with them, only as a variety to
her former life, — as a part of its vagrancy. Yet
Hannah was not entirely ungrateful. She was
moved by Miss Elspeth's benevolence, but she
could not appreciate it. Young as she was, she
had become defiant of the world, and did not trust
to any one's impulses.

Miss Dora, in the midst of the whirl of so great
a revolution, was unable to make any protest against
her sister's benevolence. In the midst of such
change, in the leaving her old home forever, all
other changes were lost. And now that her decision was made, she was only eager to carry it out.
She scarcely lent her ear to plans for the children.
She was already absorbed in calculations whether
the old carpets would fit the new rooms; in terror

lest the dear old-fashioned furniture should be injured in its passage out. She did not go out herself to the new house, to superintend these arrangements; she would not go till the very last day. Miss Elspeth did all. She made measurements of the rooms of the little house; and Miss Dora, at home, gave directions for the disposition of everything.

It was agreed that Amy should, every day, have a little school for the children, and teach them in the house for an hour or two, until they should be old enough to go to some of the schools in the neighborhood. Mrs. Badger and her friends had collected a complete little wardrobe for Hannah and Bessie; so it was hoped that Miss Elspeth might be relieved from some of the cares her benevolence had brought upon her.

It was a fine day, the day of the emigration, as Frank Rothsay called it. Miss Elspeth and Martha and Margie went out by the railroad in the morning. Miss Dora had never consented to ride on a railroad, and refused on this occasion. The Rothsays were to send their carryall and take in it, Miss Dora and Hannah and Bessie. Early in the afternoon, Frank Rothsay appeared at Miss Dora's door, with the horse and carryall, to drive her away. Hannah and Bessie stood upon the steps of the house. Many were the bundles and baskets that Miss Dora tucked into the corners of the carriage. Grimly she told Hannah to get in upon the back seat. In the midst of her preoccupation and busy thoughts, she fancied she detected in Hannah's face an intention of running away at the last moment. Miss Dora looked in again upon the little parlor. The last of its household gods had gone; but still there clung round it some of its old associations. The figures in the landscape papering seemed to move in a last farewell. Miss Dora looked round once more before she closed the last half of the shutter. Her eyes fell at last on a corner of the room where was a mutilated palm-tree, beneath which sat a dismembered Arab, over whose head waved the trunk of a bodiless elephant. It was where the little parlor had been cut in upon to make the new entrance to the house. Everything was changed even there; the old paper that used to seem so grand and fine in her eyes, had been dishonored, and nearly destroyed. She closed the shutter and the door, and was ready to go. Frank had lifted little Bessie up to the front seat, and was encouraging and amusing her with some lively talk. Miss Dora sent the key of the house into the shop. at the corner, and the carryall rolled out of the street.

Little Bessie was in a state of wonderment and delight. She had ridden once half way down a long street, in a baker's cart, and it had been one of the eras of her life; and now she looked with a sort of terror upon the wild steed that Frank was governing. It was a slow old family horse, and plodded along at a respectable pace. As she went on, Miss Dora grew eloquent upon the inroads and changes she saw in every street they passed through. As they passed the Common, Bessie almost hoped some of her young companions would see the state to which she had arrived; while she almost feared some of the great boys would snatch her out from the carryall, if they saw her. If they did, she thought Frank would whip up that splendid large horse, and they would fly like the wind.

Frank began to tell her what she would see out of town. He asked her if she had ever seen a pig, and excited her curiosity greatly when he found she never had.

Hannah was a little perturbed. The horse went on so slowly, the journey seemed so long to her impatient mind, that she began to fear she should never find her way back if she should ever want to go home, and looked on either side frequently, as if ready to jump out. Miss Dora, who was in constant dread lest something should be lost from the carriage, judiciously gave her the molasses jug to hold, and presently her cap-box. This gave Hannah some occupation; while she herself held Ralph, the cat. Frank Rothsay, meanwhile, exerted all his powers of entertainment in various ways. He must keep little Bessie from crying, if she should think of home and the baby, and she showed herself a little inclined that way, and must prevent Hannah from running away, and Miss Dora from turning

back to her beloved Boston, when they crossed
the Boston line. He looked round now and then
uneasily to the back seat, in terror lest Miss Dora,
Hannah, and the cat, should all have made their
escape while his head was turned; but no, the
journey was safely accomplished, and the carryall
drew up before the little gate, from which a path
led to the front door. On the doorstep stood Miss
Elspeth and Mrs. Rothsay, and Amy, with Martha
and Margie, came running out to meet them. They
were received with triumph. Miss Dora was helped
out, Bessie was lifted from the carriage, and this
was gradually unpacked. Hannah, after she had
descended, walked towards the horse, looked upon
it contemptuously, and said, "I could have walked
sooner." But she applied herself directly to assist
the unpacking, and went with the others to the
house.

Amy made Miss Dora linger a moment on the
step, to look down into the little garden. She
pointed out the crocuses under the window, the
violet roots, and the border, with its edge of pinks.
Miss Dora admired but little of these, and then
hastened into the house. Before the fireplace her
own armchair was drawn up, and Miss Elspeth's
rocking-chair. On the tall mantel-piece stood the
old China vases, and at either end, the large sea-
shells. In the window, upon the road, stood the
little round table, with its clawed legs. The old
sideboard stood as though it had grown into its

niche; and the antique mirror hung between the windows. On the table, beneath it, were placed the large Bible, Young's Night Thoughts, and Taylor's Holy Living.

From the fireplace gleamed a welcome blaze. Even the knitting was laid invitingly on the stool by the side of the armchair. Miss Dora seated herself, and folded her hands in her lap. "The Lord be praised," she said, "we are safely here." She would not be moved from her place that night. Her head was mazed by the confusions of the day, and its changes. Amy brought her a cup of tea; and in the evening, Mr. and Mrs. Rothsay came to talk with her. She read the Transcript, and old Mrs. Berry had died in Newburyport, and Juliana Grant was married, and the Gobbleby stocks were realizing. All of which was talked over as it would have been in the old Boston home; so that Miss Dora herself was fairly surprised, at the evening's close, to find she was really in Langdale, that the great step had been taken, that she, Miss Dora Elton, had moved from Boston.

Meanwhile, the children had taken possession of the rest of the house and the garden. They entered into the spirit of change with the delight of children. Bessie and Margie, explored every corner of the house, and admired the different doors that led out from it. They could scarcely be torn away from the corner of the garden from which they could watch Mrs. Bunce's pigs. But Frank

3

promised them he would put a bench there for them
some time, where they might take observations any
time of day. And early in the evening, Amy and
Miss Elspeth succeeded in putting the little colony
to rest.

It was one of the first of the spring days, — one
of the days that seem to be promise and fulfilment
in one. They are only of promise; for the east
wind shuts them in, behind and before. But behind the east wind is hidden the summer, and in
these early spring days we feel a little of its breath,
its warmth, and its languor, the invitation it gives
to come out from winter activities, and winter con-
finements, into its soft lassitude, and all its offers of
freedom.

CHAPTER V.

EVERYBODY said Miss Dora and Miss Elspeth did not know what it was to have a family of children in the house, and that before the first week would be over, Miss Dora's patience would be worn out. Everybody thought she would find living in the country a different thing from her house in town, where she could buy what she pleased for dinner at the provision store at the corner of the street, where she had neighbors to drop in at any hour of the day, and a brick sidewalk to walk to church upon. The living without any "help," the depending upon an inconstant butcher once or twice a week, and the having the care of half a dozen poor children, — for the world's wife exaggerated the size of their family, — all these discomforts united, it was thought, would be more than Miss Dora or Miss Elspeth could bear.

But these fears were without foundation. As Miss Dora's immovable mind was unable to grasp the extent of the shock that had come upon her old habits, she settled down into the change as quietly as she would have done to the coming of the new day in her old home. There her principal occupation had been to provide for the three meals of the day, and to keep her house in order. And these events were still the most important to her.

Ralph, the cat, had been shut up the night before, in a room by himself. Frank had insisted in bringing him out, that he should be put in a basket, his head tied in a bag, and his paws greased, according to old tradition; and the first evening of his arrival, whenever he was visited by the children, he was found busily cleaning himself. This occupation, it was supposed, would employ him till he became wonted to his new position, and he would be less likely to take the first opportunity to make his way to his old home.

It was perhaps the same enthralment of occupation that held Miss Dora. The zeal and ambition of a careful housekeeper inspired her, so that she forgot for a little while the changes round her, and set herself to duties that drove away all thought.

So, on the first morning after her arrival, she woke to the demands of breakfast, and a house in disorder. She hastened to wake Hannah and her *corps dramatique,* and set them in action. Miss Elspeth was roused to find Hannah nailing down a carpet, Martha sweeping the stairs, and Margie and Bessie busy with fetching and carrying.

"There, now," said Miss Dora, " I meant you should have slept an hour yet, you worked hard enough yesterday. I thought I would set Hannah to tacking down that carpet; I saw it wasn't finished yesterday. I sent the child in with the hammer and nails, and it took her half an hour to find out she didn't know what I meant. There's enough to do, to be sure, but it is a pity you couldn't sleep longer."

Sleep! Miss Elspeth might as easily have slept in a cotton mill; there was the clatter of tongues and the clatter of footsteps. Miss Dora's voice sounded above all, and Miss Elspeth's noiseless will was needed. For, though Miss Dora was wont to give the loud word of command and the song of victory at the end, it was Miss Elspeth who led on the silent attack upon the enemy.

There was china to set up in the very position it used to stand in the old house; there were stores to be put away in inaccessible closets; old furniture, that had just strength enough to stand, to be settled into new places. The children had to be taught the names of everything. For a long time Hannah was sure to bring the wrong thing when she was told. Miss Dora found it very difficult to teach her precisely the centre of the room, where the table was to stand, and how she must always place it in a straight line, and how the chairs had each its particular position to which each one must return whenever it had been displaced.

The younger children enjoyed this highly. Bessie brandished high with delight the candlestick
she was to carry into the parlor. Martha, more
slowly, and with due reverence, bore along Miss
Dora's old workbox, to set it on the spider-legged
table. Little Margie wanted to be useful, and was
laden with one of the old books that Miss Elspeth
treasured; but she was found, some time after,
sitting on the lower stair, gazing at one of the old
pictures it contained, and spelling out its black
letters. Bessie was charmed with the tall peacock-
feather dustbrush, and waved it about, to the great
danger of the china ornaments on the dining-room
mantel-piece, which caused her dusting zeal to be
speedily checked. Presently, she was heard crying out for help. She had tumbled into a high,
India clothes-basket, whose contents she had been
investigating.

"Lucky it wasn't the flour barrel," said Martha.

Bessie, indeed, was everywhere. Under Miss
Elspeth's feet as she carried along a high pile of
valuable china cups she had been washing; upsetting poor Hannah's tacks, as she was nailing down
the last carpet; knocking over a little stand in the
kitchen, where a pan of milk had been incautiously
placed; pulling the andirons out from under the
little wood fire that had been built in the parlor,
to see if the back legs had claws like the front
ones; and at last was found even examining Miss
Dora's knitting that lay within her reach. She

had an inquiring mind, and everything was new to her; she could not resist touching all that she saw, and tasting all that looked good to eat. But everybody was too busy to scold her, except Miss Dora, and she scolded everybody. Bessie, too, kept wisely out of Miss Dora's way. At last, Miss Elspeth seated her by Margie's side, and bade Margie tell her all about the pictures.

All day Hannah was kept busy. She was willing to work, and did not object to an occupation new to her, especially an occupation that sent her from one duty to another. It entertained her. She was interested in finding out why there were so many teapots, and so many pitchers, and such different utensils for cooking. Poor Hannah's dinner had always been cooked in one pot; and that the cooking-stove should need so many iron things, was a mystery that was long in being solved. Miss Dora was a valuable teacher for her in this way, for Miss Dora was fond of laying down the law, and liked to repeat her directions. She followed Hannah round to see if she did what she told her, and to reproach her if she failed. Hannah was not dismayed by such an inexorable taskmistress. She had fancied she was going into bondage when she promised herself to Miss Elspeth for five years, and she did not think enough to consider whether it was harder than she expected. She faithfully performed all that Miss Dora demanded of her, more faithfully than Miss

Elspeth had dared to hope. Miss Elspeth's kindness, indeed, surprised Hannah far more than Miss Dora's inflexibility.

Hannah was happy in Bessie's joy. Sometimes Bessie wondered what Steevie was doing, and what game "the boys" were playing without her, but her thoughts were so occupied with the excitements of her new home, that she had little time to recall what she had left behind. "Meat for dinner," she whispered with wonder to Hannah at dinner-time. Then there were all the joys of the garden, and untold pleasure there she might look forward to. She went to sleep that night tired out with excitement, her cheek flushing, and her veins throbbing.

Hannah left her and went down to the garden. It was the first pause of the day, and she stood leaning over the garden gate, looking up and down the quiet country road. The first day of her bondage had passed away, and she was free to leave it behind already. ' She had only to open the gate and walk down the winding road. She would not be missed for awhile; she could hide herself easily. But Hannah was already, in some degree, fenced in. For there are different kinds of fences, those we read of in the tropical regions, where prickly cactuses grow up rankly, and present an armed hedge against enemies, and there are bars and bolts that shut in prisoners, and little rustic fences that are strong enough to keep us civilized

people out from our neighbor's garden. But none
of these would have restrained Hannah if she had
felt determined to .go back to her old home and
haunts. The bolts and bars might have held her
in a little while, but she would have only cherished more warmly behind them the love, of liberty
that they kept her from. Just now she was
bounded by the thought of the five years for
which she had promised herself to Miss Elspeth.
Nobody had commanded her to make that promise.
It was her own act, so it was by her own free will
she stayed there a night longer. Without acknowl-
edging to herself its nature, somehow she was
unconsciously bound by that promise. After those
five years she would do what she pleased. She
fancied before that time she could "run away,"
and she almost began to plan how she could
accomplish this. She was eager to show herself
that it might be done any time, and so she looked
wistfully down the road she had come. They had
driven out so slowly from Boston, everything was
so different here from there, she began to think it
would be quite a long journey back. Still, she
knew she must remember the way. So, instead of
thinking of the soft evening air, just lifting the
fresh leaves budding on the trees, or listening to
the low twitter of the early birds, she brought
back the remembrance of every stone upon the
way. Miss Dora summoned her in. "Some kin-
dlings for the kitchen fire to-morrow, Hannah."

CHAPTER VI.

THE NEIGHBORS.

LANGDALE, though its name sounded suspiciously new, was not one of the modern-made railroad towns. The station lay at a little distance from its centre; and, though the tide of business was sweeping into its quiet street, its houses still stood with broad gardens all around them, and old trees shading their dooryards. It was a pretty view, up and down the village street, from Miss Dora's gate. In the summer, the drooping branches of the trees shaded more closely the bend of the street either way. One or two houses stood directly on the street, a little way down; but clambering honey-suckles and trumpet-flowers hid their deep porches and gave them a secluded air. In one of them was a milliner's shop, where Mrs. Paxton's and Mrs. Bunce's caps were made, and where ribbons might be bought. Farther down the street, out of sight, was the post-office, and the old tavern, that used to be so much frequented before the days of railroads, when there was a stage road directly through Langdale. There was a grocery store here, too, that had many attractions. Crockery of various patterns, tumblers, pewter toys, disputed their place in the window, with tobacco pipes and lemons.

But, up the quiet street, in the neighborhood of Miss Dora's house, there were no such tokens of trade. Mrs. Paxton's house stood far back from the street, just below, and close shrubbery shaded it from the public view. It was pleasant to Miss Dora to visit so respectable a family. Tall borders of box along the flower-beds showed how many years the flower-garden had been laid out. The old trees looked down protectingly upon the house that was young when they were. The gravelled walks were always carefully rolled, and the plaster figures of Flora, and the gardener's boy, were kept thoroughly clean, and frequently repainted.

Within the house, everything wore a very elegant air. Every spring, when Eleonor Paxton came home from New York, the drawing-rooms were reopened and rearranged; and through the summer she presided there, dressed for callers that seldom came, among the fine furniture, or looked at herself in the long mirrors, or sat as quietly in one of the deep chairs.

On one side of Miss Dora lived Mrs. Bunce; on the other, the Rothsays. Mrs. Bunce's house was small and low; and the little green in front of it was not separated from the street by any fence or paling. The green moss covered its sloping roof, and woodbine hid one side of the house; and it seemed itself like the natural growth of the street under the high elms. But no moss grew in the steps of its owner. She was busy, always, but mostly in her neighbors' concerns. To this Miss Dora did not object. She liked to listen to Mrs. Bunce, to get a little peep into her neighbors' affairs, if she could get it without trouble; and she had that agreeable complacency of respectable people, that led her to think that no one could find anything ill to say about her. To be sure, Mrs. Bunce troubled her with some close questionings about her affairs, with regard to the children, for instance. "How long did they expect to keep them? Did Martha and Margie's father do anything for them, etc.?" Miss Dora referred them all to Miss Elspeth's inscrutability. "It's Elspeth's business," she answered, "and I have nothing to do with it. She will have to see, at the end of the year, if the two ends meet."

"They generally do," said Mrs. Bunce, encouragingly, and went on with her remarks upon the neighbors.

She did not approve of Mr. Jasper's going away. He had been preaching for them three years, and she had hoped he was settled for life. But that was a thing quite out of fashion now-a-days. The ministers, too, were all out of health in these times; she believed they enjoyed ill-health. Everybody said that Mr. Jasper needed the change, and that he was wanted in the West, where he was going. She did not believe he was needed more than he was in Langdale. "I am sure they have solemnities and casualties enough, out West, to preach for them! With a steamer bursting up before my windows every day, I'm sure I shouldn't need a sermon!"

The affairs of the Rothsays came closely under her notice. Theirs was a changing household. They were so hospitable in their ways, that their house was open to everybody, and always full. The country aunts and cousins came there, because it was so convenient to go to town from there on shopping expeditions. And the city relations came for the country air. There was such a nice garden and lawn for the children to play in, and plenty of fruit in the orchard, — pears, peaches, and apples. The invalid friends came there, because Amy cared for them so kindly, forestalled all their wants, and made the days go by so quickly for them; and Mrs. Rothsay knew so well how to prepare little nice things for an invalid's taste. Then the healthy friends liked to go to the Rothsays because the atmosphere was always bright and clear. Frank was always full of fun, and Amy always cheerful. Mr. and Mrs. Rothsay liked to have the children do what they pleased; and it was a household that did not oppress with its rules and forms. One of Mrs. Rothsay's nieces, last autumn, had been married from there. Mrs. Rothsay had been willing to turn

the house topsy-turvy for a wedding. And she had
even allowed the same rooms to serve for a funeral
ceremony, because an old aunt, in her last requests,
had begged to be laid in the burying-place of the
town where she was born.

Now and then, some one asked what Amy Rothsay did? — what her talents were? — why it was
she was so generally attractive? But Amy Rothsay had never had the time to cultivate what talents
she might have possessed. Her time was broken up
in the cause of other people. She was the centre
spring in the working of the house; she filled up
all its missing links. She was at hand whenever
she was called for, not only in the house, but in the
village. In short, her work was what comes under
the head of " woman's work," so indescribable, so
undefinable. She did what the others shrunk from
doing, — the things that nobody else wanted to do.
She filled the gap made by those who refuse to
work, and who are insufficient for their position.
And if she had talents for a higher vocation, she
sacrificed them silently, perhaps unknowingly, to
perform lower duties that others should have done,
doing them so quickly and graciously that they
became grand.

In Langdale, the question was, how Amy Rothsay could accomplish so much. And Mrs. Bunce
wondered where she could find time to teach Miss
Elspeth's children. For this became a settled
arrangement. Amy agreed to have a little school

for them for two or three hours every morning.
She declared she should make time in this way;
because if she had a settled occupation every morning, she should learn to divide her time more
punctually, and know whether she had any time in
the day or not.

It was an inexpressible comfort to Miss Elspeth
to have the ready help of Amy. Miss Dora was so
unsympathizing, so discouraging towards every
new effort, that quiet Miss Elspeth, timid in her
ways, might often have shrunk from carrying out
what she knew to be her duty, if it had not been
for the ready help of her younger friend. Miss
Dora was fond of an institution only after it had
become old and established; she did not love it in
its original sense of a beginning. Her life was
already settling down into its old habits. But one
of her old habits had been that of complaining, —
an indulgence that formed part of her happiness.
She fairly liked to complain, and threw out the
worst part of her nature in her complaints. She
was one of that class of people who never think of
putting, cheerfulness and gratitude in their list of
virtues. In summer, they dislike the heat, because
it is oppressive; the cold, because it is unseasonable. Autumn always seems gloomy to them; and
spring suggests nothing but a cutting east wind;
and the winter is always long and dreary. Ill-
humor is a happy expression for this disposition of
mind, for it is the outward appearance of disease

within. It must be a diseased eye that conveys
only sad and distasteful scenes; a diseased ear,
that listens only to discords; and still more, a diseased heart that dwells upon them, that doubles
and repeats them in complaint. If it were true that
such evils predominate in the world over the good,
then it were surely the duty of every one to avert,
or rather silently to crush them, rather than to
reproduce them with their own restless and uneasy
complainings. But the truth is, it requires some
little genius to find fault with the year's changes,
with the wonderful way it passes through its winter
and spring, and summer and autumn, to criticise
day and night, sun, moon, and stars; so the idle
ones of the earth like to take upon themselves this
duty, and will probably carry this propensity into a
" new heavens " and a " new earth."

CHAPTER VII.

THE CHILDREN.

HANNAH learned very slowly to read, but Miss Dora found her in time a valuable acquisition to her housework. Bessie was everybody's favorite. It was hard to keep her still enough to teach her anything, but it was easy to influence her by example. Martha, who was so sedate and quiet, and who was a little older than Bessie, could take better care of her than any one else. Little Margie was a dreamy child. Her large eyes were moved round in wonderment upon everything, but she was easily pleased and easily cared for.

The garden was their playground, and each of the children had a bit of the border for her own private garden. Martha furnished radishes from hers before any of the neighbors had raised them, and flowers grew wonderfully in Bessie's, in spite of a deal of digging and the row of sticks that she had put down to show what she had planted. Margie had a great melon in her garden. Frank had brought her some melon-seeds which she had put into the earth with a variety of flower and

4

vegetable seeds, and the melon had gained the
mastery. She was quite satisfied with this, and
spent her spare time sitting on a stone by its side,
hoping some day to see it grow.

Frank worked, too, in Miss Elspeth's garden.
His mother's garden at home, he said, had been
established so long that it grew of itself, and there
was not any work left for him. He was fond of
playing with the children, and made rustic seats
for them under the apple-tree, and in secluded
corners of the garden. He often brought George
Arnold, too, who went every day into town with
him to school. George was never so active as
Frank, and he was not a student, either; but Amy
and Frank considered him a born artist. The
margins of all his school-books were filled with
sketches, caricatures of the schoolmaster, and the
"digs" among the boys. He often sketched
groups of the children, — even stiff Miss Elspeth
came into his pictures, and picked up a curve or a
grace there. Bessie never enjoyed anything so
much as to sit and watch George while he was
drawing, while Frank told them a story. They
would sit on the doorsteps, Frank whittling, Amy
and Martha sewing, and Margie, with her doll in
her lap, looking earnestly into Frank's face, as he
told some wonderful tale.

Miss Elspeth sometimes persuaded Miss Dora to
let Hannah sit upon the doorstep with her work,
but more often Hannah would prefer to go on with

her dusting and sweeping of the parlor or dining-room, stopping now and then with her brush at the window, to listen to the climax of the story. George and Frank were fond of playing with and amusing the children; but every day, almost, they went off on some long expedition of their own, and then came Bessie's time of trouble. She did not like the regular school-hours; she did not like anything regular, and was every day tempted out after the butterflies. Miss Dora was shocked at her very thinking of going off with the boys. Amy took the children almost every day to walk, and soon they learned their way to a pretty grove not far away, where they were allowed to play at times.

Miss Elspeth had promised Hannah that she should have frequent intelligence of her family, and Mrs. Badger agreed to go often to see Mrs. O'Connor. The first news served to diminish Hannah's interest in home affairs. Steevie had disappeared. The very day after Hannah went away, he had left home with the vague words about never being seen again. The next intelligence was that Mrs. O'Connor herself was in the House of Correction. One of the poor twins had died, and Mrs. Badger had found some one to adopt the other, and Mrs. O'Connor's "sister's son" had been sent to a farmer in the country. Hannah received quietly all this account of the family and the breaking up of the establishment at

Board Court. She made some exclamations when she heard of Steevie's departure, and again to Miss Elspeth, when she heard that nothing more was known of him. In the evening, when Amy went to see her and asked her some questions about it, she burst into tears. It was the first time she had been moved about anything. "Oh! Miss Amy," she said, presently, "I loved Steevie better than anybody. How could he ever go away without coming to let me know, — without coming to see me and Bessie! Will I never know where he has gone? Oh! Miss Amy, isn't there a hope if I followed him out into the wide world I could find him?"

"He knows where you are, Hannah; he will come to find you, perhaps," said Amy, comfortingly.

"Oh! Miss Amy, if he could only be taught well, he might learn to be a good boy. I had been thinking, that when I got old enough, I would teach him something. Such bad ways as he has been living in! I know it now, I didn't know it before. And perhaps he is going on to worse. Oh! I would rather be back on the cold stones in Boston than lose Steevie. I can't bear to stay here the night through, and think of him away."

"But you could not find him," said Amy, "if you went out to look for him; "and Hannah, you can't leave Bessie behind. Think how she needs you, and how much you do for her!"

"There's plenty to love Bessie," said Hannah;

"I think it was because Steevie loved Bessie so, that he must go away from home when she was not there. What with me gone,—and I used to bring something home every day for them to eat,—and Bessie gone, too, who used to make them laugh,—no wonder that Steevie couldn't stay. Miss Amy, is it doing good, what Miss Elspeth has done, to send him away from his own home?"

"Miss Elspeth has done you good and Bessie," said Amy, "and you could none of you have stayed at home when your mother was taken away. Perhaps, sometime, you'll be able to do Steevie a great good if you take care of yourself and Bessie too."

"The world is very large out there, isn't it?" said Hannah, pointing up the street.

"Don't think of going into it," said Amy, anxiously; "we will all do our best to find Steevie, and you could never find him alone by yourself."

Hannah stood awhile thoughtfully, and then broke off the conversation, saying, "Miss Dora'll be calling me in to fill the water pitchers, and it's late."

It was by no means a smooth stream in Miss Dora's household. Hannah's and Bessie's ignorance of right and wrong frequently upset the tenor of its ways. Martha was perhaps over-conscientious for so young a girl. Margie led such a dreamy life, she was willing its outer actions

should be ordered by others, but often she was
shocked, as well as Martha, by Bessie's quick
impulses.   From the beginning there had been
great trouble in checking Bessie's fondness for
helping herself to anything she fancied.   With all
Miss Dora's watchfulness, there were wonderful
disappearances from her stores.   Bessie was the
suspected one at first, but it was found that
Hannah must share the blame with her.   Miss
Elspeth was sorely troubled at this discovery.
There was some excuse for these two children,
for, coming into what appeared to them a land of
plenty and liberality, they could not understand
why they should be checked in this way.   So, at
least, Bessie pleaded ; " Miss Elspeth let her eat as
much bread and milk as she pleased at meal times,
and what harm was there in eating a little more
when she chose ? "   Miss Elspeth told her she
gave her as much as was best for her when she
ate her meals, and tried to teach her the laws of
" mine and thine."   She had help from Martha in
teaching Bessie what it was to tell a lie, or to take
what did not belong to her.

Martha was very much shocked at the discovery
of these derelictions of Bessie.   One day, after
school, while the children were playing in their
favorite corner of the garden, Bessie went into the
house.   She came back with a very mysterious
air, with something hid in her apron.

• " I've brought something for a feast," she exclaimed; "it's some of Miss Dora's fresh sponge-cake."

"Oh! how good of Miss Dora," cried Martha; "did she give it to you?"

"See how nice it looks," said Bessie, as she unfolded her apron.

"But did Miss Dora give it to you?" asked Martha, anxiously; "Oh! she never would have given us so much of her nice cake. Bessie, I'm afraid you took it."

"Well, I did," said Bessie, "only Miss Dora will never find out. It was all done up in a basket for Hannah to take to Mrs. Fay, when she goes down street. I got a knife and cut this off, and Mrs. Fay won't know how big the piece was."

"O Bessie, you would not want to steal, and from Miss Dora, too!" exclaimed Martha, taking the cake out of Bessie's hands; "I'll take it back to Miss Elspeth, and she will put it into the basket again."

"I thought you'd like to have the cake," said Bessie, beginning to cry.

"O Bessie, I'd rather never eat any cake, or anything, than steal," said Martha.

"Miss Dora read in the paper," said Margie, "about a boy that was put in prison because he stole."

"Oh, but he stole a whole houseful of things," said Bessie, "and this is nothing but a piece of cake."

"That does not make the difference," said Martha; "I think if anybody stole your pink, your pretty pink, you would think it was a very naughty thing, and it's only a flower, and did not cost you so much trouble as it did Miss Dora to make this cake."

"I guess if anybody stole my melon," said Margie, "if I had one, and it came ripe, I'd like to have him put in the State's Prison."

"Well, then," said Bessie, angrily, "take it back to Miss Dora, and tell her all about it, and have me scolded and punished. At home, if I had got it for Steevie, he'd have been glad, and have taken it and have eaten it."

Martha stopped, doubtfully. "I wish you would take it back yourself, Bessie," she said.

"You won't persuade me, — " began Bessie, but she was interrupted by the appearance of Hannah. She had been weeding the peas at a little distance, and had heard the whole conversation.

"Give me the cake," she said, "and I'll put it back without telling anybody, and nobody will ever know."

Martha gave it up reluctantly. It was wrong not to tell Miss Dora, or at least, Miss Elspeth, she thought, but she could not bear to have Bessie scolded, so she let it go.

That evening Hannah was leaning in her favorite place over the gateway. Amy stopped to talk with her, as she liked to do at such times. She wanted Hannah to talk more,—Hannah was so quiet always. She had often a sulky air, but at this hour she seemed more approachable. This evening, Hannah told her directly the talk of the children, which she had overheard in the garden.

"I think," said Amy, when she had done, " that you had better have talked with Bessie a little about it, and told her how wrong it was to take even a little thing that is not her own, and asked her to tell Miss Dora about it."

"Martha wanted her to tell about it," said Hannah.

"And you said nothing of it," said Amy. "I wish you would tell Bessie to speak of it; it would be a lesson for her. You might do her a great deal of good."

"I! Miss Amy," exclaimed Hannah, "how could I tell her, when I am often doing just the same?"

Amy saw the confession was a difficult one for Hannah to make. "The best way," she said, "would be to tell Bessie that you see that it is wrong, and that you do not mean to do such things any more, and that you want to teach her the right."

"It's a little thing,—it's such a very little thing," said Hannah.

"Then it must be a little thing to keep from doing; but by and by, if you have taught yourself to take little things that don't belong to you, you

won't know when to stop. If here, where you
have plenty to eat, you are in the way of taking
what does not belong to you, what would happen
if you ever really needed it? That poor boy that
was taken up for stealing was very destitute.
He stole all that silver, very likely, just to get
something to eat."

"Oh! don't speak of that boy, said Hannah,
seizing Amy's arm, "for I thought of Steevie. I
know it isn't he; but then, where is he?"

She looked anxiously up the road, and after a
moment, she said, "It's hard to live, Miss Amy,
isn't it? I did not think it would be so. I
thought, if I only grew up, it would be easy
enough. There are so many rules and laws. Miss
Dora talks so much about speaking the truth, and
Martha about stealing. In Board Court we didn't
trouble ourselves much, any way. We did not
live very happily. They used to quarrel sometimes, and then the boys would fight; but we did
not have to think what would come the next day.
That's what troubles me, Miss Amy. I don't like
to sweep and wash and work, but I'm willing to
do it all day long, rather than think what we'll all
do, and what we'll all come to."

"Miss Dora and Miss Elspeth are taking care of
you now," said Amy; "you have only to think
how you'll please them best."

Hannah assented, and gloomily promised to
speak to Bessie before she went to sleep.

CHAPTER VIII.

THE PICNIC.

THERE came a lovely day in the course of the summer. There had been heavy rains for a few days, and all the grass and trees were refreshed, and the air was soft and delicious. Before Miss Dora's gate stood a carryall and an open wagon; and on the doorsteps were baskets covered with napkins. And the younger children were jumping up and down the steps, and dancing through the alleys with delight. There was so much excitement going on, that Mrs. Bunce could not resist putting her cape bonnet on, and going over to see what was happening.

"We're all going on a picnic," said Amy, who stood by the gate.

"We're going to pick whortleberries," exclaimed Bessie. "And we're going to take our dinner," said Margie, quite moved. "And Miss Dora and Miss Elspeth are going, too," said Amy.

"Miss Dora going to a picnic! I should as soon think of the steeple's going!" exclaimed Mrs. Bunce.

"And we children are going in the open wagon, with Amy and Frank, and George, if we'can only stow in," said Martha.

Frank and Amy had planned the picnic for the children. When Amy proposed it to Hannah, she demurred; she did not think Miss Dora would want her to leave, and she could not go unless Miss Dora did. "We will make Miss Dora go," said Amy, suddenly; and she ran home and persuaded her father to give up one day of business and town, and go to the picnic. She came back triumphantly with him, and Mr. Rothsay went into the house to invite Miss Dora and Miss Elspeth to go too.

"I never like picnics," said Miss Dora, discouragingly. "I don't like sitting on stumps and rocks; and as for sitting on the ground, it reminds me always of when I shall lie under it."

"Oh, that's dreadful!" exclaimed Amy; "but we will take you a chair. We will carry one of our straw armchairs in the back of the wagon. Frank and George can fix that, if that's all."

There were a great many other objections; but Amy had smoothed them off, and Miss Elspeth helped to remove them too. "You don't mind sitting on a rock, Miss Elspeth, do you?" said Amy; "and we can take out the carriage cushions, too, for you to sit on. And you will admire the glen."

"Oh, a glen!" exclaimed Miss Dora. "I don't like glens; I shall be sure to tumble in, and you all will. How can you take the children there?"

"But this is a very mild glen," answered Amy. "It's none of your White Mountain ones. We don't have such ·in these civilized regions. It's the easiest place to get at you can imagine."

So the whole household were to go. Miss Dora packed up plates, knives, and forks. She said she did not like eating with her fingers, nor using green leaves for plates. If the rest wanted to be so romantic, they might; but, at any rate, they should have the choice of a china plate. Hannah chopped ham with vigor; and Martha spread the bread for sandwiches. Bessie tried to pack up Ralph in a basket, to take too, but Miss Dora would not allow that. "Ralph wouldn't enjoy a picnic!" Mrs. Bunce was astonished. "What would Eleonora Paxton say? The Irish girls are going to the picnic, too!"

"I'm glad if it will amuse her," laughed Amy. "Poor Nora does not have much to entertain her."

Mr. Rothsay drove off in the carryall with Margie, who was a little afraid of the wagon; and the rest of the children, with Amy, Frank, and George, and Amy's friend, Bertha Carlton, were packed into its seats. Frank sat behind in the straw chair devoted to Miss Dora, and George drove the two horses. Bertha Carlton's seat was made as comfortable as possible, for she was fragile and delicate, and Amy was anxious not to tire her. She was older than Amy, and an early school friend of hers. She had a clear, transparent complexion, and blue eyes full of thought, with soft, gentle manners, and a low voice.

The party were very merry in the wagon. Martha and Bessie were wild with delight at the cows in the meadows, the haymakers in the fields, at the busy farmhouses, and the birds in the trees. Frank pointed out to them every creeping and flying thing they passed, and told all sorts of strange stories about all they saw. They came to an opening in the fringe of trees that skirted one side of the road.

"Oh, what a view!" exclaimed George, as he drew up the horses. A broad slope led down to where a little river wound through the meadows. Graceful elms stood scattered through the fields, and a row of low hills rose up the other side, showing a waving line against the blue sky.

"Now, girls," said Frank, "we are to stop here all day. George has fallen in love with the view, and we must wait till he has put it into his sketchbook. Bertha will have to scramble out of the wagon and sit under that elm, and we must needs all look as pastoral as possible. The finest trout I ever caught I lost again, because George insisted on my holding it so long over the stream while he made a picture of me."

"It was but right to immortalize Frank's only trout," said George.

It was not long before they reached the appointed spot. Miss Dora and Miss Elspeth were

carefully handed down the path that led to a
pretty stream dashing among the rocks. Then
the girls were taken out of the wagon with the
rest of its contents, — all Miss Dora's store closet,
Frank declared, was there.

It was a beautiful spot they rested in, on the
bank of a quiet basin that lay at the foot of a
sparkling waterfall. It was so shaded below, that
green moss covered the rocks and stones, and the
trunks of the old fallen trees. Above, the sun
gleamed in through the tall pines and the shining-
leaved oaks and waving birches, and glistened on
the spray of the waterfall, and lay in streaks over
its paths. Miss Elspeth stood before it in silent
pleasure awhile, then she said to Amy,

"This makes me all young again. It seems to
wash out as many as twenty years of town life and
dry, droning existence."

"O, dear Miss Elspeth, you are beginning all
over again. You are starting all fresh with us
and the children," said Amy.

Frank, meanwhile, was arranging Miss Dora's
chair. There were few even spots in the ground,
but at last he placed it under a spreading hemlock,
where there was a pretty view of the waterfall.
Miss Dora tried this seat, but she thought the
moss was a little damp for her feet, so she moved
it. At last she was seated with her back to the
flowing stream, a bare rock shutting out all view,
but she was more comfortable, and professed her-

self pleased with her position. Hannah busied
herself in putting the baskets and packets in
shady nooks, and then came to stand by the edge
of the water. The children were charmed. Bessie pleaded to be allowed to take off her shoes and
stockings, and walk in. Martha actually shouted
with pleasure at the way the spray danced in the
sunlight, and Margie found directly one gay colum-
bine, nodding over the edge of the rocks.

"Oh! this is better than my garden," she ex-
exclaimed to Amy. Then the children scrambled
round among the rocks with the help of the elder
ones, and presently left the little glen for a field
on the hillside, where they were to find their
berries. Miss Dora took out her knitting under
the hemlock, and one of the party, who happened
back for a moment, found her fast asleep, with a
yellow butterfly perched on her knitting-needles,
and a bird singing away just over her head. Mr.
Rothsay was reading his book, stretched on the
ground, with a rock for his pillow.

Frank, by and by, left the berry-gatherers, to
find a place for their dinner. He came back to
consult Amy. "Here is a rock on the very
water's edge, if we can only get Miss Dora there.
It would make such a charming table, and I think
she would rather eat from a table than the ground."

Amy went to look at it, and was pleased with
the place. There were rocks for seats all round,
and room was found, too, for Miss Dora's chair.

"Where's Hannah, then?" said Frank; "we'll hurry up dinner. We'll have a tablecloth thrown over the rock in grand style."

A merry dinner it was. There was a dish of the berries, and Amy insisted it must be lined with the leaves of the wild grape that hung so near. There was cream, which Frank declared he had just milked from the cow in the pasture close by, but Martha was very sure Amy had taken it out from the tin can that came in the wagon. Then there never were such sandwiches, nor such light buns; and Amy's cake, that Amy made herself, was perfection. Even Miss Dora was anxious to have the receipt for it. Bessie liked nothing better than bringing the fresh water in the silver mugs. The waterfall made such a nice pump she thought, and pumped itself, too.

Mr. Rothsay declared he had never eaten such a meal. He told, too, what he had for dinner when he dined with Queen Victoria, and what the Shah of Persia treated him to, — nothing, he declared, equalled this. Martha whispered to Margie she was sure he had never been out of America. Miss Dora looked a little uncertainly round upon the repast. It was not till her seat was squarely placed, and a plate set before her, with her knife and fork and napkin duly arranged, that she could eat with any comfort, and allow that she enjoyed the entertainment. A gleam of delight at length came over Miss Dora's face, as she exclaimed,

5

"This does seem like dinner!" The salt was not forgotten, nor the mustard, for those who did not find spice enough in the entertainment itself. There was great talking and laughing. The children could hardly sit still with laughter, nor Amy, nor Bertha, Mr. Rothsay was so funny. Bertha sat leaning against a tree, her brown hair falling each side of her face, and an unwonted color in her cheeks. Hannah whispered to Amy,

"It would be pleasant to live so without any houses."

"That is the way the gypsies live," said Amy, and she sung a gypsy song.

"If we lived that way," said Frank, "after every meal, to save clearing up, we'd take the corners of the cloth, just so, and toss all the things into the stream."

As he suited action to the words, Miss Dora started up to prevent him from precipitating her choice household treasures into the waterfall.

"My tankard! my silver tumblers!" she exclaimed.

'The afternoon passed away quietly and quickly. Miss Dora took her seat again, and her knitting, under the hemlock, and George drew a sketch of her. Mr. Rothsay busied himself with Bessie in building a dam of stones in the water of the pool. Frank tried to make a swing for Martha and Margie in the branch of a tree. Bertha and Amy seated themselves with Miss Elspeth, and talked quietly with her by the murmuring sound of the waterfall.

Miss Dora made the first move to go. Everybody exclaimed that it was so early, and there would be a beautiful sunset, and why should they hurry away. But Miss Dora was immovable.

"There's Ralph," at last she said, "I only left milk enough for his dinner, and he'll be getting uneasy."

"Does Miss Dora keep a boy?" asked Bertha.

"No," laughed Amy, "it's her cat. We all wondered she could come without him, but I don't suppose Ralph would enjoy a picnic."

So the pretty place was left behind, all the baskets were carefully filled again, the silver counted and packed, and a supply of berries was borne away, too.

"If Mr. Jasper had been here, he could have come with us," said Amy.

"We do miss him; it's a shame he's gone away," said Frank, "but it's just like ministers to be sick all the time."

"Oh! don't say so," said Bertha, "it is so hard not to be well."

"Well, you are sick, working so much and taking care of all those boys," replied Frank; "it has done you good already to be away from them a whole day."

CHAPTER IX.

MISS ELSPETH'S TROUBLES.

THERE was still more or less talk in the village about Miss Dora and Miss Elspeth and the children. Mrs. Bunce kept up so constant a surveillance of her neighbors' affairs, that no one was left entirely in ignorance of the little commotions that took place, or what tempests rose and fell in the little teapot.

"I wish people wouldn't ask me so many questions," said Miss Elspeth one day to Amy, "for they are questions I do not like to put to myself. What am I going to do with the children when they grow up? Shall I always keep them with me? I have not answered these questions satisfactorily to myself, and I don't care to at present. It is easy enough to put people off with the answer that I have not decided, which is true. But the constant questioning is all the time renewing the subject with me, when I would rather let it rest awhile."

"What a pity it is when people don't have business enough of their own to occupy them," said Amy, "instead of going off to their neighbors. Do you have trouble with anybody but Mrs. Bunce?"

" Oh yes, only the other day Mrs. and Miss Paxton called. Both Margie and Martha were sitting in the room, and Mrs. Paxton expressed her fear that I should find trouble since the children all grew up together so, in keeping them in their places when they should be older."

" Dear me ! " said Amy, " Eleonora Paxton always looks to me as if she were afraid of tumbling out of her ' place.' I don't think I should like to live so high, on so narrow a point, that I can't move my chair back without tipping over ! "

" I have always felt," said Miss Elspeth, " as if Martha and Margie were my own children. When their mother died she left them to me, and I meant from that moment, whenever I could make an opportunity, to take them home for my own. And I hope to live long enough to bring them up as my own, to treat them as my children, and if they will stay with me, never part with them. Then when I saw Hannah, I wanted to take her from her sad position. I thought I might teach her to be a good servant, that I would teach her to be useful, so that she might one day be independent. But if this position proved too low for her, I would never think of keeping her down in it. I must do by them as I best can. God giveth the increase ! "

" Oh, Miss Elspeth," said Amy with tears in her eyes, " I am sure you will have help."

" Bessie is my greatest care," continued Miss Elspeth, " I fear for her more than the others ; she

is so pretty, I am afraid her beauty may lift her up
from whatever position she -stands in, even if she
is fitted for no other."

"Oh, Bessie is such a flower," said Amy, "now
she has light and air enough, surely she must grow
up pure and healthful."

In the evenings of autumn, Hannah often begged
leave to go out to walk. Miss Elspeth was pleased
to have her suggest going beyond the bounds of
the garden sometimes, she had usually been so close
to her duties. After awhile Hannah picked up a
new friend with whom she walked up and down the
street till quite late in the evening. This was
Janet, a girl who lived at Mrs. Paxton's. Miss
Elspeth was disturbed at the discovery of this new
friendship. She did not like Janet's appearance.
She had a bold look, and was very forward in her
manners, yet she hesitated to check Hannah, who
had never been in the habit of displaying an attachment to any one.

One cold evening late in the autumn, Miss Dora
came to Miss Elspeth. "Has anybody put away
my bonnet and mantle? I left them in the dining-
room till after tea, because I am going to walk in
and see how old Mr. Rothsay is to-night; my gloves
are there, but my velvet mantle and my scarf and
bonnet are gone." Now nobody ever ventured to
put away anything of Miss Dora's, for she was the
one who cleared away what other people left about.
She never liked to see any clutter, as she called it,

on the tables and chairs. She would not have her
parlor look like the Paxtons' drawing-rooms for the
world. At the Paxtons there was the centre-table
in the corner of the room, and so many tables she
couldn't find the middle of the room; the chairs
where anybody would run against them who came
in, and the room so dark, she couldn't see whether
she was walking over a footstool or the piano which
took up half one side of the room. Then, when she
did see the tables, they were all covered up with
crockery and gimcracks. The first day she went
there she supposed they had just been having the
house cleaned, and had laid out on the tables whatever belonged on the closet shelves.

No such display of bijouterie was found on Miss
Dora's tables. No luckless cape-bonnet found a
resting-place in any hall chair. She not only gave
out her law that everything should have its place,
and should be kept in its place, but she was on the
spot herself to execute her own law if it should be
neglected. So baskets, and books, and dolls, all
that the children played with, returned to their
stated shelves or cupboards, when their time was
over. The dolls went in and out so often, they
might almost know their own way. Three books
only kept their places on Miss Dora's table; the
rest could be found in the dining-room bookcase
unless they were actually in the hands of some
reader.

But Miss Dora seldom went out, and the making

a visit was so unusual an event that it required an hour or two's preparation. The velvet mantle was neatly folded and laid on a chair, the bonnet placed upon that, with the camel's-hair scarf, and the gloves rested on the crown of the bonnet, all ready for Miss Dora when the time came for her to go. So her dismay was great and not unfounded, when she discovered these were all missing. "Is it possible Hannah can have taken them?" she asked whisperingly of Miss Elspeth.

"No indeed," exclaimed Miss Elspeth, " perhaps you did not take them. out, perhaps ——" all Miss Elspeth's conjectures were unnatural, and Miss Dora's room and every known place was searched in vain for her missing property. At last Bessie, who was putting herself to bed with the other children, was questioned on the subject, and confessed that she had seen Hannah walking away with Miss Dora's things on, but that Hannah had told her she must not say anything about it, because she should be home before Miss Dora would want them. Miss Dora's indignation for awhile was beyond words. She walked down stairs again, opened all the doors and windows, leaning out her head to search for the missing Hannah. She walked down to the garden gate and returned, then went into the kitchen and put out the fire there. There was a biscuit left upon the stove, that Hannah had not eaten for her tea, but had apparently saved for a later meal. This Miss Dora put back into the closet, and the

lamp left burning in the kitchen she extinguished and
set aside. "I'm not going to keep a fire for her to
sit up by," she said as she came back, "she may
find her way to bed in the dark. I hope it will
teach her something this bitter cold night." Then
she began to pour out her words in anger. She
detailed all the faults Hannah had committed from
that very first day she saw her in Boston. She
went over the unwearied pains she had taken to
reform her. "My camel's-hair scarf!" she exclaimed. "Mrs. Paxton was right when she said
those emigrants did not know any bounds to their
insolent ways. And to be seen in them, going up
and down the street with that Janet! She had
better not see me to-night!" The garden gate was
heard to close just as the storm had reached its
climax. Miss Elspeth retired from the contest.
She believed it was hopeless to quell it, and Hannah
had indeed done very wrongly. But she need not
have feared. There was a sudden calm after this
great tempest. Miss Dora met Hannah at the
door. "You may lay those things in the dining-
room," she said; "it's awful cold to-night, and
there's no fire in the kitchen. Go into the parlor and
warm your feet. And if you want anything to eat,
take the candle there, and look in the closet; the
kitchen lamp is out." And Miss Dora said no more
upon the subject. This was often her way. Her
anger expended itself upon the bystanders who
were at hand at the moment of the offence, and
there was nothing left to pour out upon the offend-

er. But Miss Elspeth was grieved at this and with other many disobediences of Hannah, and she was the more pained because she believed she could trace the evil influence of Janet on many occasions. Whenever Miss Elspeth reproved her, Hannah looked very stubborn. She listened as if she were not hearing. Miss Elspeth told her at last she did not wish her to walk with Janet any more; that she could not consider her a good friend to her. Hannah spoke then with an indifferent tone and manner, "You have taken me away from the rest, and now you may as well take me away from her. I'll be shut up in your house with all of you, and not speak to any of them. But I don't do it to please you, but because I choose. And I will go away if I choose. No one can prevent me." "Somebody else has taught you such language," said Miss Elspeth; "you have not been so happy since you have made new friends. When you remember last summer, you will think so too."

Hannah did think about it, and perhaps agreed with Miss Elspeth. She kept for awhile at home more closely, going only where she was sent, and never stopping to talk with Janet. But she did not do this willingly. She showed ill-temper towards the children, and went through her duties stubbornly. Miss Elspeth was discouraged about her, and hoped for some change in the winter, when she meant to send her to school, where she thought Hannah might find companions with whom she could be trusted.

CHAPTER X.

THE CIRCUS.

FRANK and Amy came one day to take the children to a circus there was in town.

"Shall we really go into the big tent?" asked Margie; "I was a little afraid of it the other day; I thought there must be soldiers in it."

"Pooh! soldiers," said Bessie; "no, there are nothing but horses. Steevie went to one once,— oh! a great many times, and he told me all about it. The horses know as much as the men."

"Oh! they could not know as much as men," said Martha; "a horse never talks."

"Well, I don't know about his talking, but one of the horses ate bread and butter, and Steevie said there was a little girl about as big as me, dressed all in silver."

"Come, come," interrupted Miss Dora, "what's all this talking? The dinner things must all be put away. Hannah's going to the circus, and you don't mean she shall do all the work. I see your heads are half turned now, and I am sure they will be wholly after you come home."

Margie slowly put her chair against the side of the room, and then came to Amy to whisper,

"I don't want to go to the circus if it will turn my head round, I'm afraid of it."

Amy laughed, and encouraged Margie. "Oh, we are only going to see the horses ride. You will like to see how prettily they look, and we shall sit on benches to look at them, and they will not come near us."

"And shall we see the horse eat bread and butter?" asked Margie.

"We shall see something very funny, that will make you laugh," said Amy, "and you shall sit between me and Frank. We will take good care of you."

"We shall see the clown," said Hannah, who looked more radiant than she had done for a long time.

On the way, she walked by Amy, and said, "I am very glad we are going to the circus. Janet told me she had looked in between the curtains of the tents. She stood there all the afternoon. I had much rather go inside."

"How came you to see Janet? I thought you did not talk to her now," asked Amy.

"She comes sometimes to see me at the garden gate, and then I can't help talking to her; and I don't want to help it now. She told me she had seen a boy inside the tent carrying round oranges, and she thinks it was Steevie, and three after-

noons she has been to try to look and see if it is
he, but she don't know yet. Once I asked Miss
Elspeth if I might go too, but she would not
let me."

"O Hannah, why' didn't you tell her your reason?" said Amy; "anybody else could find out for
you better than Janet. Frank or my father would
have inquired for you. What made you think this
boy may be Steevie?"

"Janet described him to me. This boy belongs
to the circus, and sells oranges there, and Janet
heard him say he would one day be a rider, and
that is what Steevie always wanted to be," said
Hannah.

"And is this all that makes you think it may be
Steevie?" asked Amy.

"Oh! he must be somewhere, Miss Amy," said
Hannah, "and I must see him somehow."

As they approached the entrance of the circus,
Amy whispered to George what Hannah had said
and wanted. They made their way in through a
crowd, and seated themselves on one of the hard,
wooden seats. They had not been long seated,
when the cry was heard of, "Oranges! fresh
oranges!"

Hannah half rose up, and presently there made
his way along an ill-dressed boy, with yellow hair,
and an air of great business talent. George beckoned to him, but Hannah pulled Amy's sleeve.

"Oh! it isn't Steevie, that is not like Steevie," she exclaimed.

George asked him some questions.

"I'm attached to the establishment, sir," he answered; "I've taken out a patent right for the trade, and you can't get 'em cheaper. Six for ninepence," and so forth.

"But don't you have anybody to help you?" asked George, as he treated the children, who had been looking at them with longing eyes, to oranges.

"There's a feller has got lozengers down there," said the boy, pocketing his money; "there isn't another in the establishment.

"Send along the lozenge boy," said George, "we'll have some lozenges too."

The lozenge boy proved a little fellow, hardly higher than the benches, and Hannah turned her head away from him in despair. "Oh! Janet did not tell the truth. I believed her, Miss Amy," she said; "she told me just what he wore, and how dark was his hair, and his way, she told me, was just like Steevie's."

"But how could she know?" asked Amy; "she had never seen him."

"Oh, I had talked so much about him. I told her just how he looked," answered Hannah, "and she thought she must have met him once. But she was not telling me right. It wasn't the truth she was telling me. She wanted to get me away,

and make me come to the circus without Miss
Elspeth's leave, and she would like to have me
never go back there."

"But why would she like to take you away
from Miss Elspeth?" asked Amy.

"Oh, she wants to join the circus too, and says
they could teach us anything; and I thought if
Steevie was here — " Hannah paused a little.

"You did not think of leaving Miss Elspeth,
and coming here!" exclaimed Amy.

But the performances were beginning, and the
attention of the children was quite taken up with
the wonders that took place. The little ponies
were their great joy, and the way they breakfasted
at the table; and they laughed at the jokes of the
clown, though they did not understand what they
meant, but he made up such a funny face that
they could not help laughing if they had tried not
to. And there was children's laughter sounding
all about, so that the elders could not help laughing, too, even if they thought the whole thing
very silly and not worth looking at. And then
there were beautiful ladies, that must be either
queens or fairies, though Martha thought neither
queens nor fairies rode on horseback. But their
dresses shone and glittered so that Bessie believed
they might have bought them of the fairies. Bessie thought it must be very easy to jump through
a ring down upon the horse's back again, and
asked Frank if he did not think he could do it
any day.

But they were all the most enchanted with the little girl that came on with such rosy cheeks and blue muslin dress, with real roses all over it, or something that looked like real roses. Hannah fixed her eyes upon her. The little girl, she thought, looked more like a queen than all the ladies had done. She gave out her commands with a smiling royal air, and said what she would have as if she knew she would be obeyed. She looked so happy, too, and kept time with the music in all her motions.

Going home, they all agreed the little girl was the best part of the performance, — all but Margie, who would like to have the little ponies. Hannah was so taken up with her pleasure that she seemed to have forgotten for awhile her disappointment. When they reached the gate, Amy said to Hannah, "It is not too cold for me to talk a little while at the gate with you after supper, and the children have gone to bed."

"In quick to your supper, and then to bed," was Miss Dora's greeting to the children, "and don't let's have any talking. You have had enough of that!"

"Are my eyes looking at my heels?" asked Margie of Miss Elspeth. "Frank put me into the gate, and said if I did not run quick I should see them."

"Oh, Frank was only laughing," said Miss Elspeth, as she gave the children their bread and milk.

"He thought our heads would be turned," said Martha, "but mine isn't."

Bessie began to tell Miss Elspeth all about what she had seen, and Margie interrupted with her exclamations, and Martha began at the beginning, to tell how everything was, and exactly what happened.

But they were tired enough to be quiet, at last, and willing to go to bed. Miss Dora put on her mantle to go over and talk with Mrs. Bunce, and tell her where the children had been, and agree with her that she did not think it was the place for children to go to, and that it only made them wild and unmanageable the next day.

Miss Elspeth was walking up and down in the garden in the fading light, walking quickly to keep warm in the cool air of the approaching night. Amy came to the garden gate, but she did not find Hannah there, and went on to the house. She found Hannah had just lighted the candles in the parlor, and had placed them in front of the mirror, and was looking at herself in the glass. She turned round as Amy came in, and said presently, "It would not do. All the roses, and gold, and muslin dresses, would not make me beautiful. I did not think of that before. How different I am from that child! Oh, look in the glass, Miss Amy."

Amy looked, and saw there, indeed, Hannah's worn face and tired-looking eyes. She had not gained the air of healthiness the other children wore. She never had the freshness of childhood. There was the same wistful glance that had first

6

appealed to Miss Elspeth, and the same drooping
figure. "Miss Elspeth will have to nurse you, to
make you strong," said Amy. "You don't look
well, Hannah. I have thought of it before."

"It's the beautiful face I am thinking of," said
Hannah, "that never was mine and never will be.
Oh, Miss Amy, I would like to be like that child,
so beautiful and happy."

"Don't you know, Hannah," said Amy, "that the
roses were not real she wore, and what seemed like
gold was not gold. Her beauty, I think, was not
more real, Hannah, or her happiness. Perhaps
they paint her cheeks to make them look rosy
and healthy, and they teach her to laugh to make
her look happy. Oh, think, Hannah, how hard it
must be to have to laugh for one's work, to have to
dance when you feel tired, and to smile when you
feel sick and weary. And every afternoon this
poor child must come in and look the same, and
appear as happy, and all to earn bread, and something to live upon."

"It does not seem like work," said Hannah, as
she listened intently.

"If you could see the child, she would tell you
it must be," said Amy. "Perhaps they treat her
kindly, but even if they do, she must every day go.
through this same work, whether she chooses or
not. She is bound as closely as any one you know,
and has to work as hard."

CHAPTER XI.

ONE YEAR GONE.

THE winter, with its regular hours of school, had a beneficial effect upon Hannah. When the spring came, and she had been a whole year with Miss Elspeth, she showed a decided improvement in all her appearance, and though she was never joyous, wore a contented and happy air.

Miss Elspeth looked back upon the year's experiment, for she could scarcely look upon the year as otherwise than an experiment, and had reason to be deeply satisfied. It had been a year of great labor and responsibility to her. Miss Dora was no help in encouraging her here. When anything went wrong, Miss Dora would constantly speak of it as Elspeth's enterprise, and openly reproach her for the additional trouble her romantic plans had brought into their quiet household. But for all the days of Hannah's faithful service, for the entertainment that, in spite of herself, the children afforded her, for the gayer, more cheerful life that had taken the place of their former monotonous existence; for all this, Miss Dora never thought of bringing thanks to Miss Elspeth. And her influence was not very favorable for the children. They had soon discovered how much Miss Dora's scolding meant, and they found her much more indulgent to their desires, however unreasonable, than Miss Elspeth.

"Miss Dora talks so all day," Bessie would say, "that I don't mind whether she's talking at me or the door-post. And then I run off, and Hannah or somebody else stops to listen."

Miss Dora would rather say, "yes, yes," to any of their requests, than take the trouble to see if it were best to grant it. "Take it, and go, only don't stop here to tease;" was the answer usually expected by the trembling claimant. Miss Elspeth was more conscientious, and weighed, too closely perhaps, every little question,—whether it would be best for Bessie, to grant her this, or whether Margie should be encouraged to do that. But, in spite of doubt and speculation, time went on and the little household affairs, and the children gathered up here and there much good and very little ill.

- In the spring, George Arnold was to go away, all the way to China. There had been great doubt what his father would do with him. He had been kept at school the longer, because his father could not decide the question. He wanted to make his son a merchant, and George had other tastes, and preferred college, or to be educated as a scientific man. But now it was decided he was to make a voyage to China, before anything else was determined, and George was ready enough to go.

Hannah had been sent to the station on an errand. She met Amy there, who had gone to bid George good-bye. Frank was to accompany him into town, to see him on board of his vessel. They were standing on the platform —

"I shall bring home a whole portfolio of sketches, Amy," said George, as they waited, "and shall make such paintings of the storms at sea, that your hair will stand on end. I don't mean to give up my drawing and painting, whatever else I may do."

Amy tried to speak cheerfully, "You'll make your fortune, and then come home and settle down into an artist."

"I shall have to make my fortune in a year, then," said George, "for I mean to come home in a year at any rate. And if I am to be an artist, it is time I began. Oh, Amy, I see it now. It is all folly, all this time is wasted. These last few years I ought to have been doing something. Oh, why couldn't my father have let me follow out my tastes! Last week when he proposed to me to go, I thought I might go for the sake of the voyage and the experience, but it is only using up another precious year of my life. It won't make me a merchant, it will only unmake me what I am. Why did he not throw away my pencils when I was five years old, and shut me up in an office, if he wanted to stifle me there? One more year lost, Amy!

An artist, Amy! At my age an artist ought to be
an artist, but what am I?"

The whistle of the steam engine was heard sig-
nalling its approach. "Oh, it is not too late now,
George," Amy said earnestly. "You will see your
father in town. Don't go, to throw away your life!
Only speak to him, as you can speak, and I am sure
he will listen to you!"

Frank's foot was on the step of the car. He
turned back for George. George looked into Amy's
face. "If I lose my life, Amy, you know I am to
come to you to find it again."

The train had gone, and Amy turned to find
Hannah by her side, waiting to walk home with her.
Amy had meant to take the winding path home
through the woods. She wanted a little quiet time
to think. She wanted to ask how it was everything
must go so wrong for George, and whether she
might have done anything to make it different.
She had so great an influence over George, and
what had she done with it? That last shrill sound
of the steam-whistle, as he was carried away, was
ringing still in her ears, and she wanted the gentle,
soothing sounds of the whispering leaves in the
pine woods.

There was left a great vacant space around her,
now that he was gone for a whole year. She
wanted to go and lean against the shaded rock that
the pine tassels covered, and hide her face in her
hands, and think. Presently, she must go home to

work, but now she needed a few moments' solitude, a few words with herself, to reproach herself that she could not have found better words at parting, that she had not been a better friend before the parting came. She had thought it very strange George had consented so willingly to go away, without having made any appeal to his father that he might stay. The old talk of his devoting him-self to his art, of going to Europe to give himself up to study of the old masters and the new, all this had been lately forgotten or set aside. Those last words of George were very true. The last years of his life had been, as it were, wasted. He had devoted himself neither to his art nor to study of any sort. He had dreamed them, happily enough, away. Neither Amy nor he were conscious that it had been an aimless life. Sometime or other he had meant to speak to his father about his wishes, and urge him to give up this cherished plan of making a merchant of him, but the decisive moment had never come. Mr. Arnold had moved to New York from Boston, a few years before, and had left his son at school there. George only saw his father in his vacations, and not much of him then, for his vacations were frequently spent in travel-ling and wandering among the mountains. He had always supposed that, sometime or other, he should be able to show his father that he was able to do something superior to plodding on in the common ways. Amy believed this too. She thought

every year that George would find some way to
show the real talent and genius that he possessed.
But the days passed on without any change, until
Mr. Arnold made the sudden proposal that George
should go to Canton. And George, attracted by
the idea of the voyage, thinking it was only for a
year he was to be gone, agreed directly to the proposal. Amy had wondered, and had been a. little
disappointed, that he had so easily acceded. It
seemed like directly consenting to his father's plans,
without coming to any explanation with him. It
was like promising himself to him for the years
that should follow. But in the hurry of departure,
for George did not have time even to go on to New
York to bid his mother·good-bye, in the bustle of
preparation, Amy could have no serious talk with
him. The very evening before he left, some friends
came out of town to bid him good-bye, and she had
no chance to speak with him. She brought herself
to think that George was deciding that his duty
led him to follow his father's will, and that he
meant to make a sacrifice of his tastes. She was
willing to admire him for this; she only wished his
father might know how great this sacrifice was;
she only hoped it was right George should lay
aside all his high ambitions, and throw away, as it
were, the great gifts he possessed.

But these ideas of duty had not risen up in
George's mind. He had yielded to the proposal of
the moment, as all through his life he had yielded

to circumstances. Yet as they walked silently
through the wood-path to the station, the quiet
nooks that opened themselves on each side, the
broad-spreading trees that hung above rocky seats
brought back the remembrance of the old enthusiastic talks they had all had, when they used to go·
and pass long mornings there. Such great imagi·
nations as they had formed there ! George was to
go sometime to the old world, and study the inspiration of all its old stories and works of wonder,
and then he was to come back into these very woods,
bringing home a fresh love for the tall old trees,
and the new life that sprung up every year beneath
them, and then he was to show what the artist of
the new world·could be ! . All these promises and
aspirations came back suddenly and reproachfully
now. At the last moments of parting, came the
sudden thought that this was the decisive act that
was to cut him off from these old dreams, that he
was to leave them behind as dreams, and promise
himself to that other life of activity that he had
never fitted himself for.

Just one moment can suddenly reveal hidden
feelings ! Those last words had awakened Amy.
They showed her, what she had not told herself before, that she was bound to George, all her heart,
her whole soul. They showed her at the same
time that he needed her. Not in this moment did
she confess to herself that she was any way stronger
than he, nor ever would she feel this ! She believed

he was so much above her in his genius and his talent, she had always looked upon him with such admiration, had loved his great thoughts and enthusiastic hopes, that she did not see, and she never saw, that she was greater than he in her steadfastness, and that he must depend on her for his faith. Only she saw now that he did depend on her, and that she was truly to " find his life " for him. But he had gone away for a whole year, and she felt as if she were standing quite alone in a broad desert place.

She turned away, as her eyes came back along the two black lines of the railway to the station, already quiet and empty again. The noise and the rush of the cars were over, and the whistling and panting of the engine. There was an empty space in front of Amy where the cars had stood, and black cinders were scattered in among the little spires of grass that tried to grow between the rails. The sound of hurrying wheels had died away from the station. Hannah stood by Amy, and asked,

"Are you going home now? I have been to get the eggs. This pretty little basket is Miss Elspeth's egg-basket," she added, as she thought Amy looked at her inquiringly. Amy recovered herself, and walked down into the road with her as Hannah began to talk.

" Did you remember, Miss Amy, it's just a year yesterday since we all came here? Miss Dora made a cake in honor of it, and we would have brought you in a piece last night, but Miss Elspeth thought you would be busy about Mr. George's going away. I thought a year would be so very long. Do you remember, Miss Amy, you told me one year wouldn't be so very long, and that five years would soon be over?"

"Did I tell you one year would not be very long?" asked Amy, dreamily.

"Yes, and I have remembered a great deal you told me," said Hannah. "That night after the circus, when I felt so bad, — oh, you don't know how wicked!—you spoke to me about work; and another time you told me how everybody needed to work, and how it made everybody happier. It sounds better than it used to, but I don't get accustomed to it yet. Wouldn't you truly, Miss Amy, like to change places with Miss Paxton?"

"Change places with Miss Paxton!" exclaimed Amy, rousing herself.

"I do believe she lies on the sofa or sits in her chair all the day long," said Hannah; "and then she looks so handsomely, and all the day long has nothing to do."

"Nothing to do, indeed, Hannah," said Amy; "when I was there a few evenings ago, she looked to me so tired, she was leaning back in her chair so languidly, that I fancied she must have been riding on horseback, or tiring herself some way, and I asked her; but she said she had not even walked out. She had been so interested in a book she had, that she did not lay it down all the morning, and she was so sorry she had finished it, she had nothing left to do. What made her so tired, was nothing to do. O Hannah, I would rather suffer a great deal than be Miss Paxton!"

"And once you said that working for other people would make me happy," said Hannah; "you wanted me to work for Bessie, for Miss Elspeth."

When they reached the garden gate, Amy said, "That is true, Hannah; caring for others, and working for them, must be our only happiness."

"And will that make the years go by?" asked Hannah.

"We must not be willing they should go by any other way," said Amy, "whether they go slow or fast."

Amy walked directly home, and wondered if she must look back to her own words for consolation now. She wanted consolation, though she felt she had just gained a very great happiness. It was a happiness that came attended by a great care. She must have faith in the future, and was to nourish it by a cheerful life in the little details that to-day and to-morrow must bring.

Evening came, and Frank came out to say that George had sailed, and he only wished he could be going too, it was such a famous vessel and such a fine long voyage.

CHAPTER XII.

CHANGE AND NO CHANGE.

HANNAH's five years did pass away. They brought little change on the outer face of Langdale. The elm-trees rose a little higher into the heavens, and the maples had spread themselves more widely. The vine had grown thick over Miss Dora's porch, and the green moss had spread on the roof of Mrs. Bunce's house. The shrubbery was darker and closer round the Paxtons', and the border of box in the garden stood higher and stiffer, and no flowers ventured to grow in the midst of its shade. There was very little change here in the midst of the village. Further up the street, Mr. Fay's grounds had been cut up into separate building lots, and where his wide lawn lay, were as many as seven cottages of a pretty pattern,-but all exactly alike, and the grand old elm that stood in the corner had been cut down to make way for some stores, and in that part of the town there was a great air of business and life.

Within the houses, the change had been for the

most part slow and gradual. Eleonora Paxton had been married, and had gone to Europe with her husband, but her departure had left no great chasm for those outside of the Paxtons' house. Mr. Strange, in his visits to Langdale, and at the time of his marriage to Eleonora, had created a little excitement in the village. He was handsome, quite handsome enough for Eleonora. Some people thought him stiff, some elegant, in his manners. Amy thought he had very little to say for himself, or for anybody else. Though she did not say so, she felt he was very well fitted for Eleonora. If either had shown any warm, expressive feelings, they would have been checked by the icy chilliness of the other. She fancied them two stately icebergs, and wondered if they would ever be moved into the current of a warmer sea.

There was change at the Rothsays. The old grandfather had died, Mr. Rothsay had been unfortunate in business, and had been growing poorer and poorer, and the walks around the house showed the need of attention and care. There was still a home at the Rothsays for all the homeless. Besides the aunt who was so great an invalid, a widowed sister of Mr. Rothsay, Mrs. Campbell, with her two girls and her boy, came to live there. And Mrs. Rothsay herself had been very ill, and had never recovered her strength from the long fever she had. But Amy was still joyous and lovely, and one would say she looked as young as when she first welcomed Miss Elspeth to Langdale. Perhaps her gayety might be called cheerfulness, but it was as flowing and ready as when she was sixteen. She greeted her father joyously when he came out from town weary at night; she had a happy sympathy for Frank when he came home Saturdays from Cambridge. She was busy always, everywhere, and at home. She did her best to weed the borders in the large old garden that missed the daily care of a gardener. She raked away the leaves from the avenue to the door in autumn, and trained the vines round the piazza in summer. While within the house there were many duties. She was the favorite of the little cousins whom she cared for, and taught, too, and the watchful nurse of her mother and the invalid aunt. She did not neglect Miss Elspeth and her household in the many cares of her own. She was still Miss Elspeth's confidant, and adviser even, and the friend of the children.

With the children there was no marked change. Bessie was scarcely more sober or quiet. Her thick brown curls and fresh color, and her warm, loving eyes, made her still the beauty of the household, and helped to make her the pet. Martha was still very wise and good, and still kept Bessie's overflowing spirits in check. Margie's eyes were large and dreamy still. She loved to read all the books that she could find, and, even those the other children considered the dullest, she

lingered over, making of them, with her imagination, something very entrancing.

And Hannah's five years had passed away.
They had added a little to her height, and she had
grown more robust, and was more healthy in her
appearance. But in her face was still the old
expression, that eager, wistful questioning, as if
there were something within her still unsatisfied.
She had never shown, the last four years, any
uneasiness or desire to go away from Miss Elspeth,
and she had displayed more personal attachment
for both Miss Dora and Miss Elspeth as the time
passed on. But there still lingered this uncertain
expression in her face which the first ten years of
a wandering life had marked there, and that so
many days of monotonous duty had not been able
to drive away.

Miss Elspeth had talked with Hannah about her
plans after her five years should be over. Hannah
had been to school every winter, and had lessons
with Amy in the summer, but she had never shown
any particular aptitude or fondness for study.
Martha, and even Margie, were far beyond her in
many of their school acquirements. Under Miss
Elspeth's care, she had learned to sew excellently,
and, thanks to Miss Dora's surveillance, she was
very neat and methodical about all household
duties.

What should Miss Elspeth do with her ? Martha
was old enough now to take Hannah's place in the

house, in some measure, and Hannah ought, for her
own sake, to be earning some wages. This Miss
Elspeth told Hannah, and Hannah listened silently.
After a day or two, she spoke with Miss Elspeth.
" I will do what you please, Miss Elspeth," she
said ; " I had thought when the five years were
over, I would go somewhere very far away. I
believed that in five years I should be very different, somehow, with power to do what I pleased. I
thought I could .go away, and take care of myself.
But I will not go quite yet. I should like to earn
some money. I should like to have something of
my own. I am willing to work for it, if you will
tell me how."

The question was still further decided when
Amy heard what was under discussion. Then she
begged that Hannah might come to them for the
summer months. She had been thinking they
should want some help at home, through the summer, when they had so much company, and especially now, because Katy the cook was not well
and strong. " I'd work for you without wages,
you know," said Hannah to Amy. But Amy
laughed, and told Hannah she was quite too valuable for that. And very valuable Hannah's ser-
vices were. Miss Dora's training had fitted her
for many kinds of household experience. She was
to stay with the Rothsays through the summer
months, and then she was to go to the Carltons.
Hannah was quite in demand in Langdale.

7

One day she was dusting the parlor at the Roth says, tenderly, as was her wont. Here, on the tables and the mantelpiece, were many treasures of Amy's. Hannah had observed how carefully Amy treated these, and she felt very proud when she was allowed to take care of the parlor. Mrs. Rothsay complained sometimes that Hannah lingered too long over this part of her labors, but she was touched with the reverent feeling Hannah seemed to entertain for everything in the room.

Hannah was passing her duster carefully around the frame of a little picture as Amy came into the room with fresh flowers.

"It seems many years, Miss Amy," she said, "since Mr. George drew this picture. There's Miss Dora with her knitting under the hemlock. She looks as though she were sitting there now. And those pine cones in the frame! I remember when Mr. Frank brought them home as if it were only yesterday! Who would ever have thought Mr. George would stay away so long?"

"We could not have believed it when he went away," said Amy.

"And will he come home next spring?" asked Hannah.

"So we think; so we hope," answered Amy.

"I could not quite think your letter that came the other day told you Mr. George was coming home," said Hannah, "Miss Amy, you have been so still ever since, and quiet; you have not been round the house singing as you always do. I couldn't help thinking about you that something was the matter, that you did not seem like yourself."

"Sometimes," said Amy, "it makes one very quiet to be very happy. And to look forward to next spring, seems to me now almost as long as to look forward a year five years ago."

Amy was speaking now as if there were no one listening to her! She was standing before the picture Hannah had spoken of, and, as she looked at it, the tears came into her eyes. "I have had a great disappointment, and yet I am infinitely happy," she said. "Five years ago I wanted to be happy just one way. I was so full of hope that I was very sure I could only be happy that way. If I could have looked forward to know that all those hopes would have utterly faded, my heart would have died out within me. It was very merciful that I could see but one step before me."

"But you could not be unhappy, Miss Amy," exclaimed Hannah. "Oh, such as you ought to be happy every way. Can you talk of being happy only one way? It is such as I, that have been picked up in the streets, starving and homeless, that think of only one way to be happy, and that is shut out after all."

"You make me ashamed," said Amy, kindly. "I am afraid I have nourished a complaining heart!"

"You, Miss Amy," said Hannah, "that can smile

for everybody, and make the whole house so happy! Nobody ever saw a complaining heart in you. In Mrs. Campbell's sick-room, dark as it is, you make a light when you come in. And everybody is happy just to look at you."

"I have been cheerful, Hannah," said Amy, "because I taught myself it was my duty. I ought to have been cheerful, because I have had so much given me to enjoy. But look, how we are forgetting our work. We will open the piano, and let us set this vase of flowers just above the open keys, and we will let in just a gleam of light through the window here. And this little table, with its dish of gay flowers, shall stand by the easy-chair! How inviting it looks! Any one who came into such a pleasant parlor would want to stay. The room looks as if we had been happy in it! We must make that same air linger in it still. It will give us pleasure, just as a perfume brings back happy remembrances. But we must go to work, and when we get through, Hannah, we will sit on the piazza, with our sewing, till the children come home from the woods, and I will tell you what has been troubling me the last five years."

It was strange, perhaps, that Amy should choose Hannah as the one to whom she could tell all that she had scarcely whispered to herself. It was a kindly feeling that led her to do so, but she did not know herself how great was its influence. She did not know how much strength it gives to forlorn

and lonely hearts to be called upon to give strength
to others, to feel that their sympathy is esteemed
precious, or worthy to be asked for by one other.
Many persons would have been satisfied with giving Hannah her wages and her daily food, with
seeing that she was clothed well, and did not work
too hard. Amy instinctively saw that she needed,
besides, the fresh sympathy of some one near her
own age, that she felt herself alone without the
support of any special class of friends even, and
Amy was not afraid to give her the sympathy and
confidence of her own heart.

CHAPTER XIII.

DISAPPOINTMENT.

GEORGE had made the voyage to Canton, had stayed there the appointed year ; then had made his way to Calcutta ; then, quite to the surprise of his father and Amy, letters came from him from Egypt. From there he had gone to Constantinople and Greece.

" You cannot think how fascinating this travelling is," he wrote to Amy. " I begin at the East, where the world's civilization began, and am coming on towards its highest point. When I was in Egypt, studying its hieroglyphics, I can imagine myself living in the time of the Pyramids. In Athens, I find myself far advanced, and am again in the days when the grace of form was worshipped. I can dream here for hours and days, in the land where once dreams were life. This is the world for an artist, Amy, and you cannot think how I shudder at the activity of our New World, that hurries the life of ages into single days. Americans ought to live in some of the quicker worlds, in Mercury, for instance, where the works must be hurried up into such short days ; for me, my heaven will be in one of the slower planets, where the days and the years are long enough to let me remember I am living. I like to watch the slow growth of the rosebud, and am willing to throw away the full-blown rose." At last George reached Italy.

His letters were filled with sketches of the groups by the wayside of the Italian women, the peasants, the shrines of the Madonna, with kneeling figures before them. And it was not merely descriptions of what he saw, of the sky and the mountain ridges, the flowers, broad plains, or the pictures, storied buildings, and old cities, which he sent to Amy. George poured out to her too, all his newly awakened ideas of art and its great power. He no longer contented himself with theories of his own, but told of old schools with new enthusiasm as he was in turn influenced by them.

And these especially rejoiced Amy. Now she recognized the earnestness that used to inspire George in the old times, and that these last few years he had been forgetting.

She hoped all this old fervor for Art was coming back. She was glad to have him in Italy, to have him awakened and roused by the great works round him. She believed it would stir his spirit, so that he would insist upon giving up all lower aims, and devote himself to Art alone. Then he would come home and " do something." himself. She believed no other life could be happy for him. She believed no other life was right for him while he possessed such high inspirations, and might accomplish such great works.

How gladly she would be his companion then! She could relieve him of all the little cares of life, and work for him in its trifling details, while he was working in its higher fields. At least she could admire with him what was high and noble, if she could not labor with him there. She could be his companion in his hours of rest, even if she could not be with him in his higher hours of study. She busied herself in thinking how she could make it easy for him to make great and noble efforts while she was struggling with the lesser duties of life.

While she was inspired with these imaginings, all her own daily occupations became glorified. She went about them all with a new zeal and devotion. Before, she had always been cheerful and ready; now, she hastened about her work as if it were a real privilege to be allowed to work. Perhaps this devotion seemed scarcely different to those around her from her usual manner, but with herself, her hopefulness gave a wonderful ease to all she did. The happy smile and the cheerful word for others came, not because she thought them their due, but out of her willing spirit that could not be otherwise than glad. The days were like clear summer days. Even the struggles and the labor that came with them were like the easy growth of plants beneath the warm. sunshine and fed by the moist earth.

It was in the midst of these happy dreamings, giving fresh activity to her daily life, that Mr. Arnold, George's father, came to Langdale. He told Amy that he wanted to speak to her alone, and they walked out through the garden path quite into the woods where he talked to Amy about George. He said to her that George had been wasting the few last years of his life. He had no objection to George's travelling for the purpose of travelling, though he should have hesitated to grant his request for a few years' travel, if George had made such before he went away. But George's connection with business had been for a long time merely nominal. He thought such a pretended occupation was worse than doing nothing. George was no longer a boy, and it was time for him to have fitted himself for some business in life. He wrote George so, a year or two ago, when he was lounging away his time in the East Indies. He was not doing much better now, and two more years had passed away. Mr. Arnold said he knew how great was Amy's influence with George. He was very proud of it, it was his greatest hope with regard to George, and he wanted to urge her to use it to compel him to give up the aimless life he was leading. It was time, long ago, for George to begin to think of his own prospects, it was certainly his duty now. He went on at some length to show in what a position George might have been if he had stayed at Canton and made a proper use of his ad-

vantages, and fortunately it was not too late now
for him to go back to his friends there, who would
gladly help him if he would show any interest in
business, and devote himself to their affairs.

Amy listened to Mr. Arnold in the same quiet
wood where so many times she had heard George
tell over his plans for life, and paint his glorious
ambitions. As she stood there, she felt as young
as she did then, though that time was so many
years ago. She had the same warm hopes and
buoyant energy, but she saw suddenly that the
time for hoping and dreaming had passed away.
There was no longer time to say, " We will do so
in the future, or build gay castles to-morrow," —
the journey was no longer to be talked over and
planned, but already it should be begun, for the
day was far risen, and the traveller should be up
and on his way.

The old oak, whose leaves were gently swaying
in the wind, had heard all the talk of youthful
enthusiasm, and now was waiting to see the fruit
of such great plans and purposes. Amy looked
round wistfully, She wished that George himself
might appear to vindicate himself, to show at once
that these years of waiting had only been preparing him for greater duties than these that his
father would lay out for him. Since she had not
George's voice to aid her, she took up his cause
herself. She spoke of how much Italy was doing
for George now; of his letters to her that had

shown he had been awakened and roused by the sight of works of genius. She told what she hoped for George; how much such minds were needed in America; how much he might do for his native country. She spoke of his genius, and pleaded that such natures as his needed a longer time for ripening, and a different treatment from others.

"If he will only be an artist," said Mr. Arnold, "I shall be more than content. But do you not see by his letters that he is dreaming away his life, just as he did in America? I can't make out that he has touched pencil or canvas since he left home."

"But such letters as he writes!" pleaded Amy; "they show how he observes everything."

"Yes, I had some long letters from him about Egypt," said Mr. Arnold, "and I carried them to Mr. Percy, a great student in such things, and talked to him about publishing them, but he says it has all been written before, and I know very well George wouldn't have the industry to apply himself to give one lecture on the Pyramids. All his observation is of no use to him. Don't you see, he is merely amusing himself, while the rest of us are working?"

Mr. Arnold wanted her to urge a new proposal of his to George, to go directly back to Canton. Amy promised to present to him his father's wishes, and agreed that he ought to come to some decision; but she confessed that she should herself wish to urge him to give up all idea of becoming a business man, and devote himself to the life of an artist with eagerness and industry. In the end, Mr. Arnold agreed to this. He wanted George to be something, anything but an idle wanderer, and with many affectionate words to Amy, he left Langdale.

Amy wrote an earnest letter to George. She detailed her conversation with his father, and proffered carefully his plans and desires, but she showed him earnestly what were the wishes of her own heart. "But only show your father," she said, "that you have in you some of that impulse, some of the spark of the genius that you and I have loved to fancy in you. The thought of it inspires me, and I am convinced it must lift and rouse you. These last few years you have been struggling under the lead of two masters. Only determine now to follow after the one you love. I know that if only once you give yourself up to such a master, you will find happiness and success. But you must enter into his service, be willing to be trained, and to submit your life to your art. How foolish of me to be advising and counselling you! I never ventured to preach to you before. You have always been higher up than I, and have given me strength. How I should like to give you back some of that strength! Such a help as it has been to me to have one great and noble aim. It has made a joyful service out of drudgery.

"The poor little Hannah who is with us, now goes about her work every day as if there were no object but just to get it over. She must sweep the steps, must clean the knives, etc., go from one labor on to another, because it is the every-day labor. Poor child! she thinks of nothing but the work. But when I think of what I am living for, I find a special inspiration in each separate detail. It seems like arranging the flowers for a dear friend, and training the vines over the old arbor. Each trifling duty is helping to ornament the life of others,—even the caring for their daily food. I think each day, this is *my* art that I must bring to its perfection joyfully and cheerfully. It is very far down, very far below what must inspire you; nevertheless, it must be my inspiration.

"Work on a little while, only work, dear George. Send home something to show you have been laboring. However small it is, your father will be proud of it,—we shall all be proud. We shall look forward to your coming home, when you will be able to teach us. You will raise us out of our little duties, by the great works which are yours. We are all of us workers here; that won't harm us if we can only have one of the "High Art" workers among us too.

"And such words remind me of the old days under the oak-tree —"

Amy's letter had a great effect, very different from what she had imagined. She waited impatiently to hear from George, and a letter came. He was on his way back to Canton. "I am going back," he wrote, "that I may do something." "You were right Amy, in telling me to submit myself to a master. But you were wrong and I was wrong in fancying that I could follow the inspiration of a *great* master. Alas! I have not the patience nor the industry that the disciples of such a master need. I have wasted a great many years, the fault is not in my circumstances but in myself. If the true genius had been in me, long ago I should have shown it by my patient study of the art I loved. Instead of sitting and dreaming of high ideas, I should have begun to carry them out, rudely perhaps, but somehow. I have been learning this sadly, the more sadly the more I have enjoyed the inspirations of true genius. These came only to men who were willing to labor, not to those who were idly drinking in the delights of life. Your labor, Amy, that you speak of so humbly, has been high and glorious in comparison with my idle dreamings. It is the thought of that labor of yours that rouses me now into activity. I am going to work, not in the way we thought of and dreamed. No, I cannot go home a great artist. How should I dare to hope for so great a glory as that, when I have not the self-denial, nor the patience, that could devote me to so glorious a work?

" A pretty group there is below. Such a color as this sky has here, and so wonderful the atmospheric effect ! It colors up everything 'it touches !

" But then I can go home and work. If I cannot show any great works, I will show how to work. We will both of us work with an object, to make labor, and trial, and struggle grand, and full of beauty too." Then followed his plans for crossing the desert, and sketches of groups of camels being loaded, with an imaginary picture of an oasis, and himself drinking from a fountain under the trees, the fountain taking the form of the old pump in the Rothsays' yard.

This letter Amy had received some months ago. Since then she had seen Mr. Arnold again. He expressed himself pleased that George had returned to a merchant's life, and with his new determinations. He only hoped this would not prove a new freak of George's, and that he would hold on it a year at least. He expected to hear of him in Australia, next, or San Francisco. He was much obliged to Amy for her influence, and hoped George would not tire her out at last.

Amy thought it unkind that Mr. Arnold could not receive more thankfully the sacrifice that George had made. But she was not discouraged by his forebodings. She was sadly disheartened that George had been able to give up all his cherished hopes and aspirations. She feared he would repent sometime a determination he had made in a moment

of despair. If she could only have seen him, only
have known more certainly if this renunciation of
his were a willing one.

The letters that came to her afterward from
George, helped her to this certainty. They were
in a happy tone, and showed at the same time a
strength of purpose that she had not missed before,
but that gave her a new encouragement. His letters were shorter and more concise. They showed
he was becoming a business man. She confessed
to herself they were more manly in tone, while she
detected in herself a half mournful feeling at the
change. Lately he had spoken of coming home,
and there had been some talk of his coming back
in the spring. Ever since he had been gone, his
letters to Amy and to Frank had given promises of
his coming home "next spring" or "next fall."
This was enough to satisfy the frequent inquiries
of the neighbors at Langdale who wanted to know
when George Arnold was to come back, and wondered if he would marry Amy on his return, thinking it a great pity that she should wait for him.

His last letter had told Amy that he should certainly return next spring, and to stay. It was
nearly arranged that he should be settled in New
York with a branch of the firm there. There was
more certainty about this letter than any she had
received before, and she might allow herself to expect him home again. How different a return his
would be from what she had planned, and yet how

happy the thought of it made her! It was a still happiness that she believed could not be moved, because she had so many years been training herself to the thought that only that would be given her which was best for her and those she loved.

8

CHAPTER XIV.

THE RICH AND POOR.

AMY sat upon the piazza with her work. Hannah, too, was sitting on the steps of the piazza with a long seam before her, upon which she was sewing with the care and precision Miss Elspeth had taught her.

"I don't know how I am to get along after I leave here, Miss Amy," said Hannah; "those boys at the Carltons are so rude. Yesterday, when I passed the garden, they were throwing stones at the passers-by."

"I am afraid you will find it hard," said Amy: "It won't be at all like Miss Elspeth's well ordered household, nor even like our busy one. Mrs. Carlton has no command over the children, and poor Bertha is so sick now that she cannot control them."

"I don't believe I'd better go, Miss Amy," said Hannah; "I know those boys will make me angry."

"It won't be pleasant," said Amy, "but wherever you go, Hannah, you will not find every one so kind and considerate as Miss Elspeth."

"Nor any one that will talk so to me as you do, Miss Amy," said Hannah; "I remember when I used to see Janet so much, I saw that they treated her at the Paxtons' as if they thought she had not any feelings in her. I did not think much about it then, but since then the blood rises up in me to remember it. They would talk to her as if she were a stone, or no more than a brute."

"Oh, there are not many persons so unkind as that," said Amy, "but there a great many who are very thoughtless, and forget to speak gently and kindly."

"They think us a different race," Hannah broke out; "worse than that, they think us like the brute beasts, and would like to trample us down. But some day, oh, some day, I would like to get the better of them, and show them how I would look down on their pride."

"Hannah, what do you mean?" exclaimed Amy, surprised; "who are the people you are talking of?"

"Oh, the people out in the world, who are oppressing the poor, and keeping them down," said Hannah.

"Hannah, you don't know any such people; think of Miss Elspeth," Amy said.

"I do think of her, and of you, and of Miss Dora too; she speaks hard, but she does not think hard. But the Paxtons,—what right have they to live in a great house, with sofas and couches, more than they have time to lie upon, day after day; and poor ragged girls and children begging from step to step, that have not father or mother to take care of them?"

"It seems strange,—a great contrast," said Amy; "but what right have we to sit here so comfortably, with this pleasant air about us, and these vines and trees shading us,—what right have you and I, Hannah, to sit here so quietly, when there are so many working hard, or, what is worse, wanting work and food, not far away from us? It is a hard question to answer."

"You and I!" said Hannah; "what can we do?"

"And what can they do? the Paxtons, as you call them," asked Amy; "what would all the money they spend every year do for the deal of trouble just in Boston here? Alas! they do not know what to do to help all these poor people, more than you and I. I do not say they do their utmost,—people say the Paxtons are not kind and charitable to the poor. But we cannot judge. Do we do all that we can? At least, let us be charitable in our thoughts to them."

"Let them have all their splendid furniture, and mirrors, and dresses," said Hannah, "if they would only think of somebody else,—if they would not believe themselves to be at the top of the world and we all below."

"Every rich person is not of this sort, Hannah,"

said Amy; "we read in some story-books of two classes, the tyrants and the oppressed. It is not so where we live. Here are a great many different people, and most have kind feelings, though all don't show it."

"I feel as if everybody hated me and mine," said Hannah, "except some few."

"But that feeling you must give up as soon as possible, Hannah," said Amy; "it is not true, it is only in your imagination. I don't know what can have put it there. Even at the Carltons you won't find that hatred nor that sort of treatment."

"Oh, Miss Amy, with all those boys!" exclaimed Hannah.

"Five boys in one house are never very quiet, nor all gentle and considerate in their manners," answered Amy; "I know it will be hard to bear with them, but they will give you no worse treatment than they give to everybody."

"I'm afraid I shan't stand it," said Hannah.

"It is very provoking, I know," said Amy. "Last winter, when I slipped down on the ice in front of the Carltons' gate, it was provoking enough to have Freddy Carlton standing there laughing at me. He did not help me, either. My muff flew off one way, and my bundles another, and all the time he was making laughing speeches about me."

"Oh, if I had been there, Miss Amy!" exclaimed Hannah.

"Well, there was nothing to be done about it," said Amy, "so I tried to remember that he was the same boy that saved the child from drowning a little while before. They said, you know, that he stood on the ice holding up the child a long time, till help could come to him."

"I haven't forgot it, Miss Amy; and it was an Irish boy too."

"Agnes Carlton has come home from school now," continued Amy, "and she ought to be able to do something for her brothers; but she is not like Bertha. I am afraid she is thoughtless, and she has been away from home so much she has lost all home feeling."

"Miss Bertha looks to me like a picture," said Hannah, "like the picture of a beautiful angel."

"Bertha has had a hard life the last few years," said Amy; "she has been weak and sick, but has never been willing to tell any one of it. Her mother thinks of nothing but sewing all day long, and occupies herself so, she never has seen how much care Bertha has needed, till all at once Bertha has broken down, and everybody sees now how ill she is."

"She looks as if she came directly from the sky, only to go back there," said Hannah.

"O Hannah, it would be very hard for me to part with Bertha," exclaimed Amy; "I cannot think of it yet. Bertha was older than I at school. She used to help me every way. She never said

much, but helped me by being so good herself. I
like to think of your going there, Hannah, you
will be able to do so much for Bertha."

"I can go up stairs and down; I can fetch and
carry for her," said Hannah, gloomily.

"You will do more than that, Hannah," said
Amy; "it is very hard for any one like Bertha to
call for help from others. She has always thought
so little of herself that it pains her now to ask
help of any one else. If you give her a willing,
ready service, you will do her a deal of good."

"And Mrs. Carlton, she'll be wanting me for
other things."

"And the boys will order you round for this and
that," said Amy, " and Mrs. Carlton will want to
keep you at your sewing. You must be ready for
them all, —' Up stairs, and down stairs, and in my
lady's chamber,' — but if you have a heart for it,
you will find time to be caring for the fire in
Bertha's room, and making sure that all is cheerful
there. You will ask her often through the day
what you can bring her, and find out in time how
to bring her what she wants without her asking.
Even if you are kept constantly at work, sewing or
sweeping, you will find some time to help her."

"It is hard work you are laying out for me, Miss
Amy," said Hannah.

"I know it, but you have been working every
moment of the day at Miss Dora's," answered
Amy; "you can't work more than that at the

Carltons, and the work will be all the easier if you are only willing and ready."

"I know that is the way you work, Miss Amy," said Hannah; "you go into Mrs. Campbell's room to put it all to rights, and before you are half through, they call you into your mother's room, and when you are busy there, somebody wants you in the kitchen; and then the children are ready for their lessons, or Master Sammy has tumbled down stairs, and you must comfort him. Everything is done, and you have time for all, and always are smiling and making fun of it all as if it were a frolic."

"Ah, well, is not it easier so?" asked Amy.

"It is very easy for you," sighed Hannah, "but not for me."

"And why not?" said Amy.

"Because they all love you, and you love them. You are precious to them. Who will care for me at the Carltons'?" said Hannah.

"Who has cared for you all along?" asked Amy; "and listen, who are they that are shouting for you now? Bessie, and Martha, and Margie; I think they are coming for you to go to walk, and it will be good for you to air some of your gloomy thoughts. Now they are stopping a minute; Miss Dora has called them back for something. Perhaps Bessie has forgotten to lock the back door, or Miss Elspeth has summoned her for some errand. Why, Hannah! have you forgotten us all here? You are precious to all of us?"

"But *there?*" persisted Hannah.

"We shall see you often," said Amy; "and Hannah, if you are in any trouble, you must speak to Bertha. She will feel for you kindly, I know. And think, Hannah, perhaps some day it will be such a comfort to look back upon what you have done for Bertha."

There was a great uproar of voices, for Bessie, and Martha, and Margie were coming, and Bessie insisted on climbing the fence that separated the two houses, and then she came running up the grassy bank, her bonnet falling back from her head, while she shouted with delight.

"Oh! come into the woods, everybody! Miss Elspeth says we may go if Hannah will, and you'll come too, Amy."

"Hannah will go, but I must stay for the children."

CHAPTER XV.

THE little party made its way into the woods, telling over to Hannah the events of the day; how Margie had made her first pudding, how Miss Elspeth was really to have the sewing circle, and how they all meant to find something in the woods to ornament the parlor with, when that great day should come. Miss Dora had objected; but then she objected to everything; and Martha had promised, if they could have flowers in the room, she would pick up every single green thing that fell upon the carpet. Martha was the thoughtful one of the household now. She was fond of study, and hoped she might be a teacher sometime, if she could only learn enough. Meanwhile, she made the best of every moment's time, and had her volume of botany under her arm now.

"I think it's a shame," said Bessie, "to carry books into the woods. We have enough of them in the house, and I am sure there is plenty to look at when we are out among the trees."

"But I am determined," said Martha, "to find

out the name of that new flower we saw the other day. It was so withered I could not make it out from that specimen at all."

"I think 'lily' was a very good name for it," said Bessie. "I don't believe I can pronounce its long Latin name, when you find it."

"There are a great many kinds of lilies," said Martha, "and if I can find the flower's real name, I can read about it in the book, and I dare say you will be glad to hear about it."

"That it flowers the end of August," said Bessie, "and we know that already; and that it is found on the edge of swamps, and that Miss Dora knows, because I brought some of the mud into the kitchen the day we found it."

"There's one now, I declare," exclaimed Martha, as she ran away from the path, and out through the broad hemlocks.

Very soon the whole party were busy. Martha was comparing the flowers she found with the descriptions in her book. Margie had discovered a real fairy's haunt. She was sure it must be. There was the ring in the grass where they had danced the night before, and a purple mushroom in the middle, that must have been the queen's throne. She set herself to look for some remnant of the feast, for Oberon's mushroom, for she was sure he must have been there too. Bessie was quiet for some minutes. She was watching a squirrel. If she could only be still enough not to frighten him, she could find out where his hole was, and see if he had any of last winter's nuts there.

Hannah was the only one not busy. She waited a little while for the others, then walked down the path that led to the station. A train of cars from Boston had just left the station, to go on farther. Hannah fancied she recognized a girl, about her own size, who was lingering on the platform. The girl had seen her, and presently beckoned to her, and came hastening to where Hannah stood.

"Janet, is that you?" exclaimed Hannah.

"Yes, it's me," said Janet, hurrying up the bank, "and you're the person I've come to see. I wanted to see you in a hurry, too, for I'm going right into town again in the next cars."

"Where have you been all this long time, and what are you doing?" asked Hannah.

"Well, don't you think I'm getting on in the world? What do you think of my bonnet? What would Mrs. Paxton say to it?" exclaimed Janet. "Well, I'm not the same Janet that she used to order round."

"Where have you been since you went away so suddenly from Mrs. Paxton's?" asked Hannah.

"Well, I left the Paxtons without asking them," said Janet.

"Miss Nora is married," said Hannah.

"Dear me; who has she married?" said Janet.

"Nobody that you know about," said Hannah.

"Well, never mind, I want to talk to you. I've a proposal to make to you. Is not that grand?"

"But I can't stop, Janet; there are the children," said Hannah.

"Oh, never mind the children," said Janet, "they won't spoil; I can hear their voices close by. Bessie's as tall as you now. She can take care of herself."

"You can come into the woods with me," said Hannah.

"No, I can't," answered Janet; "sit down here on this stone with me. You were asking me where I had been. Well, I've been up and down; you would think I had been more down than up. I believe you think more of having a regular place to sleep in and food and all, than you do of having your own way."

"I mean to have my own way too, some time," said Hannah.

"Well, that's like you, that's spirit," said Janet, "so I thought. Now, I've been living in Board Court some of the time. It is not much of a place. But you see more of the world there than you do in Langdale in any time."

"I don't want to live in Board Court," said Hannah.

"You'd live there if Stephen were there," said Janet.

"Have you heard anything of Stephen? Have you seen him? Oh, tell me quick," exclaimed Hannah.

"I haven't seen him, only the boys say he will certainly come back to Board Court some time. They expect him to turn up there any day."

"I don't believe you know anything about him," said Hannah, getting up to hurry away.

"Don't go away, that is not what I want to talk about. But I've been very busy lately helping some ladies at the theatre. And such times as I have had! I can go and see the play almost every night. They want somebody to sew for them. And that is what I want you for. You were always so good at sewing, and I can get you just as much work as you want, and good pay for it too. Besides that, we can go to the theatre when we please."

"To the theatre!" exclaimed Hannah.

"Yes, we'll have a little establishment of our own in Board Court. And sometimes we can have a look upon the stage, that is, behind the scenes. But the best is, up stairs at the theatre. There you can look down upon all the show, upon all the fine people, and there's that nice warm gas smell, and it's so comfortable and all."

. "I went once to the theatre long ago with Steevie," said Hannah. "I have forgotten a great deal. But there came in a great ship. It was on the stage, but it came floating in just as if it were on the water, only it was more golden and splendid than any ship is. There was a sister and a brother floating together in it. Oh, how they must live, the

people that act there! It all looks so fine, even if
they do have to work hard! I wouldn't mind the
work, Janet."

"Oh, you wouldn't have to work hard," said
Janet, "just sewing, that you can do so easy, and
then so much fun all the time!"

"I didn't mean the sewing," said Hannah. "I
mean the actors can't have to work hard, not harder
than we do now."

"Oh, you are thinking of acting," answered
Janet; "perhaps it might come to that in time,—
who knows? Any how, it's a more jolly life than
you are leading now."

"But I can't leave Miss Amy," said Hannah abruptly, after a moment's thought.

"What have you to do with Miss Amy?" asked
Janet.

"I have left Miss Elspeth's. I'm living at the
Rothsays' now" answered Hannah.

"Is that it?" exclaimed Janet; "then it's easier
for you to go away than ever! Then you've left
Bessie in good quarters. Don't stop to think!
The down train will be along in fifteen minutes.
That will give you just time to go round through
the road and make up a bundle of your things and
come directly on with me."

"Oh, I can't go, I can't go with you!" said Hannah, yet with regret in her tone. "Never mind the
bundle," said Janet, "just sit and talk with me the
fifteen minutes. I'll tell you more what we will do.

You don't want to be tied down all your life to two old women. Just come into town with me to-night."

"No, I can't to-night," said Hannah. "I can't go now. Perhaps this fall, when I am at Carlton's, if I find I can't bear it there, I'll come in to you then."

"But it will be too late then," urged Janet, "your place will be filled up. They will have got somebody else in town, and what is it to do? Miss Elspeth would not object to your going out sewing?"

"I am really a help to Miss Amy now, and I can't leave her," said Hannah. "In the fall, I am to go to the Carltons to live. It will be different there, I know. That will be in a month or two."

"At the Carltons'! Are you going to live there? Why, Mrs. Carlton will keep you sewing from morning till night, and expect you to take care of the children too. I would advise you never to get into that house unless you want to be a slave all your life. In a month or two it will be too late."

"I love Miss Amy," said Hannah, "I don't love many people."

"Well, just come in with me to-night and see how it is," said Janet, "you can come out again in a day or two, and tell Miss Amy all about your new plans. It would be different if you were going to live with her always; but as you are to leave her so soon, it can't trouble her to have you go now."

"I can't go in to-night! I can't go to-night!" re-peated Hannah.

"Then I've had all my pains for nothing" ex-claimed Janet; "I expected you to be grateful at least."

"Yet you've never helped me much," said Hannah, "it wasn't the truth you told me of Stee-vie and the circus."

"I told you all I know, and you wouldn't believe me," said Janet; "I might have told you more. But you don't deserve I should let you know any-thing. But only come with me to-night."

"I can't go to-night," said Hannah resolutely, "next winter I will think about it." At this mo-ment Martha was heard crying for Hannah, and pres-ently Bessie's voice calling for help. Hannah hur-ried away up the wood-path. "I'll wait for you," said Janet. She sat down on the stone and listened to the different voices, but Hannah did not come back again. Janet lingered about the woods, till the train for town came along, and went away in it.

9

CHAPTER XVI.

MR. JASPER.

HANNAH met Martha running towards her. "Oh! Margie is up in the tree, and we can't get her down. She'll fall and break her neck! What can we do?"

Hannah hurried on, and found Bessie under an oak-tree, looking up to Margie, who was clinging to one of the outer branches. Bessie was half laughing and half frightened. "She's so foolish," she said to Hannah, explainingly; "it's easy enough to come down, but she is so frightened she won't try."

"How did she get up there?" asked Hannah, as she came under the tree, and tried to reach Margie.

"Oh, Bessie persuaded me to come up here, and helped me along, and now I am out on this branch, and I know it won't bear me, and I can't possibly get down, and I know my arms will break."

Hannah was not tall enough to reach where Margie was, and Margie would not let Bessie climb the tree to her, because she was sure she would break the branch if she came up into the tree. So the poor child swayed backward and forward on the light bough, clinging to it with trembling hands.

"Let yourself down, we will catch you," said Hannah; "you are not very far from the ground."

"Oh, no! I'm afraid," cried Margie.

"Run to the house for some one," said Hannah to Bessie.

"My arms will break off, I know," said Margie, "before you come back."

"There's a noise,—there's somebody coming," exclaimed Martha; "stop, Bessie, you needn't go. It's a man,—a gentleman."

Martha ran to him for help. He came just in time, for Margie, in trying to reach a higher bough, had strained her wrist. He lifted her down without trouble.

"How did you get there?" he asked; "why didn't you climb down as you came up?"

"I know it," said Bessie; "it's easy enough. I have been up and down in the tree half a dozen times since Margie has been on that branch."

"Bessie said it was so easy," said Margie, "and that it was just like a swing up there; and I didn't mind climbing up into the tree, but I didn't know how I ever should get down."

"Margie began to tell us a story," said Bessie; "Martha sat under the tree, and I believe Margie was frightened by her own story, for she was just telling something, oh, really dreadful—"

"And I heard a noise,— it was only a little noise," said Margie, "but it frightened me more than a great one. I was very foolish; I thought of bears, and I crept out to the end of the branch, and then it began to rock up and down, and I thought I should fall, and I felt as if my arms would break."

"And where were you?" asked their new friend, of Hannah.

"I was away on the edge of the wood," Hannah answered, "but I ought to have been here. I would not have let Margie climb the tree if I had been here. She is frightened so easily, she can't climb like Bessie."

"I'm so glad you came through the wood," said Martha to the stranger; "very few people know the way through the wood."

"I know the way," he said, "though it is over five years since I have been here. I only came to Langdale this morning, and I came across through the woods on my way to Mr. Rothsay's."

"We're going through the Rothsays' garden," said Bessie, "so we can go together."

"I had better take this little Margie in my arms," said he, "she is trembling still."

"It's my hand pains me," said Margie, "I can't tie my bonnet."

"I am afraid your wrist is sprained," said their friend.

"O dear, we shall have to send for the Doctor,"

said Bessie; "I wish it had been my wrist. But there's one comfort for you, Margie, you wont have to beat eggs with it."

The party went through the Rothsays' garden, and Amy came out to meet them.

"What is the matter? Why, Mr. Jasper, is this you with our little Margie? How came you here? Is Margie hurt?"

"She's more frightened than hurt," answered Mr. Jasper. "I came by the morning train from Boston, and I met this little party on my way through the woods. They will tell you what was the matter."

"It would have been so bad if he had not come through the woods. I don't know what would have happened to Margie," said Martha.

Bessie, at the same time, began to tell how it was her fault persuading Margie to get into the tree. They made a long story of it. Hannah was silent. At the end, Amy turned round to her inquiringly.

"It was my fault," said Hannah; then in a low tone, "I shouldn't have stayed as I did by the cars. I let the children go back into the woods alone. I ought to have gone with them."

"But we are not children now," said Bessie, impatiently.

"Miss Elspeth sent Hannah to take care of you," said Amy. "Hannah and I will go in with you to see Miss Elspeth and Miss Dora, if Mr. Jasper will bring Margie to the gate."

"I hope all Langdale is as little changed as you," said Mr. Jasper, looking at Amy. "When I found all this little party in the woods, I thought I had come into a new neighborhood, but I begin to feel at home again now."

"These are our new neighbors," said Amy; "the Miss Eltons came just as you went away."

"I have heard a little about them from the Fays this morning," said Mr. Jasper; "I went directly there, and they have refreshed me a little in Langdale news; it was a long time since I had heard from here."

"And you are really going to stay with us a little while?" said Amy.

"Yes, Mr. Peterson wrote me so earnestly to take his place here this winter, while he went away; and he sent, too, such earnest entreaties from the parish, that I could not resist coming."

"And can you bear a winter here now?" asked Amy.

"Oh, yes; don't I look as if I could bear any-thing?" said Mr. Jasper.

"A different person from what you were when you went away," said Amy; "you don't look like an invalid now."

They reached Miss Elspeth's house.

"This is Miss Elton's house, then," continued Mr. Jasper, "is it? — the little brown cottage. How the garden is grown! Miss Margie, I will set you down here. If Miss Elton will let me I will come in and doctor your wrist."

Bessie had run on before to tell Miss Elspeth what had happened, blaming herself for Margie's trouble.

"I will wait at the gate," said Mr. Jasper to Amy, "while you go in and see if I can give any surgical aid, then I will walk back with you to your house."

But no; Amy came out and said Miss Elspeth was equal to the care of Margie, and there was not much hurt done apparently.

"How pleasant it is to look up and down the street again," said Mr. Jasper; "what a pretty place it is. How the trees and vines grow and flourish here! Mrs. Bunce's little old house becomes picturesque as the green gathers round it."

"And Mrs. Bunce herself," said Amy; "see, she is looking after you over the fence, trying to make you out."

"I must go and speak to her presently," said Mr. Jasper; "that will announce my arrival in Langdale. Mrs. Bunce was always the Court Journal of Langdale. Children on your piazza! Ah, those are your little cousins of whom I have heard. Well, Amy, you have plenty to do."

As they walked up the path towards the house, Amy heard herself called back into the street. "Oh Amy, just come here a minute, I want to ask you something."

"Agnes, is it you? Won't you come in? What do you want?" asked Amy.

" Oh, haven't you any old novels you can lend us
to read ! I'm tired to death of the Club books, they
are all so stupid. Has not Frank something inter-
esting to read ? "

" I dare say, will you come in and see ? " answered
Amy.

" Oh, no matter now. That is not really what I
wanted. I brought you out here to ask you if that
isn't Mr. Jasper you were walking up with ? I
saw you in the distance, and I thought it looked
like him. But it is so long since I have seen him.
I suppose he has come to stay ? Well, I'm rejoiced.
I'm tired to death of Mr. Peterson. He preaches
over the same things. I could say off his sermons
before I went to church. He's got me into such a
habit of going to sleep, that I'm afraid Mr. Jasper
won't wake me up. No, I won't come in; it's such
a comfort to have a piece of news to tell people,
that I won't stay. The Lees will be out on their
doorsteps. What a novelty it is to have somebody
coming back ! Everybody has been going away
so ! Tom Paxton, you know, is really coming home.
They expect him every day. I do hope he'll stir
them up a little at the Paxtons. But I won't keep
you any longer. It must be a treat for you to have
somebody to talk with."

" Who is your pretty friend ? " asked Mr. Jasper
of Amy.

" That is Agnes Carlton. Did not you remember
her ? " asked Amy.

" Is that Agnes ? Why she was one of the little
girls when I went away. One of your witches,
that Mrs. Carlton was always scolding, because she
wouldn't sit still, and never came into the house
except to show that her dress was torn off her shoul-
ders, or her braids tumbling down her back."

" Agnes has come home from school a finished
young lady now," said Amy, " she's the model of
dress for all Langdale."

" She is pretty," said Mr. Jasper ; " I watched
her as she talked with you, her ribbons flying, her
tongue going, and her eyes dancing. Then she
has a fresh healthy color in her cheek."

" You should have heard what she said," said
Amy, " for she only stopped to ask about you."

" How different from Bertha !" said Mr. Jasper,
thoughtfully ; " a younger sister of Bertha !"

" She is a picture of health by the side of Bertha !" said Amy ; " and poor Bertha, so languid
now, so feeble. And she is different every way
from Bertha ! Bertha has all the soul and heart.
Agnes is full of life and animation. I can't make
myself interested in her, though I try to, for Bertha's sake, and though she excites so much admiration. Oh, she is a great contrast to Bertha ! She
is cold and shining, and Bertha is full of feeling."

" Bertha went to heaven a long time ago," said
Mr. Jasper, " her spirit went. She has not lived
on the earth, as one of us, this great while."

" But her body is as beautiful as a spirit, as frail

and transparent," said Amy; "that has been moving round with us still. Though lately, Bertha has been more shut up at home. I dread this winter for her."

"Why don't they carry her away to the South?" asked Mr. Jasper. "It is no place for her to spend the winter here."

"Mrs. Carlton is wilfully blind," said Amy; "she does not see how sick Bertha is. But indeed, Bertha would not like to go away from home. And I am afraid she could not be comfortable or happy anywhere else."

"Can she be happy or comfortable anywhere in this world?" asked Mr. Jasper; "her nature is so delicate it can't bear up against what this world brings. How terrible must be to her all the household discomforts, and the little home embitterments she is surrounded by."

"Bertha never shrank from life," said Amy; "she had too much faith for that."

"Yes, it takes more faith to live by, than to die by," said Mr. Jasper.

CHAPTER XVII.

THE SEWING CIRCLE.

MISS ELSPETH'S little rooms were crowded by the sewing circle, and Miss Dora's household arrangements had been previously so perfected that she was actually able to sit down to entertain her guests when they assembled. Hannah and Bessie had been busy in the kitchen with her all the morning. Martha had picked the prettiest flowers from the garden and the woods, and had arranged them gracefully around the rooms. There were dishes of bright scarlet flowers, and tall vases of wild flowers, and Margie's pet basket, out of which hung graceful vines. Miss Dora made some objections to covering the tables with flowers. She did not see where the work was to be put, or the candles, when it came time to light up. But Miss Elspeth showed her they had left room for the candles, and Martha had arranged the work on a table in the corner.

So there was great talking, and, of course, a great deal of work done too. For the two rooms were full, and the younger girls sat on the stairs in the entry. Mrs. Paxton was there. She could not sew because she couldn't use her eyes, and she never talked much, but then it was respectable to have her sitting there in her well-fitting gloves. Mrs. Bunce was in fine spirits. Her fingers went fast, her eyes took in all that was going on, nor did her conversation flag. "So, Miss Dora, Martha is to be a teacher," she broke in.

"So it seems," said Miss Dora; "she has been studying hard enough. She has her French lessons with Amy, and has been to school summer and winter. When she's old enough she will go to the Normal School, I suppose. I don't see the use of so much learning and studying, myself."

"Well, if she can teach, she can earn her living that way," suggested Mrs. Bunce; "that's a good thing."

"But what is it all to come to?" said Miss Dora. "Here's Martha learning just to teach a new set of children. Now, what good is it going to do all these others? Are they going to learn merely so they can teach? What are they going to do with it all, I should like to know? It would save time if none of them learnt."

"Ah, but Miss Dora, what will you do with the time when you have saved it?" asked Amy.

"That's verytrue," said Mrs. Paxton; "occupation is the great thing for young people."

"There's plenty to do without reading books all the time," said Miss Dora, "and there would be another saving of time. If nobody read their books it would save the time of the people that have to write them. It must take considerable to be scribbling it all; I've never wasted my time over it."

"Oh, Miss Dora, but don't you read the Harper, and Thackeray?" asked Annie Fay.

"And if you would only write a book, Miss Dora," said Amy; "only think how much good you'd do."

"The only book I should write," said Miss Dora, "would be a cook-book; and I should say in the beginning that it wouldn't do any good, and if they wanted to cook they must cook, and not read books."

"But, Miss Dora, then your book wouldn't help us," said Annie Fay.

"There's Margie," continued Miss Dora, "when she begins upon a story there's no chance to get her away from it. She has the book stuck up on the mantelpiece when she's dusting, and open on the table when she's sewing. There would be no meals in the family if we waited for her. You can't eat and drink the best books in the world."

"I must say," said Mrs. Bunce, "I don't often see Margie but what she has a book in her hand."

"But you haven't told us what we are to do if we don't read," said one of the Lees.

"I suppose you'd like to have us sew," said Annie Fay.

"The girls now-a-days," said Mrs. Carlton, "don't

know anything about sewing. I can't think what we shall come to. I cannot get along with my work unless I keep at my sewing steadily from morning till night. I always meant to teach my girls how to sew if they did not know anything else. But, dear me, I believe Agnes knows everything else, and I can't induce her to sew long enough to pay for hunting up her thimble."

"I never thought much of sewing steadily all day," said Miss Dora; "and Elspeth says there's poor folks enough who need the sewing work, to say nothing of machines, though I wouldn't have one in the house. But there's one thing that does come regularly, and that is three meals a day; and I think a girl ought to know how to get the meals, if she don't cook them herself."

"You are right there," said Mrs. Paxton, who had never troubled herself with more than ordering her meals.

And Miss Dora bustled away to arrange her generous tea-table.

Mr. Jasper came in the evening, and the greetings were especially cordial; every one was glad to see him back again, and everybody was fresh with delight at his last Sunday's sermons.

Mr. Jasper was talking with Amy in the entry. "That little Margie's hair will take fire," he exclaimed; "what is she doing with the candle in her hand?"

Amy went to the stairs, where Margie was showing a friend some pictures, and advised her putting down her candlestick.

"The little Margie interests me," said Mr. Jasper; "she is full of imagination. Only don't let her grow up into one of those girls that let their minds go to walk through some side door when they think they are with you all the time."

"What do you mean?" asked Amy.

"Don't you know how tiresome it is when you've been talking earnestly to any one, suddenly to find your listener, instead of being a listener, has been taking a little excursion of his own, wandering off into some delightful region, very likely, but he alone has the gate to it and the key?"

"Absent-minded people are very trying," said Amy. "I have a wicked desire, all the time, to stick pins into their minds and rouse them out of their dreams."

"Present-minded people are as unsatisfactory," said Mr. Jasper; "they are so taken up with what is going on, they think only of what they are saying now, and forget if they have any past or future. Most party talk goes no further than the candles, and dresses, and show of the evening. Look at our lively friend, Agnes Carlton. She leans against the door-post, complacently happy. Tom Paxton is on one side and Frank at the other. She is not even thinking of what she is saying now. She is thinking of the opinion that she sees you and I are passing upon her."

" I am afraid you are right," said Amy.

" Yet she can talk well," said Mr. Jasper.

" But she talks without heart. What she says is from her lips; it comes from no deeper. And is there anything deeper there ? " said Amy.

" Are you not severe ? " asked Mr. Jasper.

" And you ? " said Amy.

" Do you think me severe ? " asked Mr. Jasper.

" You have appeared to me more so than before you went away," said Amy.

" Have I ? And is not that right ? " asked Mr. Jasper. " I have lived five years and more since then. Should not that embitter me ? "

" It is not like you to say so," said Amy.

" What should I say ? " asked Mr. Jasper.

" Your old self used to say that true living could only refresh us. It must be those who let their better life die out who talk of the harshness of life," said Amy.

" It is my death then that I complain of when I complain of the bitterness of my life," said Mr. Jasper. " And all my disappointments, yes, they are the death of my better, my happier hopes. I may complain still then, only give my complaint a different name."

" Is that what discipline is to teach us ? " asked Amy. " You used to teach us differently."

" I can teach others better than I can myself, Amy," said Mr. Jasper; " and perhaps my own salvation lies that way. If I cannot heal myself, I may heal others."

"There's room for it here," said Amy. "We all need freshening and renewing."

"And there is room for it, you think, opposite, with Agnes Carlton?" asked Mr. Jasper. "You think she needs improving?"

"Yes; but how I scarcely know," said Amy. "I can hardly tell how to reach her. I am afraid she is weak; she seems very thoughtless. I would like to love her more because she is Bertha's sister, but I grow discouraged. And then I try to comfort myself with thinking perhaps she is not in my parish."

"Your parish is a large one, as it is," said Mr. Jasper, laughing. "All these four girls belong to it, I suppose."

"Oh, they take care of themselves very much," said Amy; "but I am deeply interested in them. Hannah troubles me most. The others were younger when they came here, and have made themselves at home here. Hannah cannot help feeling she is oppressed still. I am troubled about her."

"The others seem very happy," said Mr. Jasper.

"Yes; Margie, you see, has her little friend there, and Bessie has taken hers away to help her in the kitchen, and the sober, thoughtful Martha has her friends everywhere."

"But Hannah does not find her place?" asked Mr. Jasper.

10

"She is uneasy; still, she is not happy," said Amy.

"But to return to our old subject. Do you think Agnes Carlton is in *my* parish?" asked Mr. Jasper.

"Most certainly she is under your influence," said Amy; "but then I have not recommended her to you. Indeed, I have talked more about her than I like."

"But Bertha's sister ought not to be weak-minded and trivial. For Bertha's sake we might do something for her," said Mr. Jasper; "only, is not Bertha's own influence the best for her?"

"What has pained me in Agnes," said Amy, "is her apparent want of feeling towards Bertha. She might do much for her now. A joyous, light-hearted spirit, such as Agnes has, might add so much to Bertha's happiness! Oh, it is wrong of me to speak of Agnes so; but every day, when I am with Bertha, I see how she is pained by the selfishness that Agnes shows."

"You are with Bertha every day?" asked Mr. Jasper. "How happy for you, for her, you can do so much for her."

"It is she that does much for me," said Amy. "She purifies my day for me, and makes the air clearer."

"Now, Mr. Jasper," Mrs. Bunce broke in, "if this is a sermon you are preaching, I think your audience is too small. It is not fair; you have been talking to Amy the last half hour."

" It is Amy who has been preaching to me," said
Mr. Jasper. " That is a chance I don't have often,
you know."

" Well, I couldn't think of any one's venturing
to preach to you," said Mrs. Bunce. " Amy knows
how to practise. She's one of Mr. Peterson's most
devoted parishioners."

" Where did you find those cardinal flowers ?"
asked Agnes of Martha. " I wet my feet and spent
the whole afternoon yesterday trying to find some.
Somebody said there were plenty by the brook."

" Frank Rothsay brought us these," said Martha.
" He found them ever so far off, by the glen, I
believe."

" Oh, wouldn't it be fine to get up a party for
the glen ? " said Agnes. " Amy, do let us go and
find cardinal flowers. Tom Paxton is wild to go
somewhere, and he is making forty thousand plans.
He says it tired him so to see the house at home
look just as it did when he went away, and all the
people too are just the same. I should think it
would be tedious enough, when he has been
all over the world ! He has taken up the currant-
bushes already, and would like to remove the elm-
trees if they would move ! "

" Poor Mrs. Paxton must be disturbed," said
Amy.

" Oh," said Agnes, " I think she likes it. It must
be better than vegetating as she did when Nora
was at home. They might all of them have been

rooted in the garden, for all the motion they ever indulged in! I wonder Nora could travel! It must be such a bore to her to remember where she is every day, and where she is going the next!"

CHAPTER XVIII.

BEGINNING OF SERVICE.

HANNAH had one more interview with Janet. One evening at dusk, as she went out to go down in the village, she met Janet in the street.

"I have been waiting for you the last half hour and more," said Janet, " and I was just beginning to give you up. They must keep you pretty hard at work in there. At Miss Elspeth's you used to have a little quiet time in the evening at the garden gate."

"I don't like to be idle," 'said Hannah, "you know I never did."

"Where are you going now?" asked Janet.

"Only to the grocery store in the village," said Hannah.

"That grocery store," exclaimed Janet; "I wonder if those same two lemons are in the window that used to be there in my day! Langdale is a slow place. I have a new plan; I am going to New York now."

"Going to New York! Then you have given up living in Board Court, and the theatre, and all?"

"I couldn't make it go without you," said Janet; "they engaged me to do the sewing, and I couldn't do a stitch of it. You were to have done the sewing, and I was to get the place for you."

"Then I was to have done all the work," said Hannah, "and you were to have the fun you talked about. I wondered why you wanted me so much."

"You needn't be bitter about it," said Janet; "if you are so fond of work you needn't have minded it. And you must agree I was calculated to make the best impression about getting the place. I never could sit down and sew; I should soon be tired of that."

"But where are you going to in New York?" asked Hannah.

"Oh, I'm going to try my fortune there," said Janet; "I never like to live long in one place. It grows tiresome after a while. I expect to find friends there,—but I want you to go on with me."

"To do your sewing?" asked Hannah.

"You needn't take that so hard," said Janet; "you might just as well work for me as for Mrs. Carlton, or anybody else, and better too, if I can get you better wages for it."

"I don't see what you have to offer me in New York," said Hannah.

"Well, very much the same place I had for you in Boston," said Janet; "then New York is so large that there is plenty to do. And even if you went out to work there, you would have a better time. You needn't have to work half so hard, and it's a great place to live in."

Hannah went into the little store to make her purchases, and then turned back with Janet.

"I am going to the Carltons' this next week," she said, "and I have been thinking about what you have told me when I saw you before. If I find it hard, I will go on to New York and meet you somehow."

"If you come into Boston, to Board Court, they'll tell you there where I am, any time. You know your mother's dead," Janet added abruptly.

"How? What do you mean?" asked Hannah, surprised.

"Well, I thought you would have heard of it," said Janet; "you'll hear of it in time. Mrs. Badger has been fussing round in Board Court, and she will be out to tell you all about it. You can't feel very bad, after all, you went away from her."

"I have always thought, Janet," said Hannah, "that sometime or other —"

"Sometime or other is what you are always talking about," said Janet; "that is where you live, in 'sometime or other.' You always thought, I suppose, that sometime or other you would drive in from Langdale in a coach and four horses, and take your mother away, and live like great folks in a hotel."

"I believe I did think very much so," said Hannah.

"Well, you may come in, in the omnibus; I don't see how you'll come any other way from Langdale," said Janet. "I may as well bid you good-by; if I'm going to see you 'sometime or other,' I shall see you no time."

"Perhaps you will see me this winter," said Hannah; "I shall have earned enough to go to New York. I had meant to keep my earnings."

"Then you have begun to save up something," said Janet.

"Miss Elspeth keeps my savings," said Hannah. "I wish I were you, Janet; I should like very well to go round from one place to another. But I can't go now."

"Good-by, then," said Janet; "I shall see you 'sometime or other.'"

Hannah had found it hard to part with Miss Elspeth and the family, when it came time for her to go to the Carltons. It seemed more like going away than when she went to the Rothsays. Amy was the same friend to her that Miss Elspeth was. She would have been willing to work for her for love. She was now beginning to enter upon service, to work for wages.

"You won't be able to come and help us at our busy times now," said Miss Elspeth; "so, Hannah, we shall depend upon seeing you at your leisure hours. You will have Saturday evenings to yourself, and you must always come here then. It will be a quiet time to see you in."

"And don't forget what I told you about keeping tidy yourself," said Miss Dora; "whatever you do, don't forget to make things look neat. With all the boys at the Carltons, the house always looks topsy-turvy. You can see after things a little. You can be of great use in the family."

"Don't give Hannah more to do than Mrs. Carlton will find for her," said Miss Elspeth; "I don't want to have Hannah work herself to death."

Afterwards, she said to Hannah, "You must not forget to come to me if any trouble comes. Don't stay at home and think over your troubles, but let me know what they are. Very often I may help you."

Bessie said to Hannah, "One of these days I shall be going out to work too. I have been thinking about it a great deal since it has been planned you should go."

"That won't come for a great while," said Hannah.

"I don't know that," said Bessie; "I want to be earning some wages and doing something. Not that I am ready to leave here; oh, that would be hard enough! How kind Miss Dora and Miss Elspeth were to take us away. I don't remember much about the old home, Hannah, but sometimes I have bad dreams about it, and recall old faces that make me shudder. And there were such harsh words spoken there, and the people that came home at night talked so loud, it frightens me to think of them."

" Do you think of them all so ?" asked Hannah.

" Of all but Steevie," said Bessie; " I think I would like to see him again; yet I have had bad dreams even of him, and have fancied he came sometimes to take me to some dark place."

" Oh, don't think of such things," said Hannah, shuddering; " I had rather think that sometime we shall go and find him."

" Perhaps we shall," said Bessie, " though I don't like ever to think of leaving here. It has seemed so sunny ever since we came here. What bad ways I had when I first came. I am not so very good now; I do a great many things that Martha and Margie don't even think of. But then I did not know what it was to do right, and now I do wrong when I know it is not good to do it."

" You are not a bad child," said Hannah, half laughing.

" I'm not as bad as I should have been if it had not been for Miss Elspeth and Miss Dora," said Bessie; " I have such dreams of what I would like to do when I grow up."

" What is it you want to do?" asked Hannah.

" Oh, it is quite too good to come true," said Bessie, " but I like to think about it. I would like nothing better than to live always here, and take care of Miss Elspeth and Miss Dora. By-and-by they will be growing old, and Miss Dora will have to give up working. It's very selfish in me to take to myself the caring for them that would

be so pleasant, and seeing to their house and all.
But you others can all do better things. You are
a great deal wiser than I am, Hannah, and are fit
for a great deal more. Martha will be going away
to teach one of these days. Perhaps she will live
with us, and go into town every day to her school.
That would be good. And Margie could never
take care of the whole house. But I could, for I
know what Miss Dora wants, and I should not
mind if she scolded me when I did wrong."

"Miss Elspeth and Miss Dora would like nothing better, Bessie," said Hannah; "I don't know
why it should not be so."

"Oh, it's too good," said Bessie, "and I should
like first to be earning something, just to show
them that I could. But then, where would you
be? You must not be far off."

Miss Elspeth had heard of the death of Mrs.
O'Connor, from Mrs. Badger, who said that people
were glad in Board Court that her establishment
there was broken up. Hannah thought more than
ever of her talks with Janet, and was even moved
to join her and go on to New York with her. She
had been much touched by her talk with Bessie.
Bessie had spoken of a feeling toward Miss Elspeth and Miss Dora, that Hannah was conscious of
in herself. It was this feeling that had restrained
her when her old love of wandering, that had been
so long kept down, tempted her to go away. She
did now feel bound to Miss Elspeth and Miss Dora.

It would be really hard to do anything to pain them. For more than five years she had been provided with a quiet, peaceful home. She had not been troubled each day with doubts as to how she was to live to-morrow. She had been kindly and gently led and taught. At first, she had not been willing to trust to the kindness that was shown her. She had rather believe that it was not shown her from goodness of heart alone, but from some unknown selfish motive. She could not believe in such unvarying kindness, nor understand it. The suspicion and the distrust lingered still, yet Hannah was gradually and unconsciously softened by the influences round her. Five years of quiet, tame life had quieted her, though she was hardly aware of it herself. All the years before, she had lived in a roving, aimless way, and the old love of change came up often to assert its power. Often came back the old longing to live where she would not be bound to anybody, — where she might be free, even if she were only free to starve. Bessie showed greater gratitude to their kind friends than Hannah was willing to acknowledge or express. Hannah began to feel her own conscience relieved. Yes, Bessie should stay and take care of Miss Elspeth and Miss Dora, and Hannah herself would be free of that charge. She herself would go out and try the world; she would leave behind Bessie and all, as before she left the old home, — it could not be harder now.

But it was harder. For before, she had never been bound by any sense of duty, and now she was tied by it imperceptibly. When Martha and Bessie bade her good-night at Mrs. Carlton's door, Hannah waited a moment till the sound of their footsteps had died away. She did not, as she had planned, turn away from the door, to go to the station with her bundle, and take the evening train for Boston.

CHAPTER XIX.

NEW DUTIES.

MRS. CARLTON had given Hannah her directions over night. She was to be the first one up the next morning, and her first duty was to unlock the front door and wash the steps.

Hannah was standing on the threshold with her pail, having performed this task. It was a frosty morning, and the last of the dead leaves were falling to the ground. It was still and quiet, the only sound was the gentle fall of the leaves, and a little rustling in the dead branches of the vine by the door. Hannah looked up through the dark pines that stood against the clear blue sky, and again at the little path she had cleared so carefully from the whirling leaves. Whatever her thoughts were, they were suddenly interrupted by a shout behind her. It came from some voice up stairs.

"New girl, new girl, what are you about? here are my boots to clean!"

"Look out for your head, new girl," cried another voice; "you must clean mine too." "And be quick about it, for we want to put them on right off."

" Mine too," cried a small wee voice. And down came a clatter of heavy boots from over the stairs.

" Be particular to give them an extra polish," the voices began again. " And hurry up, don't move like a snail."

" I shall be down after mine before you can turn round."

A door was heard to open, and another voice exclaimed,

" What's all this noise ? Go back into the nursery, Harry ; Fred, are you not ashamed to be stirring up the house so, at this hour ? Don't let me hear one word more ! " There was a slam of the doors, then a silence, then a whispered sound, " We shall be down the back way, so fly round, new girl ! Extra fine blacking ! "

Hannah's head had fortunately escaped any blow, and she picked up the pile of boots of different sizes, that lay scattered round. She carried them to the kitchen, where Bridget could give her some directions as to what she should do with them. Here was a pair of heavy boots with thick soles and quite covered with mud ; next, came a pair a size smaller, but a close imitation of the first ; the third were smaller still, and the mud less alarming. The two others were not so shapeless, and less heavy. The smallest of more delicate form, still bore the shape of a childish foot, while the rest tried to look very mannish.

Hannah had hardly half finished blacking the

boots when there came down the back stairs a suppressed clatter. Fred was carrying the little Harry in his arms. "Where are my boots? oh, ready? well, that was smart! I'll soon have them on. I must go out, Jack, and see what Mike is doing with the cow; there's no hurry about you."

"Jack has got my boots," cried Tom; "it's just like him; he always thinks he's as big as I am."

"I hope we're going to have something good for breakfast, Bridget," said Fred.

"We didn't have anything fit to eat for supper, last night," said Tom. "I'm as hungry as a bear!"

"Where's Arthur?" said Jack. "I am going to pull him out of bed, he's so lazy."

"You'll take me out to see the cow?" said Harry; "don't go without me."

"Why, you haven't got any boots," said Fred.

"Take me on your shoulder, Fred, never mind about my boots," said Harry.

"Now, Mr. Fred, don't let him go without his boots," said Bridget anxiously; "what will his mother say?"

"It won't hurt him. It will save his boots," said Fred.

Hannah finished the blacking, Tom giving his assistance too. She felt relieved when they were all out of the house, and she was left to lay the breakfast-table in peace. She had a dread of this mob of boys, and she trembled at their voices. She did not meet with them again till she was sent into the dining-room at breakfast-time with some hot cakes. Fred had brought his dog in from the barn, and Fido was lying stretched by his side. Hannah did not see the dog, and as she came up to the table, she stumbled over him, letting her plate fall. The dog shook himself and gave a growl.

" That's clumsy ! " said one voice.

" You'll please to let my dog alone," said Fred.

" I'll thank you for the cakes," said another.

" Poor fellow, poor Fido ; here's a bone, poor fellow."

" I wish you'd look where you are stepping," said Mrs. Carlton ; " take the plate back, and bring some fresh cakes."

" She's a clumsy one," said Tom as Hannah left the room.

" Well, that dog is always in the way," said Agnes ; " that's a fact. It is no place for him, in the house ; the next thing, we shall have him on the table."

Fred took Fido up in his arms, and set him up triumphantly by Agnes's elbow.

" Put your dog down," said Mr. Carlton ; " Agnes is right ; we have noise enough in the house, without the dogs beside.

" Fido is harmless enough," said Fred ; " only if stupid Irish girls will tread on him —"

" Hush, she's coming in again," said Arthur.

" Don't tread on the dog," said Jack. Fido by this time was at the other end of the room, looking out of the window. Jack's remarks were always

11

considered witty by the others, and whenever he
spoke, the rest were ready to laugh. So an insulting suppressed titter greeted Hannah as she came
in and went out.

"Agnes has an extra flourish to her hair," said
Jack.

"She's dressed up," said Tom; "I wonder what
she's going to do so early."

"I'm going into town," said Agnes; "you needn't
wonder long."

"Will your highness have the pleasure of es-
corting me in?" said Fred.

"I shall go in the early train," said Agnes.

"Agnes, you are not going off early this morning," said Mrs. Carlton; "you know Miss Simpkins
is coming to-morrow about the boys' clothes. I
want to be ready for her to-day."

"If Miss Simpkins is coming about the boys'
clothes," said Agnes, "I don't see why you need
me; I thought she was to do the work."

"Pray, don't wear Agnes out with working, ma'a,"
said Fred; "Agnes has so much to do, she'll be used
up."

"She was so dreadful busy yesterday afternoon,"
said Tom, "she could not make the bobs to my
kite. She wouldn't make half a bob."

"You ought to have called them Roberts," said
Jack, "that would have been more elegant. Agnes
likes to be elegant."

"I know what she was doing," said Tom; "she
was on the sofa all the afternoon, reading."

"I wish Agnes had never learned to read," said Mrs. Carlton.

"Well, Arthur, what have you to say?" said Agnes, "everybody has something against me all round. It seems to me it's a harmless thing for me to go into town."

"Perhaps you'll stay," suggested Jack.

"I'm glad enough to have you go into town," said Fred, "because you may treat me to an ice or something after school."

"I'm going in with the Lees," said Agnes.

"I wish you'd tell them to have their names written on their bonnets," said Fred. "I can't tell the Lees apart. I can tell them without their bonnets. The one that has red hair is Maria."

"One of them talks so silly and mincing, I can always tell which she is," said Tom.

"Neither of the Lees has red hair," said Agnes, indignantly.

"Now I'll appeal to John," said Fred. "Don't one of the Lees have red hair?"

"It don't make any difference what Jack says," said Agnes. "Maria's hair is a reddish brown."

"Why, now," said Jack, "I've been wondering all breakfast time whether that bow on your collar was made out of red ribbon or out of one of the Lee's hair."

"You are too silly," said Agnes.

"If you are going into town, Agnes," said Mrs. Carlton, "there's some buttons and sewing silk to be got, and then I want you to match that plaid. I'll show you before you go in."

"What are you going to do in town?" said Mr. Carlton.

"I think I shall have my daguerreotype taken," said Agnes.

"I don't like to have you going to daguerreotype rooms with those girls," said Mrs. Carlton. "I wish you'd speak to Agnes, Mr. Carlton. I've sewing enough to keep her at work all day, and Agnes has spent half her time in town since she came home."

"Why, you've Hannah to sew for you," said Agnes. "That's what she's here for."

"Oh, yes; set the new girl to sewing," said Jack. "She knows dog stitch; I guess she'll know cat stitch."

"I can't tell about Agnes going into town," said Mr. Carlton. "I've just promised to buy her a season ticket."

"A season ticket!" exclaimed Mrs. Carlton. "Why, she'll be in and out every day. What are you thinking of?"

"I've been to school steadily the last five years," said Agnes. "I think I might enjoy myself a little while now. The rehearsals begin very soon, and then I must go in regularly. I may as well have the use of my season ticket now."

"There's a great deal of time wasted at those rehearsals," said Mrs. Carlton.

"I mean, to patronize the rehearsals this year," said Fred. "Half of the fellows are going, and I intend to invest in some tickets."

"You can carry up Bertha's breakfast, Agnes," said Mrs. Carlton. "It is time she had it."

"Why don't you send for Hannah?" said Agnes. "I thought she was to wait upon Bertha. I am sure I haven't time this morning. I am going to call for the Lees, and very likely they will keep me waiting."

"I begin to pity the new girl," said Tom. "She's to do all the sewing and all the waiting that Agnes don't do."

"I thought you were going to say that Agnes used to do!" said Jack. "That wouldn't be much."

"Here, Fido!" called Fred, and went out, followed by a train of the boys.

"Don't stay up in Miss Bertha's room now," said Mrs. Carlton to Hannah, when she was called in. "I want you to clear away the breakfast things when you come down."

CHAPTER XX.

MOTHER AND DAUGHTERS.

HANNAH carried her tray slowly up stairs. The little mob of boys were in the entry below, looking after their hats and caps. She fancied they were jeering at her.

"Somebody's cleared away my cap," cried one.

"And somebody has taken my hoop-stick," said another.

"You'd better look in the kitchen fire for it. Some folks are so clumsy and don't know any better," said another, and great laughter followed.

But the hubbub ceased, and the front door was slammed by the retiring army.

Hannah rested her tray on the stairs. She was bewildered and indignant. How could she submit to be treated in this way? And there was nobody to defend her. Why had not she gone off into Boston the night before? She could not stay another day to be insulted and oppressed this way. She took up her load again and found her way to Bertha's chamber. She opened the door, and what a quiet air she came into, and what a pleasant light!

There were white muslin curtains round the windows and round the bed, and the sunlight came streaming in across the carpet.

"It is too bad of me to be so indolent," said Bertha, as Hannah entered the room, "and to give everybody such trouble. To think of my having my breakfast in bed! That must seem quite too luxurious when everybody is working hard in the house. I won't keep you waiting here long. If you will set the tray down, I should like to have you bring me one thing. In the little dressing-room are my flowers. I could not keep them here through the night. Will you bring me the vase from the round table? They are the flowers Amy brought me yesterday morning. Did you see that she cut one of her own roses for me? That was like Amy, wasn't it? But you need not stay longer. I know you are busy down stairs. Perhaps when all your work is done you can come in for a little while, to sit with your sewing; it may rest you."

Hannah felt rested already as she left the room. The quiet atmosphere, Bertha's beautiful face and gentle tone, the sight of Amy's pet flowers that she had arranged for Bertha, all softened Hannah. She went down stairs, and for a little while their influence lingered with her, in the midst of a wrangling talk that was going on between Agnes and her mother.

Mrs. Carlton was very injudicious in her attempts

at management of Agnes. She unfortunately believed that all reading was folly, and all study a waste of time. She herself never spent her time in anything but sewing from morning till night. Her own mind had always been taken up with the making up of her household linen, with all the details of needlework, and she expected her daughters to follow in the same useful track. When Bertha was a child she had instructed her carefully in this branch of fine sewing. She was very much shocked when Bertha went to school and showed a desire to learn something else.

Bertha pleaded that all the other girls were permitted to read and study, but Mrs. Carlton supposed it to be the depravity of the generation, and believed it would grow wiser in time, and learn that its daughters should know only how to make shirts and sheets, and that it was not important they should know anything else. But Bertha, with her industry and her eagerness to keep up in school with the friends of her own age, had been able to gratify her mother's desires and her own. She managed to make herself a bright, intelligent scholar, and to satisfy her mother's demands at home. She sewed diligently and steadily, and read and studied as earnestly. She even won her mother's consent to read such useless books as Scott's novels, and the like. Her mother considered it a waste of time, but Bertha was generally so active and busy, she might be permitted to waste a little time. It was not so dangerous for her as for some girls who spent their time in nothing but reading. Bertha did more than this. She was always ready to help the younger children. She spent all her spare time from school with her sewing in the nursery, where the little army of boys were collected, and was at hand to help our their knots and soothe over their little quarrels. She knew how to suggest plays when they were tired of the old ones, or would tell tell them a story while she finished "this piece of work for mamma." Mrs. Carlton sat there, undisturbed by the tumult around her. She was so taken up with her stitching and her long seams, that her ears seemed to have grown indurated to all noise. The children seldom thought of appealing to her. If they did in extreme cases, the most innocent were often the most severely scolded and punished, for she had no time to inquire into the source of the trouble. Bertha was not able to bear this long. She had taken a violent cold, and then a fever followed. She thought she was well again, and tried to go through all the old duties. But often she was obliged to lean back in her chair, her head weary with the noise round her, and her pale hands folded over her work. At last she was obliged to give up school, and presently, work. It was only within the last year that Mrs. Carlton had begun to see that Bertha was really ill; that she was coughing badly; that she must not let her sit with the children; that she herself must watch to see that Bertha did not tire herself. Fred was proud of discoursing with the younger children of those happy days when Bertha was well and used to play with them. Bertha was not like Agnes, to think that boys were only great plagues. Even now Bertha ventured to sit a little while in the play-room, and while she was there the tumult would be quieted. Tom would refrain from knocking down Harry's brick house, and Jack find something better to do than upsetting Arthur and all the chairs in the room.

Mrs. Carlton had met with a great disappointment in teaching Agnes. She was not like Bertha. She was gay and wild, without any special fault, but a dislike to be pinned down to tiresome sewing. She became so unmanageable that, in a fit of despair, Mrs. Carlton sent Agnes off to a boarding-school, a school of which she knew nothing, except that "the Lees" went there. Mrs. Carlton had always professed a dislike to the Lees, as being idle girls, and likely to set Agnes a bad example, but as she had no higher object in sending Agnes away than to throw off the responsibility from herself, it was not inconsistent that she should send her to the first school that offered itself. Bertha regretted it deeply. She wanted Agnes at home. She wanted her to care for and love the boys. Her own illness, her loss of strength, prevented her from doing all she could do for them, and longed to do herself. She believed if Agnes could only grow up a little longer at home, she must learn to love these duties as she herself did; and she saw, on the other hand, that Agnes was growing even more weaned from them.

Mrs. Carlton regretted that she had not another daughter to bring up to her favorite occupation. The boys, of course, scorned the idea of sitting still for a moment. Only little Arthur, who was more delicate than the others in his organization, and shrank sometimes from their rough plays, consented to learn a little patchwork. But he was so laughed at by his brothers, who called him a "girl-boy," that Mrs. Carlton had to give him up in despair.

Now that Agnes had returned, Mrs. Carlton was very capricious and injudicious with her. She held a fresh contest with her every day. She abused every occupation Agnes showed the least interest in. She was quite as loud in reproaching Agnes for waste of time, if by chance she took up a volume of Macaulay's History to read, as if sitting idly at the window. Agnes, in the end, took her own way. She went where she pleased, and stayed out as late as she pleased. She read what she chose, and had no fixed hours for occupation any day. She was a favorite in Langdale. Everybody liked to have her with them on any party of pleasure, and as she had her own time at her disposal, she never refused any invitation. Agnes was a favorite of her father's, too. He liked to have her

go in and out of town with him. She picked up
gossip and lively stories with which she entertained him in the evening when he was tired.
Mrs. Carlton, through all the warm summer evenings, as well as by the winter fireside, would be
sitting occupied with her absorbing work, and it
was a resource when Agnes could spare time from
her numerous friends of the village, to relate her
day's experiences, set off with brilliant coloring
and due exaggeration. He liked to have her come
in upon him in his office in town. Her handsome,
gay face lighted up the dingy room, and put him
into a mood to grant whatever she chose to ask
him.

This morning, Mrs. Carlton and Agnes were
arguing again the question of her going into town
so early.

"You can be of great help to me," said Mrs.
Carlton, "if you stay till the afternoon, and go in
then to do my shopping."

"It's too late now," said Agnes; "I've put on
my bonnet, and it would be a waste of time to
take it off again. Besides, I have promised the
Lees."

"What are you going to do with your daguerreotype?" asked Mrs. Carlton; "you had two
taken last week."

"It's only a twenty-five cent one," answered
Agnes; "I don't know but I shall give it to
Tom Paxton. He wants a gallery of all the

Langdale beauties." And with this, Agnes hurried away.

Mrs. Carlton sank down, astonished. "Well, Mr. Carlton ought to do something about that; Agnes does go a little too far. This comes of teaching girls, and sending them to school."

Fred came in to put up his luncheon. He went into town to school. Tom, and Jack, and Arthur went to the school in Langdale. Mrs. Carlton did not think it worth while to teach Harry his letters yet, but she was beginning to think she must send him to school too. He made as much noise as all the rest of the boys put together, when he was left at home.

There was work for Hannah down stairs. When she was through with it, she was to take her sewing to the play-room and sit with Harry. Meanwhile, Harry amused himself in getting into all sorts of mischief. His favorite amusement was sliding down the banisters. Every time Mrs. Carlton passed through the entry, she told him warning stories of boys who had broken their heads in just such dangerous games. Harry kept on until he was allured by an inviting smell to the kitchen. But Bridget would not suffer him to stay there very long, and he came back as Mrs. Carlton was going into Bertha's room. She took Harry in with her under his promise of keeping perfectly quiet. He was allowed to take in his last new horse, which had been brought to him last night. Its tail and one leg were already broken off, so that all zest in playing with it was destroyed, but still it was a worthy object to display to Bertha. Hannah knocked at Bertha's door to tell Mrs. Carlton she had done all she had been told.

"Have you cleaned the knives, cleared away the breakfast things, swept and dusted the parlor, shaken the mats, etc.?" Mrs. Carlton asked. "You may stay here then, and do what Bertha needs of you, and then come in to your sewing. Here is the morning half gone, and I have not accomplished anything. If Agnes had not gone into town, she might have shown Hannah about, and left me a little time for my sewing. I don't know how we are ever to get on with the fall work, there are so many interruptions. We shan't do more than be ready for winter when the spring comes."

CHAPTER XXI.

A DAY AT THE CARLTONS'.

MRS. CARLTON was fond of pouring out the family troubles into Bertha's ears, and Bertha was very willing to listen. It was all she could do to help on the family wheels, and she was patient too, and very thoughtful in her suggestions.

Hannah now, under Bertha's directions, set the room in order, putting away all that gave it an invalid air. She brought the flowers to Bertha herself, that she might rearrange them, and then she drew Bertha's couch to the window. This looked out upon the quiet lawn beside the house, and beyond to an outline of distant hills. The autumn sun came in cheerfully through the almost bared branches of an elm that hung across a part of the window.

This was work that Hannah loved. She would not let a speck of dust rest anywhere, and her touch gave a finished air of neatness to the room. She did it quickly, too, lest she should be suddenly called away before all should be in proper order.

"Now will you bring me my books? I will have them on the table by my side," said Bertha.

"Can you read much, Miss Bertha?" asked Hannah.

"It tires me so that I can read but little," said Bertha, " but I love these books so much, that it seems like having friends, to see them here near me. And then I read when I am tired of thinking."

"Oh, Miss Bertha, the time must go very slow when you are so much alone," said Hannah.

"I have a great deal to think about," said Bertha, "and the sky outside and my flowers to look at. And Amy is here every day and my other friends. You will see I am not so very much alone." Bertha gave a kindly smile of thanks as Hannah left the room, and said, "My room has not looked so neat and cheerful this long time."

Hannah went into the play-room where Mrs. Carlton was sewing. Harry had made a train of cars of all the chairs in the room, except the one Mrs. Carlton occupied. A contest arose between Mrs. Carlton and Harry, she insisting that he must give up a seat to Hannah. Harry was the victor. He declared his train was full, and he could not spare a single car, and Hannah was sent into the next room for a chair. But she did not sit long in quiet, her work was constantly interrupted by Harry's demands. He was used to having the other boys to play with him, and he did not know how to amuse himself. Presently the door opened gently, and Amy appeared.

"I came in a minute to see how you and Hannah

are getting on this morning. I can't stop long, I am going in to see Bertha."

" Everything is dreadfully behindhand," said Mrs. Carlton, " we grow worse and worse every day. It is such a piece of work to get the children off to school, and then they are at home again before I have time to turn round."

"We are all well at home Hannah," said Amy, " Miss Elspeth was in this morning a little while, and she says they are all well there."

" How is Mrs. Campbell?" asked Hannah.

" She seems better this morning, I am going to take her to drive when I go home," said Amy ; " I have been teaching the children. We all miss you very much."

" You are very good to teach those children," said Mrs. Carlton, " but, as Miss Dora says, where's the use of so much teaching?"

" Oh, Mrs. Carlton; I don't think any of us learn or teach too much ; " said Amy laughing, as she hurried away to Bertha.

" I don't see where Amy finds time to do so much," said Mrs. Carlton ; "I should think things must go behindhand somewhere in the house. She is so busy with sewing circles and book clubs and those things. The sewing circles are well enough, only anybody might accomplish twice as much sewing staying at home. All this going out takes up so much time. Now Agnes —"

Mrs. Carlton's speculations were interrupted by

12

a loud bang at the front door. "The boys have come home from school," she sighed. A loud clatter of heavy boots was heard on the stairs. "The boys have come, the boys have come, I'm so glad," Harry exclaimed as he rushed to the door. "Come along, Harry," said Tom, "we are going to have a great time down in the swamp."

"Now you are not going to take Harry down there," exclaimed Mrs. Carlton; "he came in with his feet wet through this morning. His boots are not so thick as yours."

"You should get him some clumpers then," said Tom, "but we want something to eat."

"Hannah, you can get the boys some luncheon," said Mrs. Carlton, "if Bridget can find any. I declare, it seems as if we had just done breakfast. And you'll have to tell Bridget to show you about laying the dinner-table. Now, Harry, you had better stay in."

But Harry was already half way down stairs.

The house was not left long in peace. There were constant emissaries back to it. Jack wanted a hammer, that Hannah must find for him. Tom came back for some more luncheon, and Harry was constantly sent through the mud to know what time it was, and then Hannah must go in and look at the parlor clock. The dinner went through with turmoil and confusion. Agnes and Mr. Carlton not being there, the boys had the talk all to themselves. They were loud in their vociferations of what they would be helped to. Hannah was bewildered by the crossfire of demands made upon her, and any little hesitation or mistake on her part was received with laughter and reproaches. It came out by their talk what was the great work they were all so busy about.   They were building a bridge over one part of the swamp.

"We shall hurry home from school, just as fast as we can," said Tom, "so as to get as much as possible done before Fred comes out to-night."

"I shall speak to your father about it," said Mrs. Carlton; "I don't think it's a safe business to be working in the swamp so, and Harry is all mud. You might pay a little consideration to his clothes, if you won't to your own."

"If Harry is dressed girl-fashion, he had better stay at home like a girl," said Tom.

"I won't be a girl," said Harry, "and I won't stay at home. I don't care for my clothes."

"It will take me all the afternoon to wash him and make him decent," said Mrs. Carlton.

But the boys hurried through their dinner and were off at school again, and Harry kept out of his mother's way as long as possible, that he might not remind her of his disgraced appearance. Hannah was sent after him, and went through a long struggle with him. Harry imitated his older brothers in their treatment of her.

"You may take your work into Miss Bertha's room, this afternoon," said Mrs. Carlton; "that's the only place in the house that's quiet, and I want that stitching done to-day." It was quiet as always in Bertha's room.

"I have had a little visit from Mrs. Paxton, this afternoon," said Bertha; "she came to tell me that Eleonora's husband, Mr. Strange, is quite ill in Florence. Poor Nora! it must be very hard for her, so far away from home."

"What does Mrs. Paxton say about it?"-asked Mrs. Carlton.

"I tried to persuade her to go out to Nora," said Bertha, "but she thinks it would be impossi-, ble for her to get away."

Mrs. Carlton left the room to find Harry.

"Miss Nora never has had any trouble before," said Hannah.

"She has never had much pleasure, either," said Bertha; "she has, indeed, never known this kind of trouble, with her children, too, to care for."

"She always seemed so stately," said Hannah, "that I can't think of her being sorrowful."

"She has never been moved much, either way," said Bertha; "that will make it harder for her when she comes to suffer."

"It seemed as if she lived only to have a good time," said Hannah; "she has always had everything she wanted when she was at home, and then she went away to travel just where she pleased."

"Yet you never saw her look very cheerful or happy, Hannah," said Bertha. "I don't know how it has been since she was married, since she went away. She writes home letters filled with descriptions of beautiful places she has seen, but they are not very happy letters."

Agnes opened the door at this moment, and put in her head. "I thought I would tell you that I'd got home, and I've had a first-rate time."

"Oh, come in, come in, Agnes," said Bertha.

"I've seen a little of everybody," said Agnes, coming in, "and have bought me a new dress. The shops are full of such beautiful things, one wants to buy everything, though I can't think when I shall wear this. Oh, such colored ribbons, Bertha !"

"But come here a moment; come nearer to me," said Bertha; "what is this about the daguerreotype? Mother is quite worried. You don't mean to give it to Tom Paxton, with all the other girls?"

"Oh, dear, no; I just said it," said Agnes; "I did not even have it taken. There was such a crowd of people at the place, I couldn't wait. I only said it to make a fuss. Mother is worrying so all the time, I thought she might just as well have something to fuss about."

"O Agnes! why will you do so?" said Bertha, troubled.

"Well, because I am Agnes," she answered; "you know you are here to be the good one, and I may as well vary the subject by being bad."

The tears came into Bertha's eyes.

"You needn't be troubled," said Agnes; "I have to fight my battles. I'll try to keep them out of your room, that is all."

"It would be easy for you to get along without fighting," said Bertha, "it is so easy for you to please people."

"I should grow tired of clear admiration," said Agnes; "I like variety, and I don't mind being talked at. I like to have people talk at me and about me," and Agnes gave one of her favorite shakes to her head, and went out of the room.

Much to Mrs. Carlton's satisfaction, Hannah finished the appointed task of stitching, in the midst of her other duties. Mrs. Carlton praised Hannah's powers, and said Miss Elspeth was an excellent teacher. The boys all came home to a late supper from their labors in the swamp. Mr. and Mrs. Carlton left the tea-table to them, under Hannah's care. Fred pronounced the great work of the bridge to be going on admirably. Agnes came in to hear the account.

"What's the use of having a bridge into a swamp?" she asked; "nobody wants to go there but the turtles and frogs. You boys had rather wet your feet than not."

"You ought to be grateful, Agnes," said Tom; "girls are always wanting to be getting at flowers in swampy places. Now, you'll only have to cross the bridge."

"I suppose you've pulled up all the flowers, making it," said Agnes.

"Oh! it's great fun," exclaimed Harry.

"I should think so," said Agnes; "you look as if you had been up to your ears in the mud all day."

The elder boys were left to study their evening lessons in the dining-room. Hannah assisted in bearing the struggling Harry away to bed. Agnes held a conclave of the Lees at the door. Then she piled up the cushions on the sofa, and after she was comfortably arranged, amused herself by giving her father a lively account of her day's proceedings.

CHAPTER XXII.

A WEEK.

THE first day had passed away at her new home. It had seemed very long to Hannah. She was amazed at its close to find herself looking forward with some interest to the coming of another. She was excited by the little details that came along to interrupt its course, and she rose with unexpected alacrity to its new duties. She was not greeted this morning by the shower of boots that had roused her the day before. She went for them herself, and found it hard labor to free them from the mud of their work in the swamp. The duties that followed were very much those of the first day. There was the same rush and hurry of the boys, and noise and confusion while they were in the house. But in these last lingering days of autumn they were occupied out of doors almost all the time they were not at school. They brought in with them great quantities of mud, much to Mrs. Carlton's horror, whenever they came in, while Hannah persevered admirably with her sewing in their absence.

Bertha was very much alone. It was true that she had many friends who came often to see her, but it was at uncertain hours. Amy was with her a few moments every day. Agnes was very capricious in her attention to Bertha. Sometimes she seemed to exert herself as much as possible to entertain her. She would sit with her and watch her motions and offer her whatever she needed. No one could be more amusing.than Agnes was at such times, nor more tender in her manners. But she would be gone whole mornings or afternoons, scarcely seeing Bertha for the whole day. Some days, without telling any one her plans for the day, visiting the neighbors, or walking with her friends, lounging away her time in lively thoughtlessness.

Bertha liked to have the boys come in to see her, and they always behaved gently and thoughtfully while in her room. She showed them her flowers and her pictures. They brought home wonderful specimens of flowers that they had picked purposely for Bertha, which she always received cordially, and treasured.

"How can you keep those weeds to litter up the room?" Agnes exclaimed. "That sprangling golden rod, and there's a real mullein Jack has brought in to you."

"I always liked the golden rod," said Bertha. "You ought to admire its bright color with those purple asters."

"Why, you can see them all along the roadside." said Agnes.

" You forget," said Bertha, " that I can't see them. You know it is only very rarely, now that the warm days are passing away, that I can go out to see golden rod and asters. I like to have it in the room. It makes me think of the broad fields of it on the edge of the road, bowing in the wind."

" Well, I should as soon think of caring for the road fence," said Agnes.

Agnes was fond of throwing off the little labors she should have performed at home upon Hannah. She sent her upon errands, gave her work of all sorts to do, and called upon her continually. Even Mrs. Carlton remonstrated.

" It wouldn't hurt you, Agnes, to do some of your going up and down stairs yourself. Hannah has enough to be busy about."

" She's paid to do the work," said Agnes, unfeelingly, "and I am not. If she thinks the work too hard, she can go."

The consequence was, that Hannah did have to work very hard. She was called upon by everybody for every kind of service, and service that was not requested but demanded. She was sitting one morning with her work in the play-room. The morning's labors had been unusually hard and trying and she leaned back in her chair a moment, her hands resting upon her sewing. The boys had come home from school, and were all out at play, except Arthur, who stood by the window. He turned round suddenly.

"Are you tired of sewing?" he asked of Hannah.

Hannah was surprised at his observing her, and went on with her work.

"No, I am not tired of sewing. I like to sew."

"Then I suppose you are tired of running about so up and down stairs."

"I am used to that," said Hannah.

"Then you must be tired of being ordered about," said Arthur. "I hate it. That's why I've come in. I don't mind Fred's sending me round, but when it comes to Tom and Jack's ordering me about, I can't stand it."

"I don't mind that," said Hannah; "that does not tire me."

"What makes you look so tired all the time, then?"

"Do I look tired?" asked Hannah. "I didn't know it. It does not tire me to work, because I am used to it. I would like to work for some people all day long. I like to work for Miss Bertha because she is so kind; she is pleased with what I do for her."

"Other people like what you do," said Arthur. "Fred says you're a trump."

"I didn't know I ever pleased him," said Hannah. "He is talking at me all the time."

"Well, you can't expect him to be praising you up; that is girls' way," said Arthur. "But it is very easy to know when you've pleased Fred, and then the rest of the boys always think as he does."

Arthur was already tired of staying in the house, and he left Hannah, a little encouraged that she was beginning to find favor with those autocrats, " the boys." Saturday evening she went to Miss Elspeth's. Through the week, since Monday night, when she left them, she had seen Bessie, Margie, and Martha occasionally, and Amy every day for a few moments. Sunday morning, when Hannah went in with Bertha's breakfast, she lingered to speak with her. She had something to say which she found it hard to express.

" I don't know as I have any right to think about it, Miss Bertha," she began, " but Miss Elspeth encouraged me to think there was no harm, though it was a little plan I made all myself."

" What is it?" said Bertha.

Hannah brought our her plan clumsily.

" I wished I had time and knew how better to read to you, and then I thought Margie was such a good reader, and she would like to read to you so much. There are so many of your books that you are not well enough to read, Miss Bertha, and Miss Amy has not time either."

" But Margie has not time," said Bertha. " Did you think of asking her to come to me? Hannah, I should be afraid Miss Elspeth had enough for her to do, and Margie is too young to give up her play hours to me."

" Oh, I spoke to Margie about it last night," said Hannah, " and she was quite glad with pleasure at the thought of coming, and hoped you would let

her. She is so fond of reading. They say she
likes to read one book as well as another. She
begged that she might come."

"And Miss Elspeth?" asked Bertha.

"Miss Elspeth was much pleased too," said Hannah. "She said the books you would like to hear
read would do Margie good. Margie said she
would come any day or every day. I told them I
thought you were most alone in the early part of
the afternoon; that you could not always sleep
then."

"Hannah," said Bertha, "it pleases me to have
you so thoughtful of me. It pleases me as much
as it will to have Margie come and read to me.
And then you have chosen the right time too! It
is the hardest part of the day with me. I grow
tired then, and am often alone."

"Then you will let Margie come?" asked Hannah, eagerly.

"Very gladly," said Bertha. "She must not
come every day, though. We will try every other
day. I shall like to have it to look forward to."

"Then I may tell Margie this morning?" said
Hannah. "I shall see her on the way to church.
She said she should come and meet me, she was so
anxious to know."

Hannah went back to the Sunday morning's
duties, which were always especially confusing.
The boys were always late at breakfast, and then
they were to be dressed for church. In a most

distracting manner Hannah was called in every
direction. At one moment she was expected to
carry hot water to Mr. Carlton; to find a missing
shoe of Harry's; to hunt up Tom's cap, and to settle a difference between Tom and Jack as to the
ownership of the only cap that could be found.
There was great shouting up stairs and down.
Agnes was secluded a long time in her room, and
then came out in magnificent array. She stood in
the entry, laughing at the " set " of the boys' Sunday collars. Harry had a violent fit of crying from
some unknown cause. Jack upset Arthur, who
was already dressed for church.

"Dear me! I should think it was Babel instead
of Sunday morning," said Mrs. Carlton; "Agnes,
why can't you help somebody, instead of standing
there irritating the boys?"

"I'm only giving them some wholesome advice,"
said Agnes.

"Agnes looks like a peacock with its tail spread,"
said Jack; "she has on all the colors of the rainbow."

"I should think she might find my cap," said
Tom; "I can't wear my straw hat to church, the
brim is half torn off."

"Who has lost a cap?" said Fred, who had been
out to inspect the barnyard.

"It's Tom's cap; have you found it?" said Mrs.
Carlton, "it is time we started for church."

"I can't say it's much of a find," said Fred; "the

brown hen has stolen her nest in somebody's cap.
She looks as comfortable in it under the barn stairs
as if it were made for her. You will have to do
without it. It wont do to disturb her."

"Under the barn stairs! what a place for your
cap, Tom!" said Mrs. Carlton.

"I don't believe it's mine, it's just like Jack to
leave his there," said Tom, as he joined the rush to
see the brown hen's nest.

"I'm so tired by the time I get to church, Sunday mornings," said Mrs. Carlton, "that I don't
have strength to listen to the sermon; I am all in a
flutter now. You might have been in Bertha's
room the last half hour making yourself useful,
Agnes."

"I don't like to be useful Sundays," said Agnes,
setting forth as she saw the Lees passing the door.
Hannah had barely time to prepare herself for
church. She was in as great a flurry as Mrs. Carlton. It rejoiced her to meet Margie and to see her
delight when she was told that Bertha was willing
she should read to her.

"What a nice thought it was of yours!" Margie
exclaimed; "I shall thank you for it to the end of
my life! Bertha is so lovely and so beautiful it will
make me happy to be near her."

Hannah was indeed encouraged to think that she
could make a plan that should be so well thought
of. It was a new feeling with which she entered
church. It gave her an unusual confidence in her-

self, a consciousness that she was of worth to some-body. The remembrance of the little jars of the morning, its disagreements, passed away, and she felt more than ever before the solemnity of the place she had entered. Before, she was often list-less and inattentive. To-day Mr. Jasper's words were encouraging to her mood of mind.

Amy had observed a change in the style of Mr. Jasper's preaching since he went away. He was younger then, but she remembered perfectly how hopefully, with what courage, he spoke, how earn-estly he exhorted all to go forward manfully in the battle of life.

Now she thought he spoke more sadly, at times almost despondingly. Yet no one else seemed to remark this. His preaching was enthusiastically praised. "What an improvement upon old Mr. Peterson," said Agnes to Amy as she came out of church; "I was really beginning to give up going to church, when Mr. Jasper came back."

Hannah gladly stayed at home with Bertha in the afternoon. Bertha was not so well this day. She was more languid, but not at all complaining. Her strength varied from day to day. In some warmer days of November she was strong enough to go down stairs, to go out occasionally to drive.

When she came down stairs, the boys, even the younger ones, were devoted in their attentions to her.

"It will be fine when you are well enough to come down every day!" Tom said.

CHAPTER XXIII.

THOSE BOYS!

THERE was a constant warfare between Agnes and her brothers. Their jarrings and bickerings formed the excitements of each day. There was a little world of tumult seething in the house all the time. Mrs. Carlton went on steadily with her sewing, and the affairs of the house moved along smoothly enough, but only in Bertha's room did there seem to be peace and quiet. This incessant contest affected Hannah's temper too. She became sullen in her obedience, and impertinent in her replies to the boys, and even to Mrs. Carlton. She was sorry for what she had said often as soon as she had spoken. It was not natural to her to yield to any sudden passion. She was slow in her thoughts, and was more wont to brood over any trouble, and heighten it by her mistrust and suspicion, than to give vent to her feelings. Now she had not time to bury herself in long fits of doubt. One offence quickly followed upon another.

The faults of a household spread from the higher to the lower members. Agnes's talent for repartee

13

was very attractive to the boys, who were glad to
imitate it.   Without any ill-feeling toward Hannah,
they were glad to make her their butt, and expend
their wit upon her.   Bridget had a gift of the
tongue too, and the same warfare went on in the
kitchen that prevailed in the parlor.   What a little
world the four walls of each house shut in!   The
little duties of each day grow magnified till they
come to seem great aims.   The little differences
between one and another are fostered till they grow
into weighty strifes.   Sickness and suffering are
hidden in one place, and where there might be happiness in another, there is discordance and petty
turmoil.   One ruling, cheerful spirit might make a
sunny home in all!

"If Bertha were only well!" thought those who
looked a little into the interior of the Carltons'
home.   Yet her secluded life had its influence over
the turbid waves of the little sea about her.

Agnes, and her friends the Lees, came in one
day, at noon, and heard a great tittering in the
parlor.   They stopped and looked through the
door.   There was Jack lounging on the sofa, an old
bonnet of Agnes's on the back of his head.   The
bobs of his kite were strung on each side of his
face, and he shook them as though they were falling ringlets.   He was carrying on a talk, taking off
Agnes, with Tom, very much to the amusement of
Harry and Arthur, who were rolling on the floor
with delight, and to the entertainment of two of

their boy friends. "I saw such an ecstatic shawl
yesterday when I went into town," he went on,
"it threw me into supreme delight! I absolutely
fainted, and would you believe it, Tom Paxton? I
was carried into Vinton's and they had to throw
two pails of ice-cream over me before I recovered!
Fortunately, one was flavored with vanilla, which
you know I detest, and that of course roused me.
It's a happy thing my nerves are not easily shat-
tered, or I shouldn't be here now!"

"That would have been a dreadful pity," said
Tom. Jack ran on in the same strain.

"Those boys!" exclaimed Agnes. She kept in
her laughter and went off to find a great coat of
Fred's, which she put on and returned with it into
the room where the boys were. She walked in,
her hands in her pockets, imitating Jack's indifferent manner, and exaggerating it, making detestable
puns and creating quite a roar on her side.

"Well, you're a good-natured piece of elegance,"
said Jack, shouting and throwing his bonnet on the
floor. Mrs. Carlton came in at the noise.

"I should really like to know if there are young
ladies in the midst of all this uproar? Agnes,
what are you coming to next?"

"Do let her have a little fun with us," exclaimed
Tom. "It isn't often she'll consent to be amusing
to us."

"I think you are in better business in your
swamp," said Mrs. Carlton, "than cluttering up the

parlor, and making such a hideous noise in the house."

"That's a fact," said Jack. "Don't let us stay any longer in the house. Agnes, why can't you come and see our bridge?"

"You can bring along your Lees with you," said Tom.

"Dance over, my Lady Lee," whispered Jack.

"I don't care to see your bridge," said Agnes. "I don't want to wet my feet through."

"Oh, my Lady Elegance has on her new boots," said Tom.

"There's plenty of water in case she should faint at sight of mud," said Jack.

"Don't say the word mud, or she'll faint now," said Tom, "and the Miss Lees too." And the whole troop went clattering out of the house.

"I should think you might know better," said Mrs. Carlton, complainingly, "than to encourage those boys. They talk enough as it is!"

Agnes and the boys were not always at sword's points. They were very glad to join in the amusements that were got up when her friends came to spend the evening with her. They listened with delight to her talk, and were ready to join games and dances. They liked nothing better than these merry evenings, while the next day they would laugh unmercifully at her guests, caricaturing all they had said and done the night before. Even Harry was eager to sit up on such occasions. Many times he was rigidly sent to bed, but would appear again at some unexpected door, or start up from behind a chair.

Mr. Jasper came one day. He had hoped he might see Bertha. But she had not been so well for a few days, and was not down stairs. He found a coterie of Agnes's friends assembled.

"I was amazed to see you at the rehearsal, the other day," said Agnes.

"Why shouldn't I be there?" asked Mr. Jasper. "May not I enjoy music as well as any of you young folks?"

"Oh, I supposed you were one of the kind that would not enjoy music when there were other people about," said Agnes. "Some people are so disturbed if you say just a word or shake your head while music is going on. I wish they would sit inside of the organ, they could not do anything but hear there."

"And what else do you want to do?" asked Mr. Jasper.

"Oh, I want to see and to talk a little myself," said Agnes. "It is so tiresome at the rehearsals when they play those long, solemn pieces; one might as well be at church."

"And not better?" asked Mr. Jasper.

"Oh, I forgot about you," said Agnes, "and I was not thinking about your church."

"I had rather you would not think of it as *my* church," said Mr. Jasper. "I serve in it only."

" But I like to be lively when I am lively," said
Agnes, " and solemn when I'm solemn. Now the
sermon last Sunday made me sober, and I liked it."

" Did you ? " said Mr. Jasper. " You gave me
a whole half hour, or nearly that ! I thank you for
the present."

" I don't see that it was much of a present," said
Agnes. " Half hours are cheap. I am glad to be
rid of them sometimes."

" I was grateful for your attention," said Mr.
Jasper. " Do you give that often ? "

" What do you mean ? I attend to what I'm
about," said Agnes.

" What *are* you about ? " asked Mr. Jasper.

" It ought to be something very useful if I'm
talking with you, I suppose," replied Agnes. "Everybody wants to set me to work. Will you join
the crusade ? What will you have me give my
attention to beside your sermons ? "

" Miss Sally More was calling at the Fays, when
I met you there yesterday," said Mr. Jasper.

" Yes ; how she did look ! " said Agnes.

" I saw you were studying her," said Mr. Jasper. " I dare say you could tell me just how she
was dressed."

" Oh, I meant to tell it all to the girls here,"
said Agnes. " It was a plum-colored silk ; a real
old-fashioned plum-color. I had half a mind to
bring out some of the Fays' plums to see if they
would not match. Then she had an immense

parasol of a changeable green. There was a broad yellow ribbon on her bonnet, and pink roses inside, and a red scarf round her neck."

"That will do," said Mr. Jasper. "I did not intend to call out that sort of picture. I wanted to see what kind of attention you were paying to poor Miss Sally. Now, Amy Rothsay would have picked out something worthy from her; would have told me the story Miss Sally was telling."

"Oh, that is your moral," exclaimed Agnes. "There's always some such thorn concealed in what you say. Sometimes I have a very lively talk with you, and after I am at home and think it over, I find there was a dagger hidden."

"That is wrong of me," said Mr. Jasper. "I ought not to wound any one's conscience even, so long as it is alive."

"Amy Rothsay is a bit of perfection," said Agnes. "It is useless to hold her up as an example."

"What do you mean by a bit of perfection?" asked Mr. Jasper.

"I suppose I mean that there's a large lump of perfection somewhere, and she's a bit broken off from it," said Agnes.

"That is not saying enough," said Mr. Jasper. "The artists, you know, talk about a little 'bit' of a landscape, meaning a pretty piece of tree and sky, that they can take out from the rest and frame by itself. Now Amy is just such a bit. She would bear to be put in a frame by herself and make a complete picture."

"You go as far in praising as you do in finding fault," said Agnes. "The rest of us here are not worth framing, I suppose."

"A little piece of nature would always be worth that," said Mr. Jasper.

"Now, I'm tired of talking that way," said Agnes. "Won't you talk about the weather? It has been very entertaining lately."

"Is there no hope of my seeing Miss Bertha this week?" asked Mr. Jasper.

"I can't tell," said Agnes, "she varies so much. Some days she is much better, and then she is worse again. I wish she could have gone away. We wanted to send her with an aunt who was going to Havana, but Bertha thought she was not strong enough to go."

"It is your gain; I hope it is not her loss," said Mr. Jasper. "But you can do much to make her winter comfortable and not harmful."

"I can't *do* much," said Agnes. "It is not my way. I like to do as I feel. I can't keep my strings stretched all the time."

"Your Æolian harps that only wait for the wind are soon out of tune," said Mr. Jasper.

"I hope it isn't use that's to keep me in tune," said Agnes. "I know I am jangling half the time."

"Do you know," said one of the Lees, after Mr. Jasper had left, "they say Mr. Jasper wanted to marry your sister Bertha when he went away?"

"I never heard that," said Agnes.

"Well, people wouldn't talk to you about it," said Maria, "and you were so young then you couldn't tell."

"I remember," said Agnes, "thinking he was here a great deal. He used to be very lively and full of fun."

"Mr. Jasper don't object to fun now," said Maria.

"Well, let us go on with what we were about," said Agnes. "Mr. Jasper's coming has quite put it out of my head."

"You were telling about what Tom Paxton said," said one of the Lees.

"Oh, yes; how he thought he could persuade his mother to let us have their house for the theatricals. You know the handsome large parlors would be fine."

"But Mrs. Paxton would never consent to having them upturned."

"Oh, Tom can do what he pleases, you know," said Agnes.

"All those things would have to be moved out," said one of the Lees.

"And Mr. Strange is very sick too now," said another.

"You needn't raise objections," said Agnes, "Tom Paxton can arrange it all. He has had the furniture moved about in the parlor two or three times since he came home. But we must not make much talk about it, or it can't be done."

CHAPTER XXIV.

TWILIGHT.

MARGIE proved a very valuable reader to Bertha. She enjoyed the reading so much herself that she was never willing to allow anything to interfere with her afternoons in Bertha's room. She had a romantic admiration for Bertha. It was a pleasure merely to sit and watch her motions, and a greater pleasure to perform any service for her. She admired the exquisite air of everything in the room, the delicate perfume of the flowers there, the beautiful engravings, too, of which Bertha had much to tell her, the absolute neatness of everything, the whiteness of the curtains, and the uninterrupted sky view that came in at the windows. And Bertha always chose for her the pleasantest books. They were always such inviting looking books, too, the paper white and clean. She was willing Margie should read her poetry, and such poetry that they could talk about afterward, that Margie had never read, and that lingered long in Margie's mind with all her other beautiful associations with Bertha. Yet Bertha was not willing that Margie should dwell upon these alone, though she would gladly have read nothing else. She made her read gay, merry books, and others that were very serious.

"Oh, the winter afternoons are so short," Margie exclaimed, as she went home one day; "we have such a short time in them for reading, now-a-days."

Margie said this as she went into the parlor at Miss Elspeth's. Miss Elspeth and Miss Dora were sitting in the twilight by the fire, with Bessie and Martha, only the fire lighting up the room.

"But you went this afternoon to the Carltons as soon as dinner was done," said Bessie.

"Yet it became dark very quickly," said Margie, "and Bertha actually sent me away. I did not like to come, she looked so beautifully. The light of the sunset came streaming into the room over her couch, and the flowers, and her beautiful face too."

"Did you give Bertha your rose?" asked Miss Elspeth.

"Yes, but she had such lovely flowers to-day," said Margie. "Everybody sends her what is most exquisite and rare. There was one flower that I thought looked so much like her. It was shaped like the white water-lily, but instead of the pure white petals, they were pure blue. I can't tell you the color of the blue, — it was like the blue of the sky when there are a great many white clouds in it. Agnes provoked me by saying it was *French* blue."

"The color of forget-me-nots," said Bessie.

"But the most beautiful part was the inside; the yellow stamens were each tipped with this same delicate blue, and it was all cut so beautifully. I always thought the white water-lily was the most lovely flower in the world, but this, oh! this, was like Bertha."

"How you do talk, Margie!" said Miss Dora; "your tongue starts when you read to Bertha Carlton, and then you keep on."

"We had a talk this afternoon," said Margie, "about books, and imagination, and all those things. I said I did not see as there was any more harm in being occupied with my own imagination, and being taken up by it, than in reading stories that other people have written."

"What did Bertha say?" said Miss Elspeth.

"She said it was a more selfish occupation," said Margie, "because other people were interested, too, in the books we read, but that we did not share the pleasure we had in our own thoughts. She said she had so many hours to herself, that there was great danger she should forget the people round her, and forget to sympathize with them, and care what happened to them. She need never be afraid of that. She shows more interest in everybody than I do, walking round with them every day."

"There's some sense in reading stories to Bertha Carlton," said Miss Dora; "I don't see as she can do much else now, and Margie does as much work as when she was not away three afternoons in a week."

"It is a great privilege for Margie to be with Bertha Carlton," said Miss Elspeth.

"Are we not going to have the candles?" asked Miss Dora.

"Oh, don't let us have them yet," said Bessie; "it is so much pleasanter talking by this light. Margie never talks so much. She sits looking into the coals, and forgets we are here. Do go on about Bertha."

"I wish I could draw and paint," said Margie; "I could make such a beautiful picture of Bertha; oh! I think I could. Words always seem very clumsy to say what I want to, and I do like color so much. She looks so thoughtful always, and not joyful, as Amy Rothsay does."

"Did you see Hannah?" asked Miss Dora.

"Only for a few minutes," said Margie; "I have not talked with her lately. She used to sit in the room regularly, but Mrs. Carlton and Agnes find so much for her to do, it is too bad."

"Let me take your stocking and set the heel," said Bessie, seeing Miss Dora troubled at an intricate part of her knitting."

"I can see well enough," said Miss Dora, "only I think it's time to have the candles. I don't know what's the matter with my spectacles, — they don't suit me as well as they used to."

"I'll get the candles," said Martha; "this talking by firelight is very pleasant, but then there are my French exercises."

"And, oh dear! I have some work to finish too," said Bessie.

At the same hour, at the Rothsays' house, Amy was sitting by the firelight, in the parlor. She was waiting her father's return from town. Mr. Jasper came in.

"I have been in to talk with Mrs. Campbell," he said, "and now I want to have a little talk with you."

He drew a comfortable chair to the fireside, and sat awhile, thinking. "I want to ask you to do something for me," said he, at last; "I want very much to see Bertha. Will you ask her if she will see me?"

"I think she will be glad to," said Amy; "some days she seems very well, and I think nothing is better for her than to see her friends."

"I have spoken to Agnes about it, but I had rather you would ask Bertha," said Mr. Jasper; "I think she may not wish it."

"But she has seen a great many of her friends," said Amy; "Annie Lane came the other day purposely to see her, and papa has seen her once or twice, and Frank."

"Do you remember that spring when Bertha was first ill?" asked Mr. Jasper.

"Oh, yes," said Amy, "and the violent attack

upon her lungs. She told me about it herself.
I never shall forget that time,—it came upon
me with a shock. She told me all the doctor
said."

"She was better a little while after," said Mr.
Jasper.

"Yes, very much better," said Amy, "and I felt
very much encouraged, and tried to forget it
all,—to forget that the doctor had said she might
never be well. And we had together some pleasant spring drives, and some walks too."

"And do you remember," said Mr. Jasper, "the
place we used to walk to, not far away, on the bank
of the stream, where there is a willow that bends
over and dips into the water?"

"Yes, indeed," said Amy; "it is beautiful still
just where the stream winds round the point."

"I have never been there since that time," said
Mr. Jasper. "I went one warm spring day, Bertha thought she could walk as far. We found the
first anemones that day. Frank, your brother
Frank, said he would meet us at the turn of the
road, and would drive Bertha home. So we kept
on as far as the stream. It was there, beneath
the willow, that I told Bertha what she knew
before, that I loved her, that I wanted her to
marry me."

"And Bertha?" asked Amy.

"She could not marry me," said Mr. Jasper.

"She thought she should not live long,—was it

so ? " said Amy, after a pause. " I remember we talked of that often, or rather it was Bertha who talked to me of it. She was told she might live a few years longer, with great care, but that perhaps she might not live the summer through. I could not bear to think of it, scarcely to hear her speak of it. But I know it was in her mind constantly, and that she was quietly preparing herself for it."

Mr. Jasper walked up and down the room, and said at last, " I would not like to give her pain. I would not like to excite her with thoughts that would harass her. If, indeed, she has her face fixed toward heaven, I would not like to call her back again to earth. And yet, I long to see her. No weary prisoner ever longed to see the light again as I have longed to see Bertha's face once more. It used to give me strength and hopefulness, and when it was shut out from me, it left me dispirited, in the dark. God forgive me if it is a selfish wish, — if I forget what she may suffer in thinking of all that I shall gain in seeing her once more."

" Bertha will tell me truly," said Amy, after a while; " if she thinks it is beyond her strength, she will tell me so. But I do not think she is so easily excited as I have sometimes feared she would be. One great thought fills her mind, and everything else is swayed by that. Oh, I would like to have you see her. I know it would bring you peace."

"More than five years I have been away from her," said Mr. Jasper, "and yet her image has been closely near me. I have almost fancied every day it might be her spirit, and that I should hear it had been freed, and so was able to come and keep me from being alone."

Mr. Jasper bade Amy good-night suddenly, and went away. Amy sank back again into thought. "Then Mr. Jasper banished himself from here," she thought, "and these last few years have made a separation between him and Bertha. How little while it seems since they were both here, and in this very room George sat too. How much more hopeful is my separation from him, — more hopeful as far as this world is concerned. And did Bertha love Mr. Jasper? He influenced her most powerfully,—that she has often acknowledged to me ; and I know that with her it would be possible to keep such a love quite hidden in her heart. But yet, would she let him go away from her? What reason could she have that would be powerful enough? And how much she must have suffered if it were so! She is far more heavenly minded than I am. I am thinking so intently of my future happiness here, and she has built hers in another world."

It was not often that Amy was allowed the quiet time for a reverie by the fireside, and now her thoughts were interrupted. The little Campbells broke into the room.

14

"Cousin Amy, Katie has let us have tea in the kitchen, it was so late."

"And what do you think we had for supper?"

"May we sit in your lap and tell you all we had for supper?"

CHAPTER XXV.

BERTHA'S ROOM.

THE first snow came and fell heavily on the
ground. It interrupted the labors of the boys,
and Mrs. Carlton expressed loudly her pleasure at
this, as the very day before she had been thrown
into alarm by an accident that befell Harry. Arthur came hurrying into the house, crying out for
somebody's help, saying that Harry was lost in the
swamp. Hannah was the first to hasten to the
scene of trouble. She went out through the yard
and the meadow, behind the house, to the skirt of
the wood, along which a broad space of swampy
ground stretched. It was here the boys were
working upon their bridge. Harry had been
amusing himself in a favorite sport of jumping
from one little tuft of grass to another, till he had
lost his footing, and suddenly cried out to the boys
that he was sinking in the mud. Hannah found
that Jack had gone to rescue him, but was in
trouble himself. He had lost his own boot in his
efforts, and seemed uncertain whether to devote
himself to rescuing that or Harry. Tom was try-

ing to encourage Harry, who was screaming loudly. Hannah looked round to see how she might be of service. She brought from the wood a strong branch of a tree, and at length, with Tom and Jack's help, she succeeded in drawing Harry out of his perilous position. He was wet through, however, and shivering with cold. By the time that they were turned back towards the house they met a party of men, whom Arthur's entreaties and representations had brought down to Harry's help. Mrs. Carlton was at the door to receive them.

"I expected no more than this," she exclaimed. "I only wonder it has not happened before. Harry will be sick a week after it, and that suit of clothes is entirely ruined. Tom and Jack are not fit to be trusted with the care of Harry."

"There wasn't anything the matter to make such a fuss about," said Tom. "We should have got Harry out in time, only Arthur is always frightened the first thing. He wants to run into the house if a leaf rustles."

"And where's Jack?" said Mrs. Carlton. "In more mischief?"

"He's fishing out his boot," said Tom. "One of the men is helping him."

"Tell him to come directly into the house," said Mrs. Carlton. "I am going to speak to Mr. Carlton to-day and tell him to put an end to all this working in the swamp. It ruins the carpets, all the mud that is brought into the house! It might have been the death of Harry, and it's impossible to keep his clothes decent, or any of you fit to be seen."

The snow came to assist Mrs. Carlton in her determination. It began to fall towards night, and the next morning lay thickly piled· upon the ground. The boys were up as early as Hannah, full of excitement.

"We are going to help you this morning," they exclaimed. "We'll clear your steps for you. Fred is going to find our snow shovels; he knows where they are."

Harry, too, was eager to bear his part, and begged the kitchen shovel of Bridget.

Agnes groaned that the snow should make the walking so bad, and hoped Tom Paxton would get up a sleigh-ride. She went into Bertha's room for consolation.

"I declare, you look cosy here," she exclaimed. "Your little crackling fire sounds comfortably. And how pretty the snow-wreaths round the window are. You always manage to make the chamber bright and cheerful."

"Hannah, here, does it all," said Bertha. "She knows how to give a 'touch' to a room."

"I wish she would give a touch to mine a little oftener," said Agnes. "And before you begin dusting the shelves, Hannah, suppose you take those books out of the easy chair and draw it up

to the fire. I may as well sit comfortably while I
am here. I have not told you about the party at
the Fays' last night, Bertha."

"Was everybody there?" asked Bertha.

"Almost everybody. We had rather a slow
time, on the whole," said Agnes. "I had a long
talk with Mr. Jasper, as usual. They tried to get
up a dance, but it did not succeed very well."

"I suppose Amy went?" said Bertha.

"Yes, Amy was there. She wore her new
dress," said Agnes. "They say it's quite certain
George Arnold comes home in the spring, and I
suppose Amy will be married then. Does she
ever talk to you about it?"

"Not much," said Bertha. "I think Amy feels
very happily about it. She thinks it is best for
George to be away."

"I think it is quite useless to be so virtuous,"
said Agnes. "It would have been a great deal
pleasanter to have had George Arnold here, among
us all. He was before my time, but I remember
those funny sketches he used to draw. I don't
believe there's anybody half so entertaining now.
Frank Rothsay has grown stiff, and studies so
hard, one can't get a word out of him."

"I thought Frank seemed as full of fun as ever,
when I saw him the other day," said Bertha.

"He can be as amusing as anybody," said Agnes. "Now, Thanksgiving night it was a perfect
refreshment to have him come in here. That, to

be sure, was by way of contrast, after the stupid
time we had been having. It is the stupidest day
in the whole year, one grows so tired of one's
relations."

"That's ungrateful, when you are the favorite
of the family," said Bertha.

"Oh, well, I like them all separately, but they
are tiresome to take them in a lump, and all day
long too! I'm afraid our plan of theatricals is to-
fall through!"

"You were very sanguine about it yesterday,"
said Bertha.

"I know it," said Bertha, "but last night Tom
Paxton told me he was afraid he should not bring
his mother to consent to it. He has been talking
to her about it."

"I don't wonder," said Bertha, "that she should
be unwilling to have them in her house, when she
is feeling so anxiously about Mrs. Strange."

"She don't feel anxious enough to care to go
abroad and see her," replied Agnes. "She might at
least consent to have a little fun going on. The
Lees thought they might have them in their house,
though Mrs. Lee don't like the trouble. And Tom
Paxton says he don't care to have them if they are
not at his house and if I don't take a part."

"Have you decided not to take a part?" said
Bertha, surprised.

"I never meant to," said Agnes, "though I did
not say much about it for fear they would give it

up, and I like the amusement of getting them up.
But do think what a world of trouble it would be!
How many pages I should have to learn! It
would be as bad as school-days, because I did not
care if I missed then; now, it would be rather dis-
agreeable to forget one's part before all Langdale."

"You are consistent," said Bertha, laughing.
"You are not willing to put yourself out, or take
any trouble about the theatricals, even."

"I meant to put all the trouble off on the other
girls," said Agnes. "They were to make the curtains and the dresses and all that."

"It is a habit you have," said Bertha. "If you
had been willing to work in the school-days, it
would not come hard to work now."

"But where's the use," said Agnes, beginning to
walk up and down the room; "lately I have had a
great many talks with Mr. Jasper. I talk to him
just as I do to other people, whatever happens to
come uppermost; and I do believe he likes it. I
think he is interested in talking to me. Yet he is
always stumbling against some one or other of my
faults, and showing it off to me. I wish there was
such a thing as being liked in spite of one's faults."

"Oh, there is," said Bertha; "nobody is perfect,
and so we love our friends, whatever their faults
are; the more deeply, the more anxious their
faults make us."

"That is not what I mean," said Agnes, impatiently; "angelic people can do all that. I sup-

pose patience is one of their virtues. I don't
know anything about that. I never was patient.
But I was thinking about Mr. Jasper. I tell you I
think he likes me. But I do shock him very often,
and I know my faults stand in the way of his
liking me any better. He would like to do me
some good; that is his vocation, and he likes me
out of the hope he has that I shall be better some
day. I don't care for that. I want to be liked all
for myself, because I am what I am and no other.
I want to be loved with all my faults heaped on
me!"

"There is only one friend loves that way; only
one," said Bertha, seriously.

Agnes turned and looked at Bertha, whose eyes
were fixed upon the clear view that stretched
beyond the window.

"You can say that," said Agnes, "because you
have left all earthly feelings behind. You are
more spiritual than I. I cannot understand what
you mean."

A deep color came into Bertha's cheeks. "It
shows how little you know me," she said, "to say
that of me. I needed this long quiet preparation
for the new home that waits me; I needed it, because I was so cumbered with the weight of many
things here. God gives us the discipline we need.
He will give you the friend you ask, or be to you
the better friend himself."

"I ought often to ask you to speak to me this

way," said Agnes. "You look inspired just now, Bertha, like some pre-Raphaelite picture, as Mr. Jasper would say."

"He never spoke so of me," said Bertha, quickly.

"Oh no; he speaks seldom of you," said Agnes. 'When he does, it is with a sort of reverence. I have never told you that he wants to see you some day,— some day when you feel really well."

"He would like to see me," repeated Bertha. "Are you very sure that he wanted to see me. Perhaps he suggested it from kindness."

"Oh no; I think he was quite earnest about it," said Agnes.

"You should have told me some of those days that I was down stairs," said Bertha. "Now the winter is come, I may not go down again. Don't give him an answer yet. I must think about it. If I feel strong enough I should like to see Mr. Jasper again."

"Oh well, don't trouble yourself about it," said Agnes. "Perhaps I shan't see him to-day. I have half a mind to go into town this morning. If I can only reach the station through the snow, I shall find the sidewalks cleared in town."

"What would you do there?" asked Bertha.

"Oh, a world of things, beginning with nothing," said Agnes. "If we are to give up the theatricals, I must put something else into my head to think about."

Bertha leaned back upon her cushions as Agnes

went away. Hannah was still in the room. Mrs.
Carlton had given her some sewing to occupy her
there through the morning. Hannah thought Bertha looked tired by her talk with Agnes. She
closed her eyes, but the lids were pained and disturbed. Later in the day Hannah was in the room
again.

"I wanted to speak to you," she said to Bertha,
"about what Miss Agnes said this morning. You
looked tired after she went out, and I thought I
would not say more then, but oh, I do wish people
would not trouble us so with our faults."

"Very often," said Bertha, smiling, "our friends,
our elder friends, may say too much about them.
They ought to consider to whom they are speaking. Some people are already very sensitive to
their faults. But Mr. Jasper, perhaps, thinks that
Agnes does not think often enough of hers."

"I was not thinking of Miss Agnes," said Hannah. "I was thinking of myself. I work so much
easier when people are encouraging and tell me
often that I am right, than when they find out all I
have done wrong. You never talk to me about
my faults, nor Miss Amy, and yet I know very well
when I don't do your work right; but you always
see whatever I do that is good."

"Poor Hannah," said Bertha, "I am afraid you
hear too much fault-finding in the house! The
boys are very thoughtless and careless. I have

spoken to Fred about it some times. I think you are very patient with them."

"I am beginning to be used to the boys," said Hannah, "and they are so merry always. I wish I could please Miss Agnes and Mrs. Carlton oftener."

CHAPTER XXVI.

CONTEST AND PEACE.

THE winter passed on. The new year had come. The constant snow had made it very gay in Langdale. There had been a succession of sleighing parties and other entertainments. The boys were especially happy, particularly when Agnes and all her friends had patronized the skating on the meadow. Fred, and Tom, and Jack were devoted in their gallantry to Agnes, the Lees, and the Fays. The private theatricals had taken place, after all, at the Lees'. Agnes had made all the others work in the arrangements for them, while she sat by, without taking to herself any share of the trouble. She only offered her taste, and gave the rest her suggestions. She ridiculed all the plays they proposed acting, and finally selected one herself. All the parts were given out under her dictation, and at the last she took one of the minor parts herself, where she did not have to say many words, but made a brilliant appearance.

"It was the best part of the whole play," Tom Paxton declared afterward to Agnes.

"Oh, I didn't want to take any other," said Agnes; "I don't care about personating one of your slow heroines. Indeed, I think the whole thing is a humbug. I had rather go into the Boston Theatre, any night." .

Agnes was a favorite on these occasions, though she always threw all labor and responsibility away from herself. She was a favorite, because she was never out of spirits. She was very fastidious and selfish in taking to herself whatever she fancied, but the Lees and the others admired her exceedingly, and were willing to submit to all her whims.

"Do you observe," said Fred to Tom, "that at whatever angle Agnes tips her bonnet on the back of her head, the Lees have an exact measurement of it, and wear theirs in precisely the same slant?"

"Do you observe," retorted Agnes, "that in whatever slang Fred indulges himself, it is copied exactly by his train of Tom and Jack, to say nothing of Dick and Harry? If he would only set a respectable example. But his talk is enough to kill one!"

"Why is Fred like David?" says Jack. "Give it up? Because one kills with his slang, and the other with his sling."

"Jack, you grow worse and worse every day," exclaimed Agnes; "I wish the institution of putting boys in barrels prevailed."

"Ho! we are so useful you would have to take us out every day," said Tom.

" Who would you send on your errands ? " said Jack.

" Who would bring you out of town after dark ? " said Fred.

" Who would carry your bundles," said Tom.

" Who would you scold round generally ? " said Jack.

" And what a fermentation there'd be in the barrels," said Tom.

Agnes came home from the post-office one day. " Here's a letter for Hannah," she exclaimed, as she entered the house. " Hannah has a correspondent. Where is Hannah ? Such beautiful writing on the letter ! Your friend, Hannah, is so clear about his or her spelling. ' Care of Mrs. Jon Carlton.' That's the new phonographic style. I think I will take lessons, it must save trouble."

Hannah took her letter, wondering who could write to her. It was from Janet, who wrote to tell of her happy life in New York. Janet had not so much command of her pen as her tongue, and she was not able to fill quite one page, but she wanted to assure Hannah that she had not forgotten her.

" How I should like to see the inside of that letter," said Agnes, waiting till Hannah should finish reading it; " if it equals its appearance outside, it must be a treasure. I hope your friend writes often."

" You never had the patience to write a whole

letter," said Fred, who overheard what Agnes was
saying; "if you did, nobody would have the patience to read it. Why can't you let Hannah read
her letter in peace?"

"I expected some thanks for bringing it all the
way from the post-office," said Agnes.

Hannah had lately thrust Janet out of her mind.
She was beginning to grow ashamed of her intercourse with her, and of the influence which Janet
had really possessed over her. She was hoping
she should not hear from her again, and she did
not welcome a letter that brought up the subject
once more. Agnes's ridicule roused in her a spirit
of defiance.

"Just because a poor girl has never been taught
better, Miss Agnes," she said, "you think you can
laugh at her. If my friend, as you call her, could
have gone to school five years, as some others
have, she might be more useful than they are."

Agnes was going away, but she turned back.
"I did not mean to be insulting, Hannah," she
said; "I dare say your friend is very useful, but
from her handwriting, I should not call her orna-
mental." .

When some warm, clear days came again, Bertha ventured to go down stairs once more. Her
father stayed out of town in the morning to carry
her down into the comfortable parlor. There she
was very glad to lie on the cushioned sofa, by the
glowing fire, with her flowers and books by her

side, and where her friends might come in to talk to her.

One morning, after she had been established in this way, Bertha was left alone for awhile. She heard presently the front door opened, and then Mr. Jasper entered the room.

"Bertha, you are here," he exclaimed; "I met Agnes, who asked me to come in to see you, but I did not think to find you in this room, to come in upon you so suddenly."

"I thought you would come to-day," said Bertha. "When I heard some one at the door, I believed that it was you. It did not surprise me."

"So like the Bertha from whom I parted," said Mr. Jasper; "to stand in front of you, to look down upon you, makes all the years that have passed between, dwindle away. Was it only yesterday, Bertha? What has become of all that long time! Only once have I felt sorrow in your presence. It has always been to me light and joy. That one time was when I knew I must leave you."

The color came into Bertha's cheeks. She half raised herself. "It seems, indeed, so natural to see you here, it could hardly give me a shock of surprise. I am glad to see you once more. I have so often thought over what I would say to you." She paused a moment, and then went on. "I have been thinking that I was wrong in what I said to you that last time I saw you. So many

15

times my strength of heart has failed since then. A great many times I have repeated to myself that I was wrong in shutting out so great a happiness. I told you that it was a great happiness."

"O Bertha, how could you send me away?" interrupted Mr. Jasper.

"There were so many who needed you," said Bertha. "You were strong, you had a great work before you,— you were to work for the world. And I, I was so weak, I should have kept you back. Do not turn away, nor look so doubtfully. If I did wrong, I have suffered. But I could not bear to tie you down to me, when I thought I might live on as I have done. More than five years I have been a care to those around me. I have been very dependent. Those who loved me most have suffered most for me."

"Oh, you are wrong, Bertha," said Mr. Jasper; "do you forget that we love you? Is any care heavy that we take for those we love?"

"I am not excusing myself," said Bertha, "yet I would like to have you clearly know how, in what I did, I meant to have helped you. Oh! we are all so weak; when we would help each other, the most we have is so little to offer."

"Forgive me, Bertha," said Mr. Jasper; "how cruel I am to come to trouble you so. But you are so unchanged, so like the Bertha I left behind, I cannot think of you as ill and suffering. How thoughtless I am to add anything to all you have to bear."

"Do not think of that," said Bertha; "I have wished you should have a better opinion of me. When you left me, you thought or attempted to think that I was cold and without feeling. I tried to hope you might think so. It would make the parting easier for you to believe me less worthy."

"One hour away from you," said Mr. Jasper, "and all such idle suspicions, anything that could cloud my trust in you, vanished."

Bertha went on, — "When I was told that my days were numbered, — that for the life that had grown so precious to me, the end was already appointed, — I was stupefied with a deep sorrow. I loved everything in the world. I wanted to be everything for everybody. I thought that I would make Agnes love me dearly; that I would watch over her, would check the faults in her that had grown in me like rude weeds. I thought I could see the source of my own faults, but she was so much younger I would work for her, so that when she grew up she should not have such faults in herself to contend with. I thought I would be the dear elder sister of the boys, the softener of all that was rough in them."

"All this you were, all this you have been," interrupted Mr. Jasper, "and why would you not bless me also?"

"That would have been the most glorious joy of all," said Bertha; "to live for others, — to live for you, — it was a happiness, indeed, too great for me. Then came the sudden shock, when my strength was suddenly cut down. A new way was appointed for me. Instead of laboring for others, I was to suffer, and they were to labor for me. Oh! every way I looked upon it, to try to bring my heart into a willing state. I wished I could have a little time, a little longer time, and stretched my arms back into life imploringly. And then it was I made the great mistake. I wanted to suffer alone. I wanted to put upon myself the whole weight of my trial. I tried to persuade myself that I had mistaken your feeling towards me; that it was not so deep as I had fancied,— that you might be easily weaned from me. I taught myself that if I were only firm enough, I could shut myself out from you; that you would soon have higher aims, that would take the place of the lower love you felt for me. I thought that I alone should suffer in the separation. With you, it would be a momentary pang of deep sorrow, a sad remembrance, perhaps, while you would be left free. On the other hand, I shrank from binding you down to one whose strength and life were failing as mine were. The longer that I should live here,— the longer that I should linger weak and suffering,— the closer I should bind you to my side, and keep you away from other duties. I wanted you to be great for the world; not to give your life to one weak invalid, and I that one. I had a false idea of duty, that made me believe if

the duty were a hard one for me, it must be right.
I thought as long as I suffered, there was no fear
but that I was unselfish, and so I must be right." -

"Five years; five long years!" said Mr. Jasper.

"When they told me you had come back," said
Bertha; "when Amy said you appeared to her not
so cheerful as when you went away; when she
told me that the little duties of the parish weighed
upon you now, as they never weighed before,—
then I began to see, perhaps it was all wrong. I
saw that you had been living an incomplete life.
Something had been wanting to you. Oh! then I
felt that there was no such thing as breaking a tie
like that which bound us to each other. There
was a promise that had never been spoken in
words, yet it never could be broken. Though you
had been far away, I, weak and suffering, had
bound you still."

Mr. Jasper was sitting by Bertha, his face bur-
ied in his hands. "What God has joined together,
man cannot break asunder," he said.

"The suffering had not been wholly mine," continued Bertha; "I could not take away your
share, and it was the heavier for both of us,
because we were separated from each other. Will
you forgive me that I brought upon you this great
suffering? Will you forgive me that I sent you
out alone when you needed human help; forgive
me that I shut up in myself all those warm feelings, all that love, that might have soothed and
encouraged you?

"I have seen others die near me, whose hold on life seemed far surer than mine, who have passed out suddenly from the midst of warm love and healthy action. The battle is not always to the strong, nor the race to the swift. I have learned, too, that though the world needs sorely active workers, yet it is not for mere usefulness that one may be loved. A long illness has taught me that there may be a virtue in leaving to others the work we long to do ourselves; that even in being dependent upon others, we may find a pleasure in their willing service, may give a pleasure in receiving it with a willing heart. I could not give you active love, that hastens to move all obstacles from the path of those it loves, that wearies not in well-doing, but I was wrong in shutting out from you the sympathy that belonged to you, that was your due. I should have waited till God called me, instead of leaving behind the world in which he planted me, in order to go to meet him. I am glad to see you again, to tell you what I am in love to you for the rest of the life God gives me here; to tell you I have blamed myself for this five years' separation."

"Bertha," said Mr. Jasper, "there is nothing for me to blame in you. The blame must fall upon me. You only miscalculated my strength. I was not so brave as you. I did not take up manfully the duty you appointed me. We might have been happier if we had not parted, but there was no excuse for me. Had I been stronger, I might have grown into greater insight; I might have taught myself that my place was by you. You took upon yourself the heavier share of the burden, only to stand and wait in the presence of God. You have triumphantly performed your work; I come home one of the vanquished."

"We cannot tell about triumph or defeat," said Bertha, "not yet. Perhaps it is all right, that I needed this lonely time to wean me from the world. Yet, indeed, it is a great mistake to think that sickness can wean us from the world. Truly, the best way to prepare for another life, must be to live this one thoroughly and truly. And sickness is near to death only because our powers are deadened by which we live here, and we know not yet how to unfold what we shall need in another life. If only those who are well could realize that a sick-room is truly no preparation for that other world!"

"There is a color in your cheeks, and spirit in your eye, and the spring is coming," said Mr. Jasper, "but, Bertha, you must rest now."

CHAPTER XXVII.

WINTER TALKS.

MARTHA left Langdale to go to the Normal School. Her absence left a gap in Miss Elspeth's household. She was very quiet always, but always thoughtful for others. Even Miss Dora said, "Martha is a sensible girl. She is worth her weight, in common sense." Miss Dora had hoped to make a first-rate housekeeper of Martha, because she was so docile, and so eager to render herself useful; but she was disappointed when Martha, as she grew up, showed a decided taste for studying, in preference to the cares of the house.

"I should not have expected it," said Miss Dora, "of one of Martha's sense. But it is all Elspeth's fault. She would send her to the best schools, and there's nothing so catching as book learning." Miss Dora, too, was very indignant at the proposition of her going to the Normal School. She thought it was the height of folly; that there should be a school for schoolmasters. "Pray who were to teach the teachers of the Normal School! By and by people would get into such a whirl, they

would not know whether they were teachers or
scholars themselves."

"That's the true principle," said Martha; "we
are all learners and all teachers."

"Fiddlestick!" said Miss Dora; "I don't like
this idea of girls going to school all their life long.
I went ten months to learn how to work a piece,
and I considered myself finished then. What's the
use of my learning French, when I shouldn't want
to say anything to a Frenchman if I saw one. I
think it's blasphemous, this trying to learn so many
languages. What were people made to talk differently for, if they were not meant to talk differently.
One of these days, by way of warning, there'll be
another Babel, just as you have learnt all your
languages!"

"Oh dear," said Margie, laughing, "and shall we
have to learn a new set of languages!"

"Miss Dora will wake up and find herself talking
German!" said Bessie.

"I might as well talk German now," said Miss
Dora, "for all the attention I get. There's the
sugar-bucket standing outside the cupboard this
minute, that I told you, Bessie, to put away, full
half an hour ago."

"Oh, but dear Miss Dora," said Bessie, "you
know I only waited to see what you had to say
about languages."

"How pleasant the parlor looks!" said Hannah,
as she came in at twilight with Margie, the day
after Martha left.

"Oh, isn't it pleasant," said Bessie; "doesn't Miss Dora look like a picture, with the light falling on her just so? There's something for Margie to paint!"

"If we had more light," said Miss Dora, "I suppose you think I shouldn't make so much of a picture! Well, Hannah, so Martha's gone."

"I bade her good-night at the cars," said Hannah. "I hoped I might come round last night or this morning to help her, but we were too busy."

"All Martha thought of was packing her books," said Miss Dora. "I should think she was going to dress in books, instead of gowns and collars."

"You must not complain of Martha," said Miss Elspeth; "we shall miss her badly enough."

"Margie and I mean to be so lively," said Bessie, "that you'll think there are four girls in the house, instead of two. Only, I expect to act very badly, because Martha always kept me in order."

"Well, we shall miss Martha," said Miss Dora, "in taking care of you."

"Oh, she has helped me out of so many scrapes," said Bessie, "it is so much easier to confess scrapes when they are well over. Do you remember that time when I burnt all the cake that we were to have for tea? Mrs. Bunce was coming to tea. I left the cake in the oven and went out to cool myself in the garden, when there came up a story that Mrs. Bunce's pig had escaped. I ran to help in the chase, and forgot all about my cake!"

"I remember," said Miss Dora. "I didn't know anything about it till it was all over. I scolded you well then, and you deserved it."

"I know it," said Bessie. "Martha helped me out then. She went into the Rothsays and borrowed some fresh cake they had just been baking. You were putting on your best dress, and we did not have a chance to tell you till Mrs. Bunce had gone."

"I smelt the cake burning, though," said Miss Dora. "I supposed you had spoilt half the batch, if you hadn't the whole. You didn't have a chance to tell me! I guess you might have made a chance."

"Oh, Martha couldn't have kept it secret," said Bessie; "she was burning to tell you, and she did tell Miss Elspeth, but Mrs. Bunce talked so fast she couldn't put in a word."

"I remember how Martha mended your barége dress," said Hannah.

"Yes," said Bessie; "the very day I was going to the Rothsays, I tore it slipping off the ladder, as I came down from the cherry tree."

"A pretty place to be in the cherry tree, in your barége dress!" said Miss Dora.

"Well, Martha mended it so beautifully," said Bessie, "that I was more proud of it than I ever was before."

"I always used to forget to take the right books to school," said Margie, "and when I got to school I always found Martha had brought them for me."

" She always reminded me to study my lessons," said Hannah.

" What a pity Martha is not here to hear her praises sung!" said Miss Elspeth.

" I guess she wishes she were here now," said Bessie. " I wonder what she is about; talking stiff to some poky people, I suppose."

" Bertha Carlton said she knew the Mays, with whom Martha is to board," said Margie, " and she says they are very pleasant people."

" How is Bertha to-day ?" asked Miss Elspeth.

" I think her strength is failing," said Hannah. " It tires her more to talk than it used to."

" Oh, but she says so much in so few words," said Margie. " We were talking this afternoon about that book, 'More Worlds than One.' Annie Lane was there."

" What does that mean?" said Miss Dora. " Aren't people contented with one world? What with California and Australia, I should think there was room enough here!"

" Annie Lane said she liked to think of all the stars being inhabited," said Margie, " and what an occupation it would be to go from one to the other, and how grand it was to think there was so much to know."

" I think there's enough to know here, and travelling enough here," said Miss Dora. " I want to get to a place where I can be quiet."

"That is not very different from what Bertha said," said Margie. "She said she was afraid sometimes of forgetting all there was to enjoy in this world, in thinking of all the different glory that might come in another. I think she spoke for my sake, as she often has before. She thought we might pass by the beauty of this world, if we were wondering all the time at the splendors of another. Then when we reached that, we should be looking after another, still neglecting what lay nearest to us, and what had a greater claim upon us."

"There is so much to think of in this world," said Miss Elspeth.

"And it is so easy to be taken up with just one little set of thoughts and cares," said Margie.

"I should not like to live as those Miss Rosses," said Bessie. "I showed them the way into the woods the other day, and wanted to have them see how pretty the wood-paths were, and what splendid great rocks were scattered about, and what a magnificent tree the oak was! But they were so intent on picking up little straws they were going to paste on paper and make into houses and fences, that they did not once look round."

"I like to have people keep their eyes open," said Miss Dora.

"I believe Bertha thinks I am always in a maze, and that she would like to wake me out of it," said Margie.

"I hope she'll succeed," said Miss Dora. "I

dare say now, you forgot to buy the split peas as
you came along."

"I did forget all about it," said Margie, starting
up.

"I'll go for them," said Hannah.

"It's too late now," said Miss Dora. "I suppose
we shall forget to have dinner now Martha has
gone."

"We shan't need much, there are so few of us,"
said Bessie.

"Martha wasn't much of an eater," said Miss
Dora. "But I dont see how you could forget the
peas, Margie; I told you the very last thing!"

"I could have got them," said Bessie. "No
wonder Margie forgot about it."

"No wonder, indeed," said Miss Dora; "talking
about all the worlds."

"Oh dear," said Margie, "I never shall learn to
be good for anything. I came near crushing Miss
Lane's bonnet this afternoon. It was in the chair
I usually sit in. But all the way there I was thinking about Martha's going away, and all the way
home I was thinking of what they had been talking
about, Bertha and Annie Lane."

"You must have been a pleasant companion for
Hannah," said Miss Elspeth.

"Oh, I knew what she was thinking about," said
Hannah. "It makes everybody thoughtful to go
in and see Miss Bertha,—and a happy sort of
thinking, too, it gives everybody,— for Miss Bertha

seems happier to me since she has seen Mr. Jasper. He comes every day to talk with her; every day that she is well enough."

"I hope you keep up your early rising," said Miss Dora. "They say the Carltons are late people; but there's no need of your being late. I have no doubt of your finding enough to do, if you get up at early hours all the winter long."

"There's no danger of that," said Hannah. "Mrs. Carlton gives me plenty to do; she likes to have Bridget and me up, and she is up herself, too, sewing before breakfast."

Margie and Bessie went out with Hannah when she went away. Hannah lingered at the gate, as she always used to do.

"It seems so natural to stand here," she said.

It was a clear, cold, winter's night, and the stars shone brightly in the deep blue sky.

"How many worlds there are up there!" exclaimed Margie.

"I wonder if there are girls standing at the garden gates, in those other worlds," said Bessie.

"And I wonder if we shall ever know them," said Margie.

"I had rather know more about this world," said Hannah.

"How much more we might know here," said Margie. "Perhaps in the very next street is standing somebody whom we might help, or who might help us,— some friend who could be very friendly to us."

"Perhaps Steevie is waiting somewhere, wanting us," said Hannah. "If we could only go to him,— if we could only know where he is."

"He knows where we are," said Bessie. "I think some day he will come to us."

"Good night."

CHAPTER XXVIII.

A DEPARTURE.

AND the spring came again. There were some warm days in early March. They bore a deceitful promise of spring, and even a warm summer glow. The sun shone fervently down upon the moistened earth, and in the edges of the woods the little vines here and there ventured to throw off their warm winter shelter of leaves. There was a languid softness in the air, and late in the afternoon there lingered a dreamy haziness about the atmosphere. Occasionally a bird was seen here and there, the buds were swelling on the trees, there was a few days' forgetfulness that it was March, that the stormy March had come, and not spring herself.

Some complainers bemoaned of the unseasonableness of the weather; they liked better a steady cold. Mrs. Bunce said that as long as she had not put away her winter things, and was expecting to keep fires in the house, she did not mind its being cold. She had rather have it now than in the middle of June. And yet, Mrs. Bunce was one of

16

those who found something unseasonable in every month in the year. Her listeners always wondered what was the standard of climate that she had laid down. Langdale certainly never came up to it.

The few warm days were encouraging to the poor people, whose means for fuel were small or none, because some of the charitable societies did not give out fuel in March, their standard of the season's warmth and cold being different from that of Mrs. Bunce.

It was happy for the poor that the windows could be opened, and a fresh air let into the small, poor houses where the winter's cold had been an enemy, and a few sticks or a little coal could be saved up for the winter days that might yet come, and for the occasional meal when a fire could be afforded. To those who were obliged to labor all day, there was something oppressive in the air that exhausted and dispirited them. They would have enjoyed so much a little moment of rest, when they could fold their hands and look out upon the fresh activity that was waking up in nature. The school-girls found their books weighing heavily as they carried them to school, and panted for the air as they came out of the close schoolroom and walked lazily home in the warm noonday sun.

Agnes returned from a visit in town, languid and dispirited too. She came home complaining that she was forced to come back to Langdale in this dreary season when the roads were so muddy that she could not walk nor go out of the house, and when it was so gay and lively in town. Her complaints were hushed when she entered the house, for she found there a subdued atmosphere. There was no longer any strife or bickering. Even Mrs. Carlton's querulousness was for awhile subdued. The boys' noisy gayety was calmed. They moved about the house quietly and gently. They came in, closing the doors carefully. They were unwilling to begin upon any amusement until they had knocked at Bertha's door to know if she were better, or to ask if she would see them. Even Harry, who could scarcely know what it was that made them all so quiet, sat in the parlor with his picture books, so that his noise might not disturb any one, and imitated his brothers, often asking if he was not wanted for anything, and could not do something for Bertha. All the village, too, was quiet. The neighbors were all thoughtful in their attentions to Bertha. Bertha was loved by everybody, and so warmly, that what she suffered was suffered by all.

But Bertha was not suffering. She was sinking away as gently to repose as sank these warm, summer-like days into the glowing sunset. She looked out through the opened window upon the clear outline of the hills beyond. She said once to Amy, " How peaceful it looks there. It reminds me of that place to which we shall come from all doubt and sorrow; from all doubt of ourselves whether we are right or wrong. I think often, Amy, of those beautiful lines,—

" 'And thou shalt walk in soft, white light, with kings and priests abroad,
    And thou shalt summer high in bliss upon the hills of God.'

" I often think of them as I look upon that clear line against the sky. The beautiful hills! The sky always seems to rest gently over them clear and blue, and the clouds there are always lighted up, or softened by some glow."

But Bertha's words were growing fewer as her breath grew fainter, while from her room the friends that loved her most, carried some precious words that lingered with them afterwards to sustain and uphold them. They saw the spirit was passing away already, leaving a glow round the beautiful face that to the last moment was lighted up by a peaceful happiness.

Before the cold spring winds had returned to chill the opening earth, Bertha had passed out from this world into the new life. It seemed as if the unwonted loveliness of those March days had been sent to hang as a beautiful halo round the moment of her departure. On the day that was called the day of her death here, the air was soft and mild, the budding willows waved gently over the sunny spot where was laid the beautiful form to which her spirit had given life.

There was a heavy sorrow and silence in Langdale at Bertha's departure. She had been loved so warmly by all, that her absence left a great space among them. The change was not hurried over and forgotten, as it might have been in larger places, where the tumult and bustle and changes of one day hurry out the remembrance of the day before. There was time enough to recall all she had been in life, to feel that her memory was living still and fresh. For some months, though she had not been present in the little circle, her influence had been warmly felt, and now it seemed as if she had scarcely been taken farther away from them.

Amy wondered at the strength and cheerfulness with which Mr. Jasper went through his duties. He was more active than ever. She met him one day in one of the poorer houses in the outskirts of Langdale.

"Are you strong enough for all this?" asked Amy. "Are you not working too hard?"

"I believe the hard work helps me," said Mr. Jasper. "Sometimes I feel like stopping to think. I feel like shutting myself up with my own thoughts, and having my sorrow out. That might be better for some people, and at such times I think with a half envy of those who believe they purify themselves in leaving the world, its cares as well as its temptations. I feel as if I heard those beautiful words: 'Never did Nature or Art offer thee pleasure so great, as did that beautiful form in which I was enclosed, that now lies scattered in the earth. And if thy highest pleasure so failed thee at my death, what mortal thing ought to lure thee to its love? Thou oughtest, at that first stroke, to have lifted thyself above all that is deceitful, directly to me, who was no longer among such things.'"

"Bertha did not say those words?" asked Amy.

"Beatrice reproaches Dante with them," said Mr. Jasper. "No, Bertha did not use such words. It is the purity and beauty of her life and thoughts that lift me that way to her. I think Bertha would have dreaded using any words that should have seemed to move me away from whatever duties there are waiting for me in the world."

"Oh, I think," said Amy, "that she used to reproach herself for what she used to call her sin of Other-worldliness. She said that for many years she had thought too much of another world, and had tried to live too little in this."

"In all her last words," continued Mr. Jasper, "she was urgent in praising all the work of this life. I think by her death she sang a song of life."

"She must have had," said Amy, "a constitutional shrinking from all the real struggle of life. It would have been hard for her to have been out in the battle of life, contending with many who were uncongenial to her. And yet how brave and courageous she was in all the struggles she did go through; how patient in her want of sympathy,

which must have been at home, a continual want
for her."

" It is strange to think," said Mr. Jasper, " that
she already knows what we still doubt of, and
question; that her faith has passed out into certainty, or higher questionings have risen upon the
lower mists that trouble us here."

Hannah found the house very lonely and desolate. The younger children were oppressed with
a feeling of sadness, the whole weight of which
they did not understand. Fred and Tom went
about the house without occupation, and unwilling
to begin upon any amusement, finding no one to
sympathize with them. Mr. Carlton involved himself more than ever in his business. Mrs. Carlton
had no resources in the hour of great sorrow, and
no comfort to bring to those around her, only her
own complainings. Agnes was sullen and capricious. She, perhaps, felt deeply her loss in Bertha,
and was disturbed by a self-reproach that she had
not been more to her while she lived. But this
she would not show to Bertha's friends. She was
unwilling to give way to any feeling before them,
and wore an air of indifference, though no longer
of gayety. Hannah missed the expression of sorrow. It was hard to go back to the old routine of
duties, only those duties wanting that were the
lightest to perform, that gave strength for others.

CHAPTER XXIX.

A RETURN.

THE same spring that bore away one of Amy's friends, brought back George Arnold. He returned in April to Langdale.

Frank brought to Amy the telegraphic dispatch that announced George would arrive in Boston by the morning train from New York. He would come directly to Langdale. Amy went into the garden to await him. She walked up and down its alleys. She listened eagerly for the whistle of the engine that would prepare her for George's approach. She looked down the path into the woods. A leafless branch that hung across the entrance, waved often deceitfully as though it were moved by some one passing by. She had heard the hurry and the bustle of the cars; certainly it never took any one so long to come through that little path. She turned away again from watching it. Suddenly she heard a voice behind her. George was standing by her side. She looked at him doubtfully a moment. He was changed indeed in so many years. He had certainly grown manly, he was taller, his figure broader. Then his complexion was bronzed, and the dark moustache gave him a different expression. But his voice was the same. "You don't know me, Amy," he said, "you do not feel quite sure that it is I? But I have no doubt of you. I knew the sunny brown hair, I saw the well-known figure in the distance as I came through the woods. Through the branches of the low bushes it shone upon me like sunlight! A little more slender, perhaps! But the face is quite the same. The hair hangs a little lower, either side the checks, and the mouth falls into a sadder curve, though it smiles, and tears are in the eyes. But you are my Amy still? Will you speak to me and tell me so? Or shall I begin freshly to plead my cause?"

"I cannot tell if I am dreaming," said Amy, "my eyes swim, I cannot see if it is you, if it is George."

"Sit down in the old seat here," said George; "let the sun come through the lattice, the warm, welcoming sun. All through the woods I heard voices speaking to me. The oak would like to have talked to me, but I hurried by too fast. Am I the same? Not quite the same, though these old voices will call me back into the past. Not the same, — better, I hope. You are willing I should change in order to be stronger, Amy, than I was?"

"I have been almost afraid," said Amy, "I loved the old so much, till this moment I have been almost afraid to see you, George. I wanted no change."

"Not even for the better, Amy?" asked George. "Perhaps, indeed, you'll not be disappointed; perhaps I have grown no better."

"You are quite the same," said Amy. "I'm so very happy."

"Perhaps you saw in me what was best," said George, "and I have been working to make myself worthy of you; to raise myself to the ideal you had formed of me! After all, I have brought home little that I did not carry away. I was to come home an artist. I have brought home no great works for you to be proud of."

"I did not want to be proud of your great works, but of you," said Amy. "George, that did disappoint me!"

"I saw it did," said George. "I knew that it must be your fancy had given me greater powers than I possessed. I was not so great as you, and I dreamed that I was, under the oak-tree. I woke out of the illusion before I had dreamed away my life."

"I cannot yet think those were all dreams and illusions," said Amy; "though while I hear you speak I find myself willing to believe all you say."

"As you believed what I said then," said George, "it is well I am no longer the will-o'-the-wisp, the ignis fatuus I was, to lead you after me, over marshes and briars. Now, I am come home a solid man. I no longer go astray in fields of art. I sit down and count my gains and ponder fresh ones."

"That I will not believe," said Amy.

"Well, then, Amy, I will tell you I have had some struggles," said George. "At first I did indulge in complainings. I found myself reproaching the way I had been brought up, my early life. If I had only been permitted to bring out my early tastes; if what talent I had, had been cherished; if my youth had not been thrown away,—I amused and tortured myself with such exclamations as these. But they were idle and foolish. An artist needs more strength of mind, more earnestness and singleness of purpose than any other laborer; more than I possessed. If I had been trained earlier to work, to work about something, if it had only been in a sawmill, I should have been better fitted for an artist, than I was when I began to look around me and ask myself what I was ready to do. It was a time of despair then! As I gave up the hope of helping to make the world glorious in art, so I must lose all hope. I was not fitted even to be a shoemaker. I had not the power of application which would make me worthy the lowest profession or trade. This was when your letter came to me,—the one that decided me."

"My poor letter," said Amy. "It was written with a very different purpose."

"It was written to infuse strength into my poor wavering spirit," said George. I determined to make myself fit for living somehow, and I chose the easiest way. The clank of dollars and cents would drown the voice of the syrens. I might forget the forms of the sculpture round the temple, at sight of the gold and silver, and in the company of those who bought and sold."

" Oh, don't go on in that way," said Amy. "If it were not for the tones of your voice I should think you were speaking in bitterness."

"And you would not have me speak bitterly of the trade that I have chosen, of the profession that I am going to follow?" said George. "It would not be fair in me, I have found such friends among my fellow-laborers; it would be dishonorable of me. Indeed, there is no need of the fingers being soiled by the base metal that passes through them. I have seen brave deeds done, Amy, with dollars and cents, equal in beauty to a copper statue or a vase of silver. I have only changed the tools of my trade. I am going to work on in the same cause for art and beauty still."

" That sounds natural," said Amy. " The words come out with the old earnestness."

"I have only come home to carry out the old theories," said George, "and your favorite theory, too. Do you remember the day you taught me that even to sweep a room was 'divine.' I have a sketch of you I made from recollection, a white

handkerchief pointed over your head, a dark dress
with a white apron which floated in front, a fresh
color in your cheek, and a broom that was exceedingly picturesque in your hand. After all, the
beautiful lies in the actual. What we admire, is
the way the spirit expresses itself. It is the expression that gives the charm to the form, and a
beautiful spirit must give beauty to the form."

"So you have time to theorize a little over the
dollars and cents," said Amy.

"I am another Benvenuto Cellini," said George.
"I work in silver and gold for merchant princes.
My vessels bring the raw material from the mines
in California. We put it into a crucible and it
comes out silks and burlaps, and teas and coffees.
My works of Art ornament and refresh the world,
only I do not carve my name on their pedestals."

"These theories, then, don't interfere with the
great labors," said Amy.

"You will be sceptical, still," said George.
"You think I can do nothing still but talk. I will
show you solid proofs of my power,— testimonials
of the esteem in which I am held by the magnates
in my field of Art. No, I have not a great picture
to bring home, a great historical work, done in
my own school of color, an American work of
genius! I am not a member of the great Academy
of Art! But I have a whole shipload consigned
to me, and papers and documents to show that I
am partner in the great firm of Shelburne, Arnold,
& Shelburne! Are you satisfied?"

"I must be satisfied," said Amy, "since you are here."

"But I shall have greater demands to make of you," said George. "We used to have old dreams, of a home among the mountains, in the midst of grand, glorious scenery. We would only leave it to go to more glorious places still, to see the great ocean, or to cross it for Italy and Greece and Spain. Wherever we went, wherever we lived, we were to live for the sake of Art. I was to devote myself to its study, and you were to admire all that I labored upon. These were great plans, and it was in the archway of such a glorious life that you promised yourself to me. I have turned away from that path. Will you come into the home that I am going to build now,—a little narrow house,— a brick house, in a brick street in Boston? The view of the sky will be telescopic only,— the outline from the windows will be the jagged outline of brick chimneys. The walks will not lead through pine tasselled woods, but over dusty pavements, and there will be noise and clatter of wheels, instead of murmurings in trees. The thought of Art, the study of Beauty will be my rest, and not my labor. There will be around our house, not even such beauty as hangs round Langdale. Can you look upon such a home with the same hopefulness you had in the old days, and give me the same promise you gave me then?"

"While you speak to me, while you are by my

side," said Amy, "I hear and see nothing else. Even Langdale fades out of my sight. How can I care what air surrounds me, what walls shut me in, so that we have each other to live and hope for!"

In the evening Bessie went hastily to the Carltons'.

"O Hannah, we want you to come home to spend the evening. George Arnold has come home! and we want to talk with you about it. Mr. George Arnold! You would not know him. And they are all so happy! And we have so much to tell.

CHAPTER XXX.

GOING AWAY.

MRS. CARLTON was becoming more capricious and rigorous in her treatment of Hannah. One morning, after Hannah had spent an evening at Miss Elspeth's, Mrs. Carlton lectured her severely upon her love of going out.

" Bridget, too, is out every night," she went on, " and I am half the time left to sit down stairs alone in the house. Last night I heard a noise at the back part of house; I went to the door, but there was nobody there! I called Mr. Carlton, who was asleep over the newspaper, and he looked round in the yard and did not see anybody. But I am convinced some one had been there from the noise I heard. Either it was burglars trying to get into the house, or else it was yours or Bridget's friends."

" I have no friends to come and see me at that time," said Hannah.

" I don't wish to be contradicted," said Mrs. Carlton. " I dare say you have as many friends as anybody, and I have no doubt they are a poor set.

I don't wish to have them lingering about the house. Agnes says you have a friend that writes to you who does not know how to spell. They had better keep away from here."

"There's no danger that any one will come to see me," said Hannah, about to leave the room.

"All the Irish are banded together," said Mrs. Carlton; "and they all know one another, and they all uphold one another, and if you trust yourself to one, you trust yourself to all."

For some time longer Mrs. Carlton kept up this tone of conversation with Hannah. She was always making some complaint of the way in which she did her work.

"I've been expecting it," said Bridget to Hannah. "Mrs. Carlton don't ever keep her girls more than one winter. I supposed she'd quarrel us off before the spring came. And I'm about ready to go, for my part. I'd as lief live in the big bell of Bow, as hear the sound of Mrs. Carlton's tongue all day."

But Hannah did not feel this willingness to go. She was attached to the memory of Bertha that lingered round the house. She was even fond of the boys now. Little Harry was more obedient to her than any one else. Arthur liked to read stories to her when she was sewing. The other boys, it is true, were always appealing to her for help, but they had learned to be grateful in their

17

acknowledgments, and it was pleasant to her to think that she was useful.

At last there came an outburst. Mrs. Carlton found a favorite cream-pitcher broken. She called in Hannah and accused her of breaking it. Hannah said that she knew nothing of it; she did not know it was broken.

"How can you deny it, Hannah?" Mrs. Carlton said. "You know you are more awkward than any one else in the house, and that no one else could have broken it."

"I know I am awkward, Mrs. Carlton," Hannah said, "and that it would be very likely I might break it, but I never would deny it if I had broken it."

"I don't wish to listen to your fine language," said Mrs. Carlton. "If you can't speak the truth you may as well not speak."

"Perhaps I had better not stay in the house," began Hannah, slowly.

"You are quite right," interrupted Mrs. Carlton. "And Mrs. Fales told me this morning of the two sisters of her cook who are in want of a place. They are American girls. I've been dissatisfied with Bridget a long time —" She stopped without finishing her sentence.

"I was going on to say," said Hannah, "that I would rather stay here till I could find out who did break the pitcher; that I would rather not go till I could show you I did speak the truth this time; but if you have already found some one for my place —"

"What is this about breaking the pitcher?" said Agnes, sauntering into the room. "What a loud talk about nothing! You need not lecture Hannah, ma'am, about the pitcher. I broke it myself and picked up the pieces!"

"You might have told me of it," said Mrs. Carlton; "but it makes no difference. Hannah and I were talking of her going away. Hannah herself seems to think she had better leave, and we have not got along well together for some time."

"You won't find anybody that will do so much work," said Agnes. "I would advise you not to let Hannah go."

"I shall not try to find any one to do all your work, Agnes," said Mrs. Carlton. "It is time that you begun to work for yourself. I am tired of having disputes with Hannah, and we had better part."

"Perhaps it is better so," said Hannah, turning slowly to leave the room, but she came back quickly. "Mrs. Carlton, I had rather not go," said she. "I will stay and work hard for you. It is like working for Miss Bertha still. It will be like parting from her again to go away. I will do all you ask me. I will promise to see no friends of mine."

"I see you are willing enough to stay," said Mrs. Carlton, coldly. "I supposed it would be so. When it comes to the point you don't care to leave a good place. And it wouldn't do for Miss Elspeth to know that you didn't suit me any longer. But I don't like such uneasy minds."

More words followed. Agnes interposed, but her interposition only irritated Mrs. Carlton the more, and the conversation ended by Mrs. Carlton's insisting that Hannah should leave that very night.

"You had better go now and pack up your things," was her final dismissal.

Hannah met Fred at the door as she was leaving the room. He followed her.

"Has mother been quarrelling you away?" he asked. "It is a real shame, after you have been knocked about all winter! It is all the better for you. There is nobody fit to live with in the house. I wish somebody would send me off. We shan't ever have anybody we like as well as you. And nobody that is good for anything will stay in such a house. I am sure I wouldn't ask them to."

Fred turned away, and there were tears in his eyes. Not for Hannah, but for the uncomfortable home and its succession of discords and annoyances. He would keep outside of it as much as possible, and take the other boys with him. If there was nobody to think of or care for them at home, they needn't stay there.

Hannah went to her room bewildered. She shrunk from the idea of going back to Miss Elspeth. Now was the time to carry out the long-cherished plan of taking care of herself. Mrs. Carlton had promised her the back wages owing to her. This would be enough to carry her to New York. Janet's letter had given her some directions where to find her if she should ever go there. She put up her things hurriedly, determining she would not go to see Miss Elspeth. She left Bessie safe there, and now she would try for herself.

In the midst of her plans she was summoned to the parlor, and was surprised to find Mrs. Paxton there, with Agnes.

"Mrs. Paxton wants you," said Agnes, "for Mrs. Strange, to take care of Mrs. Strange's baby. She heard that mother was going to send you away, through Mrs. Fales."

"Yes," said Mrs. Paxton. "Mrs. Fales's cook told our chambermaid that her sister was coming here in Hannah's place. Miss Agnes says, Hannah, that her mother has no serious complaint to make of you. Now, Mrs. Strange is all packed up to go away to New York to-morrow, and her nursery-maid is taken sick, and we want somebody directly to take her place."

"They want you, Hannah," said Agnes, "to go on to New York to-morrow, and to take care of Mrs. Strange's baby."

"It is just the way everything happens," said Mrs. Paxton; "that Mary should be taken sick at this time. She has always been a very reliable girl, but one cannot tell what to depend upon. I don't like Eleanora's going away again so soon, but it seems very quiet to her here, and so sad and all; and she is so used to travelling, she is listless whenever she is still. Then Mr. Strange's friends are anxious to see the children. The baby is such a splendid fellow, and the little girl is a little thing, but she has such pretty ways. I should like to have gone to see Miss Elspeth. I suppose she would give Hannah a good recommendation. Anybody that she has brought up ought to be faithful with a young child."

All the while Mrs. Paxton was pouring out this and more to Agnes, Hannah was standing in doubt. And yet hardly in doubt, rather in a surprised pleasure. Here was an easy way to go to New York. Her wish was suddenly anticipated. And when Mrs. Paxton and Agnes allowed her time to speak, it was to give her consent. Indeed, Mrs. Paxton's carriage was at the door. She would take Hannah away with her if Hannah was ready. She had left Ronald crying for his nurse, and it would be a comfort to take Hannah back directly.

Hannah felt herself carried away in a whirl. She was naturally slow of thought and motion, and now gave herself up to Mrs. Paxton's quick suggestions. She thought to herself bitterly that it was but a change of masters, but she was attracted

by the novelty, and was rather pleased than otherwise, when Mrs. Paxton kept her so occupied
through the rest of the day that she had no opportunity to go to consult Miss Elspeth, or tell her of
this change in her life.

CHAPTER XXXI.

THE WHIRL OF WATERS.

THE next day, Hannah set forth upon her jour-ney, taking the station at Langdale for New York. Hannah was to have the care of the youngest child only; a French maid took charge of the little girl. As she could speak nothing but French, Hannah could have little intercourse with her. At New York they went directly to the house of old Mr. Strange.

Hannah's first view of New York, was when she went to take the child out with some other nurses of the family and neighborhood. They were all dressed in their best, the nurses and the babies. Little Master Ronald, Hannah's charge, met a full share of attention. His Paris hat and embroidered cloak were the study and delight, not only of the whole band of nurses, but of the mothers who were straying up and down the sidewalk. Many were the questions Hannah was obliged to an-swer with regard to him. She herself was won by his great blue eyes and his healthy good nature. Hannah repeated to Mrs. Strange the praises that baby had received.

"Ronald does look well," she said, languidly; "but Hannah, you must not let him crumple his ruche; you must keep his hands still."

Hannah afterwards walked down Broadway with one of the women. She was bewildered and confused by the noises, by the crush of people. She saw a great many girls dressed as she fancied Janet would be; she shrank when they came near her. She had no desire to meet Janet yet. She would wait a little while and see what a life in New York might be, and Mrs. Strange did not allow her much time to make inquiries.

And indeed, her interest in the little Ronald held her unconsciously, as well as the newness of the life around her. She seldom left the upper part of New York. Sometimes she looked down the narrower streets, anxiously and inquiringly. She saw along the sidewalks, poor, thinly dressed girls, who reminded her of herself as she was many years ago. She had started when she first met some of them when she walked in Broadway. It had needed that she should turn round to a broad window at her side to recall to herself that she was not one of them, but that the decently dressed, sober-looking figure reflected there was herself. She found herself almost dreading that Janet should meet her in some of the streets, while she was walking with the respectable-looking servants of Mr. Strange's establishment, and feared that she should be ashamed to acknowledge her if she did meet her.

Mrs. Strange had been received warmly and kindly by her husband's family. She was surrounded with all the luxury of woe, and all the attention that her widowed state required. But she was as restless here as in Langdale. Her children gave her no occupation nor pleasure, for she did not allow them to give her any care. Ronald came to her every day before he went out, that she might see that his rosettes and ribbons were properly adjusted, and then he was displayed again at dinner-time. "He looks so like his father," Mrs. Strange would say to her friends, "that it brings up most harrowing recollections to have him with me."

Elise was an hour or two a day with her mamma. She could say a few words, half French and half Italian, that entertained her and her friends. Her toilet, too, was perfect, her dress always exquisite, and a fruitful subject for admiration and discussion. Elise had already learned to cast down her eyes, to turn aside her head when her dress or herself were admired, and she knew perfectly how to keep in order her embroidered ruffles and streamers of ribbon. When the children's dresses had all been displayed, and the bijouterie that she had selected and brought home with her had been sufficiently admired, Mrs. Strange grew tired of her New York relations, and very gladly consented to the proposal of some friends she had met in her travels, to join them at Niagara, and go from there to Montreal with them.

The French maid was charmed with the prospect of finding somebody to talk French with in Canada, as she wearied a little of the society of her mistress, and found Hannah a little impracticable. Hannah, too, was glad to be travelling again. It was with the hope of seeing the world that she had entered into Mrs. Strange's service. The little Ronald, however, and herself, were firm friends. She went with him every day to the pretty squares, and was proud of all the attentions that were paid him. He was always good-natured with Hannah, and slept well and eat well. He refused to let any one else care for him, so Hannah had the almost constant charge of him.

They arrived late at night at Niagara. Mrs. Strange found her friends awaiting her. All the evening they talked over her trials, her sad affliction in Florence. Elise and Ronald were shown off.

"What a sad responsibility! What a terrible charge!" they all exclaimed.

The next day, Mrs. Strange, with her friends, went round in a carriage to see what was to be seen. In the afternoon, Adèle left Elise in Hannah's care. She wanted to go and see the wonderful falls herself, and went off with a gay party of the servants she had picked up. Hannah had no chance all day to leave the rooms that were allotted to them. The roar of the waters sounded in her ears, the doors and the windows shook in their fall, but the windows commanded only the village street, and she could see nothing but the different parties setting off from the door of the hotel.

In the evening, Mrs. Strange had Ronald brought into her parlor. Elise was talkative and noisy, and she was afraid Ronald would not sleep in the same room. Hannah sat by him as he slept on a couch in a distant corner. He could not be disturbed by the subdued conversation that was going on between Mrs. Strange and her friends. Hannah, at first, did not pay any attention to this conversation. She sat with her knitting by the sleeping Ronald, thinking of the great roar that was all the time sounding in her ears. At last she was attracted by the words of one of the gentlemen. He was more animated than the rest, and had been a great traveller. He had been talking of San Francisco.

"I suppose everybody gets along in California?" said one of the ladies present. "What an excellent place it is for all the scapegraces and ne'er-do-wells to go to."

"That's a pleasant picture of society there," said Mr. Jones, laughing. "But it is only the most spirited that manage to reach there, or to get along after they have reached there. There was a little Irish fellow I was interested in, went out in the same ship with us when I went some years ago. He got on board nobody knew how, and the captain could not throw him overboard. He raised the interest of some of the passengers. My friend Smith was struck with the mixture of foolhardiness and courage there was in the boy, and he helped him along after he reached San Francisco. The captain had threatened to put him on shore at Aspinwall, but by the time we reached there, Steevie was quite a favorite with the passengers and they would not let him go."

Hannah had been listening attentively to Mr. Jones's words, and now she came across the room.

"Oh, tell me what was his name!" she exclaimed.

"Hannah, what are you thinking of? what do you mean?" said Mrs. Strange.

"I know I ought not to speak to Mr. Jones," said Hannah; "but perhaps he is my brother. I mean the boy. Oh, sir, will you tell me his name, and how long ago it was?"

"Hannah, you surprise me," said Mrs. Strange, "to interrupt Mr. Jones in this way!"

"Never mind, Mrs. Strange," said Mr. Jones. "I remember his name, because we used to laugh at John O'Connor about him, and tell him he ought to support his own relations, and that they probably came from the same place in Ireland. John O'Connor was a young Irishman that we thought everything of; he was rich and jolly and young."

"Then it was Stephen O'Connor?" interrupted Hannah. "Tell me about him. When did he go to California? Is he there now?"

"My poor girl," said Mr. Jones, "it was so long
ago! I should be very glad to give you his history. Smith took a fancy to him and got him some
work in California, but Stephen was forever falling
into scrapes and tumbling out again. Smith kept
an eye on him. I saw him a year ago and asked
him about it. I think he said Stephen had gone
up to the mines, or to Australia."

"Oh, how long ago? When did he go?" said
Hannah.

"Let me see. It was the spring of —— " said
Mr. Jones. "I should say five or six years ago.
I can't remember which, but then it was a year
ago I met Smith, and he had lost sight of Stephen
then."

"But wouldn't he know? wouldn't he hear from
him?" asked Hannah.

"What, Smith?" asked Mr. Jones. "There
would be no hope of finding Smith. He turns up
now and then, but nobody ever knows where he
keeps himself."

"He sinks into the sea of Smiths, I suppose,"
said one of the ladies.

"Then there is no hope," said Hannah. "Stephen is lost again."

One of the gentlemen tried to comfort her by
telling her he would come home again, very likely,
after he had made his fortune.

"Well, now, I think it is only your bad pennies
that turn up again," said another.

Hannah returned to her corner, and later in the evening she had permission to go out. It was late and dark. She wandered into the street. She followed where the noise of the Falls led her, though she was so full of other thoughts that she forgot entirely where she was. She hurried along a pathway under the trees. The sound of the roar was nearer and nearer; at length, she stood on its very edge, just where the great ocean-like mass of waters plunges itself into the broad, deep basin below. The sky was heavily clouded, but a white mist rose up to show the deep precipice of waters. Hannah stood, confused, bewildered, before, in the midst of the heavy tumult. Suddenly the black sky was cleft, the broad, clear light of the moon broke through and made clear the wonderful sea of waters that lay below.

Hannah had hastened on in a tumult of passion and excitement. Within her a perfect tempest was raging. The coldness, the heartlessness, the thoughtlessness with which she had lately been treated, filled up and were exaggerated in her thoughts. They were sitting there all so comfortably; they had been talking of their journeyings, and their plans were arranged to give themselves excitement and pleasure. They had bemoaned over Mrs. Strange's great loss; they had exclaimed so loudly over their own joy at meeting again. All the time they had never given one thought of sympathy for the silent girl in the

corner of the room. Hannah had not expected
they would. She had thought it a little hard that
Mrs. Strange had not remembered that the nursery-
maid might have heard of Niagara Falls and had
never seen them. She claimed nothing more.

But she was aroused at the cold way in which
her excited questionings had been received. She
had a right to a brother and to love him, even if
she had no right to admire what was wonderful
in nature. This Mr. Jones, if he had had any
feeling, might have told her more of her brother,
might have given her hope of finding him. But
she was nothing to them. A poor straw upon the
waters, and it was no matter where she floated.
They had returned to gossip about the fashions,
and her brother, her only brother was lost again.
He was always falling into scrapes, Mr. Jones had
said; then perhaps he was doubly lost. What
could she do for him? Nothing. What was there
left for her to live for? But the great thunder of
the waters woke her out of her passion. The
tumult and the rush, the whirl of the waves stilled
the tempest in her breast. She stood in a presence of great majesty. Her own self became
small before the wonderful scene around her. It
was greater than her eye or thought could take in,
and so she stood confounded before it.

A long time she stood there, motionless, fasci-
nated by the never-ending motion before her. She
forgot herself and her own cares in the presence
of One great being.

"The waters stood above the mountains. At his rebuke they fled; at the voice of his thunder they hasted away."

On her way there, she had thought to herself, as she heard the roaring and the rushing around her, she had groaned to herself, "If it could only bear me away too; if it could hurry me on into its immense abyss. I am small, I am nothing; what matters it if I am swept away? My cry will not be heard in the midst of the great tumult!" But now she stood checked and silenced. It was the voice of God in the great waters that spoke to her and calmed her. The moon shone clearly on the mass of water that went to whirl itself below, and lighted up, too, the glistening spray that danced above it. Her soul stood terrified, as it were, in the presence of God. She shrank before the abyss that had opened in her own spirit, at the same time her heart throbbed to remember she was the child of God, watched over by him, as was the single drop of spray among the great waters.

She turned homewards, and the mighty sound that had seemed to her despairing, revengeful, now rung in her ears like the organ notes of a grand psalm, that is claiming and praying for the return of a soul to God!

18

CHAPTER XXXII.

THE RIVER'S BANK.

THE next morning Mrs. Strange decided she would leave Niagara. The noise of the Falls had kept her awake all night, and made her nervous. She knew she should not be able to sleep a wink as long as she remained there. Her friends had been some days at Niagara, and were willing to leave, and were urgent that Mrs. Strange should come directly to their home just out of Montreal. It had been determined that when Mrs. Strange went there, she should send the children to her mother-in-law, who was by this time at her country seat on the Hudson.

At noon, then, the very day after her arrival, Hannah found herself leaving Niagara Falls with little Ronald under her charge, Elise and Adèle, and Mrs. Strange's trusty man-servant. She had been so busily employed in repacking, in all Mrs. Strange's different requirements, that she had been allowed no opportunity to leave the hotel. Mrs. Strange sent away the children, expecting to meet them again in a few weeks. She had brought them with her to show them to her friends,—that they might see how Elise had preserved the French accent in the few words she could say, during the few weeks she had been at home, and how Ronald's hair was beginning to curl.

Adèle, for want of her mistress to converse with, made some efforts at talk with Hannah, and the journey was quickly accomplished.

The house of old Mrs. Strange was beautifully situated on the banks of the Hudson. It was a large house, stretching across a broad lawn. In the summer it was the home of any of the children and grandchildren that chose to come there; so beneath its roof were collected several families of young people and children, with maids and nurses. These were left to take care of themselves, — to do as they pleased; the children played in the grounds, or in the broad hall; the young people wandered in the garden, or made excursions through the country round. Their elders met in the library, or took sober drives to visit their neighbors. Below the house, not far from its balconied front, stretched the Hudson,—behind, was a line of hills of the Catskill range. Everything was comfortable and luxurious about the house. There were easy lounges in the airy summer rooms and in the cosy library, and in the stables there were horses and carriages for those who wished to ride or drive. It was a haven of rest for Hannah even. A rest for her body, but her thoughts were full of uneasiness.

The night that she heard news of Stephen at Niagara, all her old passions had been roused and excited. She was filled with hatred and distrust of all the rest of the world. Even for a moment she had believed she would gladly leave it, since it was so cold, so harsh, so cruel to her. In the midst of this mood she had stood beside the torrent of Niagara, and its wild tumult had hushed for a little while the passion within her; it had brought gentler thoughts back to her soul; it had reminded her of one great Protector, because it had filled her with an awe that had driven her to him alone for protection. That night, as she tried to sleep in the midst of the great roar of the waters, gentle sounds had mingled with her dreams. She fancied she heard Bertha's voice,— she recalled her soothing tones. She was conscious of a spiritual help, such as Bertha's faith had taught her of already, and that came to uphold her now.

But for poor Hannah these were high and great visions. She could not strain herself up to rest in them. The little vain trifling talk that Adèle kept up with her, brought her down from the higher feelings that might sustain her. What right had she, a poor, abused, unconsidered servant-girl, to nourish such thoughts as these? She listened to the little squabbles and jealous quarrels that Adèle confided to her, that she was carrying on with the servants, and found her own jealousies and distrusts nourished as she listened.

The children were received with warm pleasure by their grandmother and the rest of the family. Hannah found that her charge was taken very much out of her hands. His little cousins Alice and Lily took a fancy to Ronald. They were about twelve and fourteen years old, always together, and alike in their tastes. Whatever one did, the other must do also. They could not rest without having Ronald to play with. On the pleasant days, they would take him out upon the lawn. Hannah was made to sit under the trees while they had a lively frolic with him. Then, whenever they went to drive, Hannah must take Ronald with them. He was such a good-natured little fellow, and laughed whenever they shook their curls at him.

Elise was a pet of the older girls. They were fond of making her mimic young-lady airs and graces, and she was a very apt scholar, and liked nothing better than to be praised and laughed at for her bright sayings. The French words coming out from her little mouth sounded so charmingly, and then they had such an excellent opportunity to talk French with the nurse! Ronald was charmed with the attention he received. On rainy days he would walk up and down the hall with Hannah, and Alice and Lily would play hide and seek with him behind the statuary that stood there. It was a grand hall that went through the house, and Ronald and Hannah both admired much

the marble figures with which it was adorned.
They liked best the little Cupid on the Dolphin,
and Hannah held Ronald in her arms to look at it
again and again. Sometimes they ventured into
the conservatory, but not often, for if the gardener
was there he scolded them away. He did not like
to have the children there, — they broke off the
flowers, or perhaps even knocked down the pots.

Everywhere else Hannah, with Ronald in her
arms, was welcomed. Grandpapa Strange laid
down his book if they came into the library, and
took off his spectacles to look at Ronald, and then
would lift him on his knee awhile, but give him
back to Hannah with a sigh, " He looks so like his
father, as he was, so many years ago."

And in the drawing-room they compared the
hearty, rosy Ronald with the delicate, dainty little
Elise, and the girls were quite willing he should
pull down their hair, he was such a handsome little
darling.

One day, after a noisy play with Ronald on the
lawn, Alice came near where Hannah was sitting,
and threw herself all out of breath on the grass by
her side.

" Don't you think this is a pretty place ?" she
asked of Hannah, as soon as she could recover herself; " isn't this a pretty place ? I wish we had at
home such a wide lawn. We have only a little bit
of a garden, and the walks in it are so narrow that
I can't run through it, or my skirts will knock off

the heads of the tulips. But it is such a fine place here! Don't you think so, Hannah?"

"Yes, Miss Alice," said Hannah. "I never saw such a beautiful place."

"And don't you like to be here?" asked Alice.

"I like to be with Master Ronald," said Hannah.

"But don't you like to be here?" persisted Alice. "Do you want to go anywhere else? You look tired always; you look as if you wanted something else."

"Do I look tired?" asked Hannah. "Everybody says so; I don't know why they look at me."

"I don't suppose they do look much," said Alice; "only I was wondering if it was so very tiresome to take care of Ronald. Now I think I should like to take care of him all day."

"Master Ronald isn't any care," said Hannah. "He isn't enough care."

"Why, I shouldn't want any more," said Alice. "He is such a little plaything, — just enough to take up all one's time. Perhaps you don't like to have us take him away from you."

"Oh no, Miss Alice," said Hannah. "I like to see you playing with him, and very often it makes me forget all about myself."

"Oh, you have unpleasant things to think of then," suggested Alice. "I suppose people do, as they grow up. Sometimes when I go to ask mamma something, she says, 'Don't worry me, I'm thinking.' But I shouldn't imagine any one could worry here."

Hannah did not reply to this.

"Perhaps," Alice went on, "you have been un-happy in your former life. Oh, I wish you would tell me all about it. I like to read about people who have had a former life, who have suffered much through their early days, and then something turns up that makes it all very happy for them."

"I have had kind friends who have kept me from suffering," said Hannah.

"Did you leave an old father in Ireland?" said Alice. "Did he send you here to try your fortune?"

"I had a brother that I loved, Miss Alice," said Hannah, at last, "and he went away to try his fortune, and I think I shall never see him again."

"And hasn't he written to you?" said Alice; "and don't you think he'll come home sometime with a very magnificent fortune? Oh, I shouldn't think you would be tired, thinking and wondering and fancying what has become of him, and how he will come home."

"Perhaps he never will come home," sighed Hannah.

Lily came running up with Ronald in her arms. There was a summons into the house. It was time to dress for dinner. All through the rest of Hannah's stay, however, Alice pleased herself with talking with Hannah about what had become of her brother. She was pleased to know something that the rest of the family had never heard of, so she kept Hannah's confidence all to herself. She raised wild speculations, and asked of Hannah a great many questions. She was very sure she should meet with Stephen herself in some very romantic way, and then she would befriend him and speak to him of Hannah and send him home to her.

"Oh, Miss Alice," said Hannah, once, "I am tired of thinking of that. I have been over and over it again, a great many times, and have planned in my mind many ways in which I should see him; and I have wondered how I should meet him, till I have begun to fear to see him again!"

Mrs. Strange returned from her visit to Montreal and took her place in the family circle. Hannah perceived that she did not bring much pleasure there. She showed no sympathy for her cousins and nieces, or sisters-in-law. Even old Mr. Strange could not interest her in anything. Everybody was very attentive and kind to her, but she was not satisfied with any attention or kindness. She did not care for the books they were reading, nor admire the collars they were embroidering. She was listless, and expressed no pleasure in the beauty of the scenery. It dazzled her eyes to see the sunlight on the water, and she thought the sight of the mountains was gloomy and dismal. They reminded her of that sad winter she had been passing. She drew down the curtains over the windows, and shut out the sunlight and the view, and then she had no power to make any sunlight within.

She objected to Ronald's playing so much with Alice and Lily. She was very sure some accident would happen if he was left so much with those wild girls. It was Hannah's business to take care of him. She was quiet and steady, and Mrs. Strange decidedly prohibited his constant frolics with the others. Ronald did not like being restrained, nor to return to Hannah's sober society after he had tasted something more cheerful. Poor Hannah had trouble in keeping him quiet, while Alice and Lily were obliged to find amusement somewhere else, and set off on long expeditions with their uncles into the mountains.

But Mrs. Strange could not decide to spend the summer here; she determined to go back to Langdale. Ronald had a violent fit of crying, because he did not wish to go away. His mother did not listen to him, but with her whole family went down on one afternoon in the boat to New York, and stayed there a few days before returning to Langdale.

CHAPTER XXXIII.

THE OLD HAUNTS.

EARLY in the morning they reached Langdale. Hannah was kept busy over the trunks and with Ronald till the afternoon, when she asked Mrs. Strange if she could spare her for a little while.

"You look tired," said Mrs. Strange, for once observing Hannah's appearance, "and I suppose you would like to go and see Miss Elspeth. You shall have the afternoon to rest yourself, and Mary shall take care of Ronald."

Hannah did look worn and anxious. She dressed herself, took a hurried good-by of Ronald, and went into the street. Here she stopped and looked up and down, as she used to do in the early days when she first went to Langdale. As she looked up the street, she could see just beyond the row of trees that stretched along the sidewalk, the gate that led to Miss Elspeth's house. As she looked down, she saw the curve shut in by the drooping branches of the elms, that always closed the prospect there.

She turned her steps down the street, and

passed the little grocery shop, and the tavern, and
went out of the village. Farther than this she
had never walked before. She had never been in
Boston since the day she drove away from it with
Miss Dora and Frank. For the first year or two
Miss Elspeth had purposely kept her from going
there, as she wanted to break up her associations
with the place, and afterwards the family wants
from there had been so small, that Miss Elspeth
could always supply them herself. So, for the first
time, Hannah trod the road that had seemed so
long to her six years before. Now she hurried
along it, and as she passed on and drew nearer
Boston, the way grew more and more familiar.
She recognized some of the large houses, to
which broad avenues led, that had seemed to her
like palaces when she passed them before. She
remembered the different places Frank had pointed
out to Bessie to amuse her. As she walked on she
came to the long ropewalk that had astonished
Bessie, and she had asked Frank what it was, and
if a ropewalk were anything like a sidewalk. Boston rose up before her. The brick houses shutting
in the narrow streets, towering up and crowned
by the dome of the State House. She saw the
water again, and the many bridges stretching
across it, over which she used to wander so long
ago. She hastened along so fast that she was surprised to find it so near. "Has it always been so
near to me?" she exclaimed to herself. In her

hurry and excitement she felt no fatigue, and pressed on more and more ardently. Just as she entered upon the dusty streets, a little girl touched her. "Will you give me a cent, ma'am?" she asked. Hannah did not venture to look at her. She dared not see this image of herself as she once was. She pushed by and went on. She crossed the Common, that seemed little changed, though she hardly cast her eyes around. There were children playing there, who looked as the children did there six years ago. An apple-woman sat beneath a tree. Hannah could not help observing her. "Is that old Mrs. Grundy sitting there still and looking just the same, sewing on the same work, with one eye still upon her apples? Mrs. Grundy, they used to say, was rich, and had saved up money in the bank, or somewhere. She saved it so that Jem might be taught book-learning. Where is Jem now? He never liked anything so well as playing marbles in the streets. And poor Mrs. Grundy sits there still, sewing on the coarse, blue pantaloons." But Hannah did not stop here. She even walked on faster. She would not have Mrs. Grundy see her and recognize her. So she hurried on till the streets grew narrower and narrower. There were new buildings here that almost confused her. The old landmarks were gone, and high rows of stores, with broad-paned windows, filled with brilliant silks and ribbons, rose up where before were old wooden houses, that Hannah herself used to frequent. She turned the corner of one of these, and came in sight of the entrance to Board Court. She passed on and reached the very corner, and looked down the little, narrow court. There everything was quite unchanged. The old gates in front of the doorways still hung loosely on their hinges. Old barrels stood along in front of the houses. Rubbish, broken baskets, stoves, laid heaped up, all along the court. There were groups of children, noisy children, that were quarrelling there, as they used to do long ago. There were women hanging out clothes along the lines spread across their door-yards. They were talking to each other in loud tones, the strains of which sounded familiar to Hannah's ears. Two boys were fighting over the broken hoop of a barrel, and a dog was joining in the contest, and some girls were struggling about a torn straw bonnet. Yes, it was all familiar to Hannah's eyes; the sight of it made her dizzy, the sounds stunned her. She stood a moment fixed. She had meant to go down there, to have inquired about the people that used to live there. She thought some of them might tell her news of Stephen. She had a vague idea that there would be somebody there who would receive her warmly and cordially. She remembered that they used to love one another there, and she came back to find an old home-feeling she fancied she could meet nowhere else.

But she stood still, shocked, overwhelmed. She had thought so much of her own people, of her earlier friends, that her fancy had thrown a mist over them that elevated them in her remembrance. At one moment all this went away. At one moment she saw what she was, in comparison with what she might have been. She saw, coming towards her, a girl struggling under the weight of a heavy basket of chips. It was just so she used to come home from her daily wanderings. It pictured herself. She realized it now more than she had done in the crowds of New York. Now she stood puzzled between the Hannah that was, and the Hannah of seventeen years of age, standing there, well-cared for, and in comfortable dress; and within, how different!

The thought of this last difference made her shudder afresh. She suddenly began to fear she might be recognized, might be drawn back into that abyss. For she suddenly saw how she herself had been made over; how within her were new standards of right and wrong, such as she had been quite unconscious of before; such as she was partly unconscious of now. She could not now say to herself, I believe that there is a right and wrong; that it is my duty to follow in the path to God; she did not know this, but she felt herself shuddering before that other path.

She turned away quickly; she dreaded lest they should know her; lest somehow she should be tempted back to that old life that only from this moment she loathed. Faster than she had come there, if possible, she hastened away; only one thought was in her mind. "Miss Elspeth, Miss Elspeth! She saved me. But for her, I should be there still; or where, indeed, should I be?"

She pressed through the crowded streets. The high houses that looked down upon her were crowded too. Those just around her had once been grand mansions, but had been deserted for more fashionable quarters, and were given over to the lowest of the poor. They still had their stately entrances, and iron balconies, and stone facings to the large windows. Within were high-storied rooms, ornamented ceilings, and oak-carved balustrades. Now the houses swarmed with occupants. Each room held its family, perhaps more. Children and lounging men and women were crowded out upon the steps and staircase. All were struggling for life. It was like a wild field, where the native plants struggle with an overgrowth from alien seeds, for daily subsistence. It was a struggle for mere physical life; for the food of the day; for permission to breathe, and to breathe in an air that seemed to choke breath. There was little room for a struggle for spiritual life.

Two women leaned together from a window, looking equally old. They were mother and grandmother of the child looking up to them from below. . Their faces were grimed with filth, and

worn with care, and hardened and stolid in ignorance and brutality. All humanity had so faded
from the coarse, repulsive features, that one would
hesitate to call them women still. The little child
beneath looked up with laughing brown eyes, shak-
ing joyfully its curls of golden hair. Its cheeks
were hidden in dirt, but were still ruddy and fresh.
It was a picture of health, and heartiness and happiness. It is to struggle for life, as those two
poor women have done before it. Must it be only
to find food for the day, losing health of body and
soul for the sake only of food and raiment? It is to
struggle with the crowding humanity around, with
weeds and tares, while its own growth is feeble
and unassisted. Must it be left so? Must the
child harden into vice, stunted and maimed, when
it has a child's hearty claim on life, life physical
and life spiritual, — the claim of every human
being?

Some of these thoughts and questions came into
Hannah's mind as she hurried along. She was
suddenly conscious that she had been transplanted
from a close, weedy, unhealthy soil, into food,
and air, and light. Not only herself had been
saved, but Bessie, Martha, and Margie had been
rescued. For suddenly she realized what a down-
ward path there lay from such a home as she left
behind. There was love and kindness there, such
as she fancied she had been longing for these
many years; but there came before her the mem-

19

ory of evil, she shuddered to think how alluring; and the destitution that shuts out the sight of all else but the thought of supplying daily wants; and the recklessness that cares only for the moment's pleasure; and loathsome sights, and misery in all its forms, to harden the feelings or drive the heart to despair. From all this she had been saved, snatched away, brought into a higher and lighter atmosphere, to another world.

To Hannah, it seemed as if this were the moment of her own salvation, because for the first time she felt utterly grateful to Miss Elspeth for all she had done. Before, she had wild, ambitious, vain imaginings; she had believed that if only Miss Elspeth had left her to herself, she would have worked out for herself some greater position in the world. She had cherished a sullen feeling towards Miss Elspeth and Amy. She thought they had taken her away merely to make her work, to live a life of labor. While she had been with Bertha, her sullenness had been cleared away, the darkness of her atmosphere purified; a little while she had been raised above her natural range of thought. But like a vision, these better modes of mind had lately passed away.

The last few weeks, her old passions, her gloominess of disposition, had returned with new force. She had become suspicious of her old friends, distrusting those who were near her. Travelling back to Langdale, there had rushed upon her a desire to return to her old home, to her old haunts, and her old ways of life. And she had come to Boston with the firm resolution of returning to live in Board Court. If she found there one of her old friends, a single person who could welcome her, she meant to stay there. She would live as they did, and make her home with them. Miss Elspeth, Amy, Bessie, Ronald, she could leave them all behind, as once she had left Board Court. She was older now, and could take care of herself. She would live independently, free of others, and not subject to their exactions.

It was not till she saw the old place, with its desolation hanging round it, that she knew just what a home she had left there. It was not till this moment she realized the strength of the new ties that bound her. She hurried back, dizzy, her head confused with thought. In the crowded streets she seemed to see only the poor, thinly dressed girls. At all the street corners they seemed to appeal to her. She saw them clinging to the omnibus steps, seated under the church porches, coming out from the alley-ways. Again, upon the bridge she was asked for a cent, and emptied the contents of her pocket into a poor girl's hand. On she walked until she was quite out of town, till she drew near Langdale. Here she left the road, and turning into a little wood by the wayside, sat down in a sheltered spot. She hid her face in her hands and wept bitterly. They

were softening tears, they broke up the stoniness
in her heart, melted the ice there. For once, she
thanked God heartily, earnestly. He had turned
the heart of Miss Elspeth towards her, and that
had saved her.

It is so hard to melt away the influences of an
early life, to counteract all the lessons of the first
ten years, to tear up the weeds that are early
planted. There are evil inheritances to be strug-
gled with, childish prejudices and fancies banished. It requires the constant care of a warm
love, and the patience that comes with love, and
even at the last there is often disappointment.
For there comes often a moment of reaction, such
a time as came to Hannah, when she found herself
independent, or fancied herself so, when the old
life came upon her, almost irresistible with its
charm, of which its distance formed a part. At
this age and point of their lives, such girls as
Hannah, who have been saved so far, suddenly
feel a right to choose for themselves their future
life. They have no special home of their own, like
those of their own age who are fortunate enough
to have mother, father, sister, and brothers to hold
and claim them; and in contrast, a life of indepen-
dence looks attractive and tempting to them.
They are restless under restraint, they are unwilling to feel grateful, — are unconscious that they
have anything to be grateful for. It is a time of
contest. The struggle comes for a spiritual life,

and upon the nature of the influences of the last few years will depend the result. It is not enough to have kept these poor ones from the evil, to have sheltered them from harm, they must have been brought into a positive love of the good, and must be held still and restrained by the powerful arms of love.

It would be hard to say what influences were now most powerfully working upon Hannah; what it was that had remade and regenerated her. There was Miss Elspeth's untiring kindness that had never looked for an answering glance; there was Amy's warm, tender, unvarying interest; and there were the pure strong words of Bertha;—all these had made an atmosphere around her that had elevated her above early clinging habits, that had given her a higher tone of character, which she did not know of, till a sudden glimpse showed her the contrast between the old and the new. And to help the sharpness of this contrast came Miss Dora's obstinate love of order that had, one by one, weeded out the unneat habits of the first years of Hannah's life, which nothing but Miss Dora's preciseness and attention to petty detail could have destroyed.

In looking down Board Court, besides the horror of the degrading atmosphere with which she suddenly felt it was surrounded, Hannah shrank from its filth and its unthriftiness. If nothing else had kept her from the place, the sense of order and of neatness acquired in these last few years would have kept her from it. Any life, a life of hardship and of labor, were better than a home in such squalor and discomfort.

The long summer afternoon had passed away, and the sun was setting, as Hannah lifted her face from her hands, and rose to go back. A new sense had come in upon her; her first thought of gratitude. With it, a new hope, new resolutions, even plans for the future. It was no vague idea of something great to come upon her that animated her, but something that she was herself to do, an object in life.

CHAPTER XXXIV.

A MEETING..

As Hannah turned into Langdale, at a meeting of two streets, she was asked a question about the way, by some one who was passing by. Her face was bent down, so she had not observed who it was that spoke to her, but the voice roused her. She looked up to see a tall, well-built man, with sunburnt face, not different from many she met in the street; but something about him attracted her, especially when he repeated his question, " if Miss Elspeth Elton lived anywhere near."

Hannah had hardly wakened out of the dream into which her walk had thrown her, with all its remembrances of all the years of her life. Instead of answering, she stared at the stranger, and said to herself, " If it should be Stephen!"

" But it is Stephen," was the answer. " Stephen O'Connor. But I'm sure I can't say who you are, if it is not Hannah."

He was interrupted by Hannah's exclamations. Poor Hannah was never demonstrative. She had never shown in her face any feeling that warmed below. And now in the street, with an unknown Stephen before her, she scarcely knew how to bring out her expressions of delight and joy, her questionings and wonderings. She forgot all the weariness of her walk, of her long life, in the crowning pleasure she had dreamed of and pictured to herself through these many years. She was passing from one dream of life into another, into a happiness she neither knew how to realize or to express. And now no action or color or words came to Hannah after that first utterance of surprise in the reality of her happiness. There was no doubt in it either, for though the Stephen that stood before her had outgrown the Steevie of six years ago; though the reckless, ragged boy had become what Hannah's fastidious eyes had directly perceived to be "respectable" looking, there was enough of the old manner and voice and face to assure her that her brother was not lost, — that he had indeed come back again. Stephen's words did not falter.

"I do believe it is Hannah," he said. "But you look so white and pale; you can hardly stand up. Just sit down here a minute; let us look at each other. It is better than I expected, to find you in the same place all the time. It would have served me right if I had lost you entirely. It is Hannah, and Hannah grown well-looking, though you are so pale, and happier than ever you looked before. I was afraid to go to Board Court; I was afraid lest

I should find you in the old place. And Bessie, I'm afraid to ask about Bessie. Don't tell me yet about her if it's bad. I can't hear it."

Hannah had seated herself on a stone by the wayside, under the barberry bushes, the blackberry vines clambering in and about her feet, almost opposite the Lees' house, but she started up when Stephen spoke of Bessie.

"I must take you to her," she exclaimed. "I must not keep you here. I believe I thought I was dreaming, and that it would all act itself out without any moving."

Hannah hastened away with Stephen, and met at Miss Elspeth's door Bessie and Margie.

"Oh, Hannah," Bessie exclaimed, "we were coming to see if it were true that you had got home. And how could you go away without bidding us good-by? But what is the matter? You look pale and sick, and happy, and crying too! Oh, Miss Elspeth, come here; it is Hannah, and I cannot tell what is the matter with her."

Bessie was so taken up with Hannah that she could scarcely notice her companion. But Hannah succeeded at last in making her understand who it was. After she understood, it was some minutes before Bessie could welcome in the grown-up man before her, the old playfellow she could never quite forget; but at last she threw herself into his arms with sobbings and delight.

Bessie and Margie had an idea that Hannah must

have brought Stephen from Niagara or New York; it was a long time before they could understand that he was as new a treasure to Hannah as he was to Bessie, or how or where it was that Hannah had found him.

Through the summer evening, Bessie sat upon the door-steps listening to Stephen's talk as he told of all his adventures, how he had come home a "carpenter," not a "nabob" with California gold, of his narrow escapes, and wonderful stories about the sea. Margie sat by with eyes wide open in wonder and delight. Hannah listened, too, for a while, but presently went in to talk with Miss Elspeth, while Miss Dora had fallen asleep over her knitting.

"I want to ask you about yourself, Hannah," said Miss Elspeth. "You went away so hurriedly, and Mrs. Carlton has already regretted that she let you go, and would gladly have you back again. But I can't regret the journey, if it has made you look so fresh and well; or is it Stephen's return that has refreshed you so?"

"It is neither, it is neither," said Hannah, "and it is that I want to tell you. It all comes from my walk to Boston this very afternoon."

"You walked to Boston!" exclaimed Miss Elspeth. "It is not possible you walked all that way."

"Ah, I did more than that," said Hannah. And she went back to tell all the distrust and ingratitude of her last years, all the hardness of her heart, and evil suspicions. She told as well as she could of the sudden glimpse into her old life, and how it had wakened her into a feeling of what she had been, — of what she owed to Miss Elspeth.

" I came back," she said, " thinking Bessie and I could never do enough if we gave our whole lives to you, and eager to work all my life long, if I can only do some of the good you have done."

Miss Elspeth listened, wondering, in silence. She had never looked for reward. When she began her work she had never looked towards its end. She was one of those workers who would never have asked to see the end. She liked best that work whose object was so grand that its ending fell into the hands of God, though its beginning was small enough for her weak energies. Not that she ever reasoned so, nor knew that she was working in so grand a way. She took up what lay near her to do, because it was her work and she would never give it to another. That night she could scarcely close her eyes for this wondrous gratitude at her own work. She loved Hannah with a love different from that she felt for the other children. They were attractive to everybody, and won their own way; but for Hannah she had longed and waited. She had found it hard to understand her, and for this reason had yearned the more to move her.

CHAPTER XXXV.

HOME AT LAST.

MISS DORA was a little suspicious of Stephen at first. When he left, she herself locked all the doors. She did not like the idea of introducing a new man into the house. It might be Stephen, but then, again, it might not be; and if it were Stephen, what ought they to expect of him? Her prejudices were gradually removed by Stephen's constantly respectful air and deference, and by the handiness that he displayed in sundry little pieces of work about the house. It was settled that Hannah was to live with Stephen in Boston. Hannah and Bessie easily persuaded him that it was not right to take Bessie from Miss Dora and Miss Elspeth. Hannah talked with Miss Elspeth of it.

"Stephen will not listen to any other plan. He is willing that I should sew to help him earn his living. There is another plan, and Stephen is willing to help it. I thought of it that day in the wood, after I came from Boston. I thought all my life long I would work for those poor girls wandering in the streets. If I could find the one that was so like me, that I saw that day, how I would like to help her. I shall not have such a home as yours to bring her to. I am not like you. I cannot show her what goodness is. But I can take her or some child out of a sadder home. You will help me, Miss Amy will help me. Perhaps, because I have been so near those poor ones once, I may know how to help them, though I am so little in myself."

On an appointed day, Stephen met Bessie and Hannah at the station and led them to his house,— some rooms in a little, quiet street, one of a block newly built. Everything was neat about it, the steps and the stairway. Hannah opened the door of the front room and started to find it all furnished. She had partly expected this, but not to find such a finished, comfortable air over everything. She was still more surprised when Agnes and Fred Carlton came to greet her.

"Have not we done wonders?" said Agnes. "I can't say I have done much. But one day, when I was coming into town, I found Amy was concocting this plan, and I could not help having a hand in it. She was busy enough about her own house, I told her, and I asked her to let me come and arrange it with her. I suppose we ought to be out of the way now, while you look round on your new possessions; but I never did anything before that I enjoyed so much!"

"Why, how beautiful it is here!" exclaimed Hannah. "And Miss Agnes, you helped about this?"

"You know I never do much," said Agnes. "I tried this time, but it was hard work. I thought I might accomplish some sweeping, and took up the broom one day, but it made my side ache so that I had to sit down again."

Hannah was looking round, admiring all there was in the room.

"Pray, admire the carpet," said Agnes. "That was Mr. Rothsay's present. Amy was coming into town to select it the day I met her, and that she told me of her plans. So I went with her, and I do believe I prevented her from getting one of those horrid red and green ones. Amy has a good taste, but she had an idea they would be more useful. Now, look at Fred's labors in putting up those bookshelves."

"Mr. Fred has been very handy," said Stephen.

"Oh, we have had a famous time," said Agnes, seizing Hannah and spinning her round the room and seating her at last in a little sewing-chair. "That is Fred's present," she continued; "and the workbox on the table Tom and Jack sent you. Do you know they were full three days in the woodhouse, hammering up a workbox for you with shingles and nails, which they thought quite splendid? But when papa came to see it, he thought it would not do for you, so he brought them into town and took them to a shop, to pick out the prettiest they could find. And this was the result. A little gaudy, perhaps, but valuable as expressing their taste!"

" But this picture by the table here!" exclaimed Hannah. " Why, this is Miss Amy herself!"

" Ah, yes, you can see George Arnold's hand in that," said Agnes.

" She looks as I have seen her so many times," said Hannah, " standing on the doorstep."

" Yes; the broom in her hand and all," said Agnes. " Nobody would have thought of that but George Arnold. She is brushing away the leaves from the piazza, and the vines across the pillars make such a pretty archway for the picture!"

There was a sofa Mr. Carlton had sent to Hannah, to be admired and praised. The pretty round table Agnes had contributed, with its vase of flowers.

" Now look into your cupboards," said Agnes. " See how nicely Miss Elspeth has filled them!"

" What beautiful china!" exclaimed Hannah. " Stephen, what shall we do with such handsome things?"

" And this famous chest of tea, George Arnold brought home," said Agnes.

" And my store-closet furnished too!" said Hannah. " What kind friends I have!"

In her own bedroom were traces of Amy's hands, in the white window curtains and the pretty work-table she had left for Hannah.

Agnes followed Hannah into the room just as she was looking up at an engraving that hung opposite her bed.

"That beautiful picture too!" she said. "Oh, Miss Agnes, the one Miss Bertha loved so well!"

"Yes, Hannah," said Agnes, "it is the very one that used to hang in Bertha's room. I thought you would like to have it. It will seem to you like a present from Bertha."

"Miss Agnes, it is so kind of you. You are so very thoughtful," said Hannah.

"You had not expected it of me," said Agnes. "I would not have expected it of myself. Yet I am not quite ungrateful. You were more to Bertha than ever I was, and you have taught me a great deal. I would give much if I could be like you."

"Like me!" exclaimed Hannah. "You could not wish that!"

"Oh yes; you know how to work, and I think there must be pleasure in that," said Agnes. "I believe Bertha used to think it would be a very hard lesson for me to learn how to work. And it is so. My thoughts fly about in so many different ways. I am unsettled. I have no aim. I have had greater pleasure here than I ever had before. I tried to think what Bertha would have done had she been here. But as soon as I compare it all with her, I can think of nothing but a failure!"

"Oh, dear, Miss Agnes, not so," said Hannah.

" It was such a very great pleasure merely to see you and Mr. Fred here! And that you should have thought of this beautiful picture! I could love nothing more than this. We seem to see the angels that bore away our dear Miss Bertha."

Agnes hurried away. She would not stay any longer, but she ran back to tell Hannah she should stop there often to give her some valuable hints upon housekeeping, and to help her if she were in any strait about her sewing.

Hannah was left with Bessie and Stephen, to look again at all her own possessions, and exclaim again with gratitude. There were the books that Frank Rothsay had selected, and the silver spoons that Mrs. Strange had sent. The pretty water pitcher and some plaster statuettes were the gift of Bessie, Martha, and Margie. They, too, had persuaded Miss Elspeth and Miss Dora to have their daguerreotypes taken for Hannah, and Ralph, the cat, was also introduced into the picture. It had proved as difficult to get Miss Dora to the daguerreotype rooms in Langdale, as the cat. She did not like daguerreotypes, and her sourest expression was transferred to the plate. Miss Dora's gifts were found in the store-closet.

Miss Elspeth, Bessie, Martha, and Margie assembled at Hannah's house-warming, which was celebrated by a splendid tea in her new home.

20

CHAPTER XXXVI.

AMY'S LANDSCAPE.

MRS. BUNCE was very much shocked that Amy Rothsay should leave Langdale to live in a narrow street in Boston. Mrs. Bunce had been to see the house Amy was to live in, for George Arnold had asked her one day when she went into town with him in the cars, to go and look at it. It was a small house, and there was a row of brick buildings in front, and a dead brick wall behind it. To be sure, there was a horse-chestnut in front of the doorway, but it was only a mockery of a tree, growing out of the bricks, and Amy all her life had lived in the garden and in the woods, as it were, and George pretended to be so fond of sketching from nature. To be sure, she should think it would be easier to draw houses and windows, where he could rule the lines, and she always wondered anybody would try to draw trees when there was not one tree like another, if the woods were ever so large, and she never could see how anybody could think of putting them down just the same on paper. But then George and some other painters she had seen, always had a fancy for trying to draw trees and vines, and George had always insisted she should keep the creeper over her own porch, though it had grown so thick now that it quite darkened her front room. But she was sure she didn't care if there was not any light in the front room, now Amy and everybody else that she wanted to see, were going away from Langdale.

Amy herself was not at all so melancholy about her new home. There was sunlight in the house, even if the brick walls shut it out so closely. The outside of the house was like all the rest in the block, and it needed George Arnold's name on the door to guide the most intimate friend to the right entrance; but once inside, there was no doubt to whom it was to belong. Already it wore an individual air, in spite of the plan that ruled the whole row of houses, and its rooms expressed both comfort and elegance.

It was one day when almost the last finishing touch had been given to the pretty rooms that Hannah drew Amy to the front window.

"I have never yet told you," she said to Amy, "why I like these windows of yours. If you look up the street to the corner opposite, you will see the place where I first met Miss Elspeth. I remember perfectly how I stood shivering there, lingering in the cold, before I should go to my cheerless home. In front of Miss Elspeth, came along a lady very handsomely dressed. She attracted me, and at first I meant to speak to her. She wore so many satins and furs, I thought she must have a great deal of money. I was going forward to speak to her when I saw Miss Elspeth just behind. There was something about her face that looked gentle and kind. Oh! you cannot think in those days how we learned to study faces. I did not think of Miss Elspeth's dress. I only saw she looked as though she could not answer me harshly, and so I spoke to her. That first lady, dressed in the satins and furs, Miss Amy, was Mrs. Paxton, so I knew afterwards, for I had never forgotten her face. And if I had asked her for help, oh, think of it! she would have turned me away, — I should have lost my chance of speaking to Miss Elspeth. I know Mrs. Paxton would not have listened to me, and she might have given me hard words. Those hard words would have sent me back into my old life, — into that life that I loved in those days, but out of which I never could have lifted myself. I know how stern, how severe she is, and she would have made me harder and colder than I was before."

"Stop a moment," said Amy, smiling; "you are talking in the way you used to go on. Think of the kind words that have been spoken to you."

"It is those words I am thinking of, indeed," said Hannah; "but how can I help shuddering when I think what a difference just those few words might have made in me. Even a kind word might have helped me then. Miss Elspeth gave me much more, but in those days gentlé words did soften me. It was the hard treatment I received that helped to make me hard. I remember when I was quite young, I was more like Bessie when she was a child. I did not care what came the next day or the next hour. I laughed at the gay sights I saw in the street, and was full of joy on those days that I had more food to eat than others. One day I remember I stood in the street by a carriage door to watch a lady who was getting out from the carriage with her two children. I watched them as one does a pretty sight. I liked to see their gay clothing. I did not. think at all that I was a child like them, nor regret that I had not their fine clothes. But suddenly I was roused by the lady's voice. 'Child, what are you standing there idling for?' Suddenly I grew angry; I turnéd away, but wondered why it was these children should be dressed so gayly, and fed so carefully, while I was left to wander in the streets, and might not even stand to look upon their finery."

"But you were not left to wander quite alone," said Amy.

"I might not have been a better child, Miss Amy," continued Hannah, "if I had lived such a life as those children whom I envied. I could never have been better taught than by good Miss Elspeth."

"There was One who cared for you, and who led so good a friend to you," said Amy. "What a moment, indeed, it was that changed your life. How glad I am that my windows look upon so pleasant a spot. Mrs. Bunce need not be anxious about my landscape. I have found one charm in it already."

"You will make many such sunny places," said Hannah, laughing, "all through Boston, while you live here, Miss Amy."

"You and I together, Hannah," said Amy; "we will do our best."

It was an encouragement of this resolution that Mr. Jasper spoke, when he came to Amy's new home. "I have seen some households," he said, "that stand like a centre for many planets. All the members of it revolve around in their little duties, noiselessly and easily, and presently their quiet, even motion is felt beyond their small circle, and it harmonizes many wandering bodies that would seem beyond its reach, and many erratic planets, comets that have a wide orbit, come within its influence. All this time the little system is keeping on its course round the great central sun, performing its part of the grand law that ages must complete. All these words mean that the little households whose members truly perform their part have a wide influence, farther than they know or are aware of. If they only keep to their own centre, going on with an even,

equal motion, they become themselves the centre
and support of others. I say I know many such
homes that give out warmth and light beyond
their firesides, and work more good than many
great conventions and large assemblies. And this
I believe will be one, for it begins with the spirit
of love."

This was Mr. Jasper's benediction upon Amy's
home, and Hannah felt that he meant it for her, too,
for he looked kindly to her, and spoke encouraging
words to her. So when she went back into her
own home, she felt that however humble it might
be, it could still have some of that power of which
Mr. Jasper spoke. Miss Elspeth had saved her,
not with money, or by great influence, but by the
power of her own good-will, and Hannah prayed
for that kindly heart that might lead her to help
others. She felt that into her room came the spirit
of Bertha to help her, with the memory of Bertha's
loving and beautiful life. And she counted up the
many living friends who stood near her to counsel
and support her. For she needed support when
she looked out into the streets and saw so many
wanderers needing more than a home, and she felt
herself so small for so great a work. Her only
thought was, "Ah, if there were more Miss
Elspeths!"

www.ingramcontent.com/pod-product-compliance
Lightning Source LLC
Chambersburg PA
CBHW060529030726
47498CB00004B/1130